The Fabulists

Philip Casey was born to Irish parents
in London in 1950 and raised in Co.
Wexford. He lived in Barcelona from
1974 to 1977 and has travelled widely
in Israel and Europe. His publications
include *The Year of the Knife, Poems
1980-1990* (1991); his play, *Cardinal*,
was performed in Hamburg in 1990.

A member of Aosdána, he lives in
Dublin on the north bank of the Liffey.

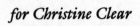

for Christine Clear

The Fabulists

PHILIP CASEY

THE LILLIPUT PRESS

First published in 1994 by
THE LILLIPUT PRESS LTD
4 Rosemount Terrace, Arbour Hill,
Dublin 7, Ireland.

in association with

SERIF
47 Strahan Road
London E3 5DA

A CIP record for this
title is available from
The British Library.

ISBN 1 874675 30 9

*Acknowledgments are due to the Arts Council (An Chomhairle
Ealaíon) for a travel grant to Germany, and to The Tyrone
Guthrie Centre at Annamakerrig where some of this novel was
written. With special thanks to Karina, Christine, Ulrike, Bríd,
Peter, Mick, David, Paddy, Eileen, Shane, Sean, Kevin, Eileen,
John, Ann, Pat, Arthur, and Grainne.*

*The Lilliput Press receives financial assistance from
An Chomairle Ealaíon/The Arts Council of Ireland*

Cover design by Ed Miliano
Set in 10.5 on 13 Galliard by
mermaid turbulence
Printed in Dublin by ßetaprint

- One -

Tess was brooding about Arthur and Brian when a large puppet bird caught her attention. Its head lunged on its unwieldy neck as it led the noisy, colourful parade along O'Connell Street. A judge rolled his eyes and absently waved a claw from his perch. His platform was dragged by lawyers, their wigs askew as they strained and groaned under the weight of the law. It was all good fun, but when she saw that the Keystone Cops were confused about guarding some men in a cage, she realized the point of the demonstration. The case of the six men had become notorious. Tess believed they were innocent, and now, by chance, she could support their cause.

She was mesmerized as one scene displaced another. Weird ranks of marchers dressed in black, with cowls or tricorn hats, carried flaming torches. Their faces were black, their masks were white. There was a choir, in red and orange cloaks. It was like the German carnival Marian had mentioned in one of her letters.

She was relieved when the drums faded, and as the support groups began to pass, she slipped in behind a union banner.

By O'Connell Bridge the groups had become less disciplined and more sociable. Even Tess had joined in the banter. She could see no one that she knew, but although he was more or less with a group behind a banner, a man was casually watching her. She had already noticed him as she joined the parade, because he had a stiff arm, but now he was lost in the shifting crowd. There were mythic animals everywhere she looked, weaving in and out of the straggling groups, keeping them moving, insulting friends from the safety of their masks. She hadn't enjoyed herself so much in a long time.

Darkness fell quickly as they marched on. At the Central Bank Plaza, the parade mustered under the moon in a clear sky, and the crowd spilled over onto Dame Street. Tess shivered. She had been fine while she was walking, but now she was glad of her long coat and boots, and her woollen cap. By the time the last of the marchers had arrived, the speeches were coming to a close. Christy Moore had sung, and there was one last chorus from the red and orange choir as a sculpture of a victory fist was set alight. Tess had got herself close enough to feel its heat dancing on her face.

She turned to leave, and saw that man glance at her again. She walked quickly behind the Bank and through Merchants' Arch to the Ha'penny Bridge. As she waited for the traffic-lights to change, he arrived beside her. In the steady flow of traffic, a bus and then a lorry passed, leaving clouds of diesel fumes in their wake. By now he was one of many who had come from the Plaza. The lights changed as they streamed across. The yellow bulbs of the bridge lamps were flickering in their black casings. She could taste the sulphur in the air as coal fires burned across the city.

Perhaps it meant nothing, but he was still walking beside her and she was uneasy. On the other side they had to wait for the lights to change once more. When they did, she hurried across and, pretending to look through the security gates of The Winding Stair Café & Bookshop, she could see that along with two others he was following her. This was ridiculous. Her heart was pounding, and she broke into a run until she reached her door. There was no sign of him, but her hand shook as she unlocked it. She ran up the stairs, out of breath, and slammed the door of her flat. Not daring to turn on the light, she went to the side of the window. It took a few moments, but then he came into view. He was separated from the others and walking at a leisurely pace, his head bowed. She didn't think he looked like someone following a woman with intent, and to her relief, he didn't check her door as he passed; but you could never tell.

She pressed her cheek against the cold pane and stared at the floodlit bridge. 'Fuck him,' she said out loud, annoyed that she had got herself into a panic. Now that she could think straight, he looked harmless. Even pleasant.

Her thoughts returned to Arthur. She had recently been struck by something he'd blurted out – something very male. It had made her realize that she dreaded the end of his childhood.

She lit the gas fire and went to the bathroom. A fungus had formed on the wall where a chronic leak had left its tracks. It would have to be seen to, but right now she hadn't the energy to think of such things. In the living-room, she drew the curtains and put on her cassette of Schubert's 'Wanderer' Fantasy. She thought about the parade. The Parade of Innocence. It had passed an hour very pleasantly. The city could do with a carnival, something to lose yourself in, if only for a while. Turning off the light, she nestled into the scruffy armchair, and in the dull heat of the gas fire she fell asleep for a few hours.

When she woke, her neck ached and, confused, she stared at the red light on the cassette-player. The air was dry and her mouth was parched. She turned on the lamp. The clock on the mantel ticked loudly; it was almost midnight. Grumbling, she looked through the curtains at the street below, wondering if she might get a take away. The Chinese would still be open, it wasn't too far, and her mouth watered at the thought of a beef curry – but it was too damn late.

Her kitchen was so narrow that if she bent down her head could brush one wall and her heels the other. In a box on the floor were carrots, Brussels sprouts, an onion, some garlic and a few potatoes. Cut up fine, they would boil in a few minutes.

She put on the other side of the Schubert as she ate. The

meal revived her, which she appreciated as food often made her feel bloated. Poverty had some compensations after all. There was a screech of tyres as a car sped against the flow of traffic outside. Later, she lay awake, listening to the music until after four, her only light the red eye of the machine.

When she woke again, she lay still for a time. There was something important she ought to think of but it didn't matter right now. She stretched out and brought the clock to view in the grey light. It was two, and she had to be at the dole office at half-past. There was just about enough time for a cup of strong tea, and a quick wash and change.

The queue had stalled because of an argument at the hatch, and several women were already grumbling and restless. There was a light steam rising off their coats, and one woman's hair was stringy from the rain. Tess took off her cap. Small mercy, her hair was dry. The young woman at the head of the queue was still arguing, her voice rising and her face red. She turned sideways, shouting from an angle at the unfortunate clerk who was now exposed to the queue. Tess stepped a little to the right so she could see everything. The clerk retreated behind an immovable bureaucracy, but Tess could see she was upset.

'Fuck this for a lark,' the woman in front of Tess swore. 'I've a kid to collect.'

'Me too,' Tess said.

The woman glanced at Tess, then roared at the clerk.

'Would you not get her a supervisor so we can get out of here today?'

Tess gnawed on her nails, and stared at a big rubber plant as she automatically shuffled along. Her turn came, she put her cap firmly back on, signed the docket and brought it to the pay-hatch queue. The notes were fresh and before she put them into her purse she flicked them for the pleasure of it. Outside, she hesitated, longing for a cup of coffee, but she would have to get the bus to Fairview.

She arrived at the school on the stroke of three, and heard the faint bell and then the clamour of the children as they rushed out. Tess glanced at a woman who nodded and they

smiled at each other. There were a few men waiting too, aloof
– embarrassed, she supposed. Only one spoke to his children;
the others turned as their children came up to them and one
walked away as soon as he saw his girl, letting the child catch
up with him along the street. He was the surly one who stared
at Tess most days but always turned away when she faced him,
as if she embodied all his humiliation, and she hated him. It
wasn't her fault that he was unemployed and humbled like this
in front of women. He was employed bringing his child home,
like everyone else here.

Arthur as usual was last, holding his satchel in front of him,
his knees bumping it forward as he walked. She always meant
to reprimand him for dragging his feet coming out of school
as if she was the last person he wanted to see, but as soon as
she saw his dreamy brown eyes, she forgot. They stayed on her
until he had almost reached her, and then his face would come
alive, in a mischievous, embracing grin. Like an actor with perfect timing, he left it to the last moment, keeping her sense of
expectation flickering.

'Hello Tess.'

'Hello Arthur.'

She gave him a quick, sideways hug. Arthur was a loving
child, but she had discovered that boys, no less than men, dis-
liked being embraced in public. They walked happily through
Fairview, oblivious to the constant roar of traffic. She glanced
down at Arthur, who seemed completely at ease, and while
envying his self-possession, she was grateful for it too.

He was obviously happier since she and Brian had split up.
There was peace in the house and he could be with both his
parents for some of the day, most days. How had two people,
who had been at each other's throats for most of their marriage – how had they produced a placid, contented boy like
Arthur? She often wondered, and supposed it to be one of
life's conundrums.

'Can I invite Annie to tea?'

'Who?'

'Annie. She's been sick.'

'Annie. Oh yes, of course … Yes of course, invite her to tea! That's a very nice thought, Arthur.'

And to think she hadn't even missed Annie. He retreated back into himself, with a hint of a smile, content. He looked as if he had his life plotted out, and his asking permission was only a polite formality.

They went into the playground in Fairview Park and she sat down, holding him before her and looking into his eyes.

'Arthur, do you miss me not being at home at night?'

He thought about it for a moment.

'Would you come and tuck me in more often? Daddy's not very good at telling stories. He reads through a book at a hundred miles an hour and turns out the light as soon as he's finished.'

'Do I tell good stories?'

'Well, you don't rush, and they come out of your head, and your eyes go all wide when you think of the good bits.'

She laughed.

'But apart from the stories, is it alright?'

'I suppose so,' he shrugged, and dropping his bag, he ran off to the slide. She watched him climb and slide several times before calling him, and he immediately trotted to her, satisfied. She wanted to get some mince.

Annie was Arthur's age, but taller. After tea, they went into the garden, playing under the tree in the precious minutes before nightfall. Tess grinned. Annie believed that she dominated Arthur, not realizing it was impossible. What would become of him? He seemed assured of his rightful place in the world, something special and fulfilling, if he wasn't hurt along the way. She gnawed at her knuckles, watching him for a while, and then set to making Brian's dinner.

Half-way through making it, she remembered that shepherd's pie used to be his favourite dinner. She had even liked making it for him, once upon a time. She sometimes thought they might still be living together, at least, if she hadn't had to go out to work to keep a roof over their heads.

Then, out of the blue, he had landed a job in a warehouse in the East Wall, just as she lost hers in Norton's clothing factory. It seemed ludicrous paying the bills for a house she didn't live in any more, but it had maintained her right to Arthur. With money in his pocket Brian was civil to her, in speech at least, but she didn't care about that anymore as long as she could see Arthur. It was, as her father put it, a queer set-up.

In a way, Brian had it made: his meals prepared for him and a free baby-sitter at least one night a week. No sex, of course, not from her anyway. She stood on a chair and took down his videos, carelessly hidden as usual on top of the kitchen unit. What did he have out this week? She examined the titles and the faked ecstasy and disintegrating flesh of the cover photos. It wasn't so much the porn or even the horror she minded. What she minded was that he never got out anything else. All he seemed to be interested in were anonymous fannies and gouged eyes. In one of the horror videos, a hypodermic needle plunged into an eyeball.

She bundled them back, leapt from the chair and retched at the sink. Of all the videos she had watched with Brian, that was the one which made her sick. And now he had it out again. Apart from the sadism, which made her squirm, all those things she would never have dreamt of doing with Brian or any man – and certainly not with a woman – all that appealed to the voyeur in her for a while. It was fascinating and some of it even turned her on; but then its cold athletics bored her and the horror stuff made her angry. The videos protruded over the kitchen unit, so she pushed them back out of sight with the brush.

Over dinner, Brian was in a good mood. He even repeated a joke one of the men had told him during the day. It was actually witty for a change, and, laughing so much, he wasn't put out when she didn't respond.

'I see you've got more of those videos,' she said, looking at the floor.

'So?'

'So you've got a seven-year-old son.'

'And you don't want him to see nude women, is that it?'

'Seeing nude women is one thing. Crude sex and torture is another.'

'He sees worse on the six o'clock news ... Okay, okay!'

She had been about to protest.

'I'm not going to let him near them, don't worry. I'm not a monster. I look after him, remember. I'm here six nights out of seven. I put him to bed, and get him out to school in the mornings.'

'I know what you do!'

'But I don't know what you do, six nights of the week, unless you're walking the streets.'

'Fuck you,' she said quietly, her voice breaking.

'And you. Though I wouldn't. Not now. Not never. And I'm sorry I ever did.'

She pushed the table away, upsetting everything on it, and ran into the hallway. She was furious, mostly with herself for leaving herself open. In the kitchen, his fork grated across his plate. Breathing heavily, she felt as if she was breaking in two, trying to cope with her fury and hurt. She wanted to shout that she wasn't going to be his skivvy any more, that he could make his own slop in future, but, biting her lip, she remembered Arthur.

Drained, she leaned against the living-room door. Arthur knelt before the television, absorbed in a loud cartoon. Tess watched him for several minutes, but he didn't move, except when his shoulders shook in mute laughter. The cartoon ended and she knelt beside him.

'I've got to go now, pet.'

He looked at her and leaned in towards her and she held him close, rocking him, moved as ever by his spontaneity.

'I love you very much,' she whispered. There was no reply, but she could feel how he bathed in her words, and gave himself completely to her, and she knew she would die for this, if she had to.

She looked around and saw that Brian was watching them. He looked empty and lonely and beaten, and for a moment she felt sorry for him and yearned that all three of them could be together in a warm embrace. But it was a wild fantasy, and, breaking the spell, he turned and went into the kitchen to put the kettle on for tea.

'I'll see you tomorrow, okay?'

Arthur looked up, nodded and rolled away onto his knees to watch a new cartoon. She went to the door, then looked around.

'Bye.'

'Bye,' he answered, without taking his eyes off the screen.

She walked back to her flat, her cheeks streaked with tears in the cold evening.

- *Two* -

A few days later, it dawned a fine morning. Mungo got the children out to school and, whistling softly, he walked up Stoneybatter to cash his disability cheque. Nothing put him in good humour like a fine morning. He had even brought Connie breakfast in bed and, although she had tried to conceal it, she was surprised and pleased. Maybe he should do it more often. He was bursting with life since giving up drink, and felt smug as he passed Moran's pub. With his exercises and then his long walk in the mornings, he was fit for anything, and his mind was coming alive again. Sometimes his walks took him well into the Phoenix Park, or as far as Stephen's Green. In the park, which he preferred, he could find a quiet stretch and burst into a jog when he was sure no one was watching, and he made trebly sure, because the idea of anyone seeing him jog in his boots, jeans and heavy overcoat was excruciating. Not to mention his arm, whose limpness, he knew, made him look odd, especially when running. His arm was all that bothered him. It ached badly. At first he had excluded it from his exercises, but then it became more difficult to do so, and now it felt like fresh, rearing blood was trying to push through veins grown accustomed to a sluggish flow. His left hand tingled, and he flexed it. That was another thing about walking: he could gently, unobtrusively, exercise his hand – flex, open, shut, flex, open, shut. He still couldn't raise the arm very well, but that would come soon, he felt sure.

In a few weeks time it would be two years since the fire. That would be a bad time for Connie. Aidan seemed to have forgotten about it and got on with his life as children do, especially as the burns had healed so well, thanks to the people in James's. Sure, the poor guy still had the dreams, but they were less frequent. Mungo was trying to be as kind as he could to all three of them. Connie still hadn't forgiven him, he knew, so he couldn't just hand her a bunch of roses, for instance. She wouldn't wear it, so he'd have to sneak in and put them in the kitchen, maybe in that white delft vase she liked.

Six red roses. Romance on the welfare she'd say, if she said anything. She hadn't spoken to him, not a word, for nearly a year after the fire, but nobody could keep that up all the time, so now she only spoke to him when necessary. Maybe she was softening. The response when he brought her breakfast in bed this morning had given him hope. He had been trying to work up the courage to do it for weeks. Perhaps there was no going back, but he just wanted to be part of the human race again.

He cashed his cheque in the hushed bank, and back home, he left the money on the table for Connie, keeping only the loose change. He sat and looked at it, that which only barely carried them through the week, though he didn't smoke or drink any more. Connie still smoked, but not a lot. He heard the bedsprings as she turned.

'Is that you?' she called.

'It's me,' he called back.

'Well get some meat if you're going out.'

At least the children were fed and clothed. Nothing fancy, but enough. The curse of Christmas was still to come, but if children couldn't have Christmas, what could they have? He took some money and left the house.

He went down Grangegorman, crossed North Brunswick Street and turned left at North King Street, flexing his fingers as he walked, and sweating a little at the effort. It took concentration. His New Year's resolution would be to get the strength back in his hand and arm. If he couldn't get a regular job then he could do nixers until the building trade took up again, and someone had told him that that wasn't far off. He had intended continuing along North King Street, but when he came to Smithfield, he set out across the cobbles which stretch almost to the river. On one side were warehouses, some of them derelict, covered in colourful, garish murals. He passed the weigh house. There were young trees planted in rows of three all the way down. On the other side was new Corporation housing and, farther down, the new Children's Court. In between were three travellers' caravans, smoke rising from the aluminium chimneys.

'Mungo! Hey, head-the-ball!'

This was as he passed the Children's Court. An old drinking crony was lounging on the steps.

'Hey Frankie! I thought you graduated from that place a while back.'

'Been rejuvenated. Mungo, you're a rich bleedin' culchie – any ciggies?'

'Sorry, pal. Don't smoke any more.'

'Ah, keep goin', so. You're no use to me.'

He walked on. That was about the size of it. Once you were one of the lads, knocking it back a couple of nights a week, money no object, you were a great fella, but hit bad times and you might as well never have existed. When he thought about it, he hadn't one real friend. It was a useful piece of knowledge.

His journey brought him past the derelict distillery on to the fruit and vegetable markets, and as the pavements were blocked by crates of produce, he followed a dray cart through the chaos of vans and lorries and whining forklifts. He realized he was thirsty, so instead of taking the more direct route along Little Mary Street, he checked the change which he kept for himself, and went down to Abbey Stores on the corner of Arran Street and Mary's Abbey. He saw the butcher talking to a customer outside his shop farther along Mary's Abbey, and thought of the meat. If he didn't get it now he'd forget it, as sure as daylight. So he went down to McNally's. The butcher, who he presumed was J. McNally himself, stayed outside, finishing his conversation in the sunshine.

'I'll be with you in a minute,' the butcher called into the bright but old-fashioned interior.

That was fine. Mungo was in no hurry. He had all the time in the world.

'Now, what can I get you, sir,' Mr McNally asked as he came back in.

'Can you give me a couple of pounds of stewing stuff?'

'Sure. Why not?'

The meat was good and it was cheap. This was the way to do things – combine a little business with a pleasant walk. Pleased with himself, Mungo doubled back to Abbey Stores. It was a tiny shop but they had nice oranges and they didn't mind if you only bought one.

'Magic,' the young shopkeeper said when Mungo handed him the exact amount.

A juggernaut from Holland was parked in the lower, residential part of Arran Street, being unloaded by a forklift. Tons of apples. Mungo happily sucked on his orange. He turned into Little Strand Street to avoid the quays. At the junction with Capel Street he paused, then gravitated to a shop window and a multiband radio which caught his eye. It cost what his family now lived on for a week, but it would give him access to any station in the world, almost; to languages he could never hope to understand, unless Spanish, perhaps. It was first year college Spanish, brushed up a little on the Costa Brava, but it would be something to build on. It was vaguely painful to know that he would never be able to buy the radio, unless he was able to work again. He tried to lift his arm, thinking it would never recover.

He turned and crossed over to Great Strand Street, away from shops and dreams. There were Corporation offices, a pub and one single shop, which sold guitars and amplifiers, but apart from a school, it was a street of light industry and dereliction in equal proportion. A granite-faced warehouse, refurbished and converted into small units, pleased him. It had been a while since he had been along here.

Just as he turned into Liffey Street, joining the streams of people walking between Abbey Street and the Ha'penny Bridge, he saw her. She gave a little start of recognition, just as he did, but he continued around the corner. Not knowing what to do, he stepped onto the road to let her pass, or whatever she might choose. She passed, but he could see that she was hesitant too. They walked almost together for a few moments, she slightly ahead; then he crossed over to one of the Pound Shops and pretended to browse, his heart pounding. She had paused too, and he knew that, like him, she was pretending to be interested in a shop window. This was his cue, but he was transfixed. She's beautiful, he thought, and this was all his mind would allow. No strategy, no opening line, only the all-consuming fact of her physicality.

Baffled, he perversely entered the shop, when all he wanted to do was catch up with her and tell her his name. That was it: My name is Mungo, what's yours? It's so simple when you can think straight, he thought, and rushed out of the shop. She was gone. It was impossible, but she was gone.

He hurried, trying not to run, to Abbey Street, and looked up and down. Nothing. Over to Upper Liffey Street. No sign. She had disappeared. Agitated, he checked again in four directions. She had to be in a shop somewhere. Perhaps at that very moment she was watching him, highly amused. This sobered him, and he reassumed his dignity.

In the shopping-centre he walked through the crowds in a daze. All the shoppers could think about was Christmas; all he could think of was how beautiful she was, and that he would never see her again because of his stupidity.

He took the library lift for a few moments privacy. Her red hair dropped a little below her shoulders. She seemed about the same height as himself, five foot seven, but with raised heels on her boots, it was hard to know exactly. What else? Her eyes he wasn't sure of – blue or green, but they were generous. She seemed ... plump, although again it was hard to know with her heavy winter clothing. He couldn't picture her legs, but remembered with pleasure that she walked gracefully. To him, grace was important.

He went straight to the travel books by force of habit, taking down the largest volume on Spain. His paper mark was undisturbed and he opened the book at page ninety, but though he read two pages without pause, not one word registered. He felt sure her carriage would be matched by her manner and voice. Her voice would immediately decide if ... Her voice would decide what? he wondered. He was a married man, after all, which was not altogether beside the point.

He hoped he hadn't spoken aloud, and moved to another reading table in case he had. His attraction to this woman had amounted to a surge of hormones, yet his imagination had leapt ahead, making assumptions and laying down conditions. The attraction disturbed him. Even if they met again, which was unlikely, it would have the same inconsequential end. A similar experience in his youth reminded him how juvenile his reactions were. It was just an attack of juvenile projection. He could read his book in peace.

He read about a traveller journeying through Castile by train. It had been snowing, but as dawn broke the sky was a steely blue and the snow was compact and silent across the plateau. Later, as the sun rose, the traveller saw a herd of black bulls, and then the eleventh-century walls of Avila.

Mungo closed the book and dreamed himself onto that train approaching Avila, the city of Saint Teresa. At first he tried to remember the details, but abandoned this and let his imagination provide. Apart from the two weeks with Connie and the children in a tourist hotel on the Costa Brava, he had never been outside Ireland, unless he counted the months on housing sites in the English Midlands, a failed student. So it was Spain that nourished his fantasies about a new life, the discovery of which would change him, as if stepping out of the skin that was his past. It would even change his past, give it a context which would lend it meaning. Then, one day he would go to Spain and not return.

The idea was still crude, but little by little it was forming. He opened the book again and went back to the beginning of the chapter. The traveller, an Irishman, had relatives in Galicia – the Celtic part of the peninsula. Mungo envied him such a background. At the same time, it would be better if he, Mungo, were completely alone to make a fresh start.

It didn't have to be Spain, but it was the country he knew most about for now, more than England – more than Ireland, perhaps. A fresh start. In reality it was impossible, he knew; but he could rehearse it in his imagination. Maybe he could disguise it as a story for the children. He returned to where he had left off, and finished the chapter.

It had been snowing, but as dawn broke the sky was cloudless and the snow was compact and silent across the plateau. Mungo repeated the lines to himself while descending the library stairs to the shopping centre.

As he turned from the stairs he almost collided with her. She smiled faintly as if in recognition, but flustered, he wasn't quite sure if it was the same woman, and side-stepped to let her pass. Could it be her? Surely not. Was it a smile of derision? He backtracked, and she had paused by the sweet shop. Staring, as if in shock, he decided it wasn't her. This woman didn't fit his luminous image. True, she had light red hair, and similar clothing, but she seemed defeated somehow, whether by age or constant misfortune he could not say. And he had remembered her as having flaming red hair, hadn't he? If only he could see her face again, he would know then. If he could see her eyes, then certainly he would know. It would give him a chance to smile, and she could smile back and they could laugh at his foolishness and say hello. She didn't turn, but as soon as she walked along the passage to Parnell Street, he knew. He stood at the sweet shop and watched her retreating figure. Yes, it was her alright, and yes, despite her graceful carriage, she seemed defeated. Suddenly, he felt the weight of defeat too, and turned to leave by the Henry Street exit, when Parnell Street would have brought him more quickly home.

'Ripe bananas, five for fifty!' 'Cigarette lighters, four for a

pound! The sing-song cries of the street-sellers greeted him on Henry Street. He lounged about for a while, browsing amongst the cheap shoes, and then in the music shop across the road. He hated wasting time like this, when he could afford neither shoes nor music, but he did it all the same, knowing he was trying to avoid thinking about the woman.

He found himself walking back along Liffey Street, half believing he might meet her again, and paused at the junction with Strand Street, where he felt something magical had brought them together for those shocking moments. At the Ha'penny Bridge, he looked down Ormond Quay and recalled that his journey home after the Parade of Innocence had left him in her wake. How she had hurried away! Of course it had been dark, and maybe without realizing it he had scared her, and he felt pity and then affection and a desire to make amends.

On the hump of the footbridge, he stopped and looked around him, as so many passed by. Then he peered up-river. He knew he was attracting curious glances, and he longed at that moment for a camera. With a camera he would have a legitimate reason – a composition, perhaps, of the copper-green domes of the Four Courts and Adam and Eve's, with the Guinness steam house in the distance, slightly left of centre, completing the picture. Without a camera he felt naked. If he was a passer-by, he too would wonder why some-one was staring into the distance from a bridge over a river at high tide. The obvious reason was furthest from the truth. He did it because he wanted to, and that was reason enough. There was no other reason. He had no purpose here, nor did he want or need one. He felt a thrill of happiness at his brief freedom, and gratitude to an anonymous woman.

- *Three* -

It was where she shopped anyway, so for a week she found an excuse to go to the shopping centre every other day at about the same time. The coincidence of meeting him twice in an hour was one thing, but the moment had passed and was lost. She shrugged. Such things happened all the time in the likes of Henry Street – didn't they? Apart from his stiff arm, what intrigued her was that he had frightened her half to death on the night of the parade, but in daylight he seemed deferential and almost timid. Anyway he looked pleasant enough. She was very lonely, but she didn't want another arsehole messing her around. She'd be in control with this one, that was certain, and for a few days she felt a surge of exhilarating hope. It was nice to fantasize about him – what he might be like, what he did, if he was married. Yes, he was married, but then so was she. Thoughts of an affair made her smile and even laugh, but the tread of her life reasserted itself and she forgot about him. Finding a decent present for Arthur on her few bob took up most of her time. She spent weeks, hesitating, counting her pennies, hoping to come across a better bargain. As a truce offering, she bought Brian a video tape.

Christmas passed more peacefully than she could have hoped. Arthur was happy with his football and boots, and his video games from Brian. Annie had spilled the beans about

Santy, but despite Tess's annoyance it had turned out to her advantage in the present arrangement, and his manic spirits kept their minds off reality. Alcohol and television and the visits to Arthur's grandparents did the rest.

They drank so much on Christmas night that they ended up fucking on the living-room floor, she not caring who he was, and she even came. It wasn't great, but it was better than fighting. The next day, appalling hangovers allowed them to pretend nothing had happened. She left that evening, relieved that Christmas and its obligations were over. She put the idea of pregnancy out of her mind. On New Year's Eve she went to Christchurch, and rang in the New Year and New Decade, dancing with strangers with as much abandon as if she believed they held a promise of happiness. She went to a party off the South Circular Road, where there were so few men that several women danced with each other. They were several drinks ahead of her and she felt awkward, so she walked home around three, ignoring the boisterous calling from passing cars. At least she hadn't been alone for the first few hours of the year. That was symbolically important. She took down the redundant calendar and burned it, hoping all her bad luck would go up in smoke.

Arthur settled back into school, and the routine was established again. On her way back from Fairview, she felt the first drops of rain as she hurried across O'Connell Street. Already the windscreen wipers were zipping on passing cars. She crossed into Abbey Street while the lights were still red, but within moments she was caught in a downpour. Her head was bare so she cursed fluently while running to a bus shelter, where she huddled with a dozen others, but then realized the rain had soaked through her coat and she walked slowly and miserably home.

Once inside the flat, she made no attempt to change her clothes but looked around the cold room, so bleak and lifeless in the naked light: the old armchair with its torn covering and collapsed springs; the red Formica table with the accumulated dirt in its steel rim impossible to dislodge; the tattered nylon carpet which made her skin creep; the discoloured chipwood wallpaper; the thin grey curtains ... A tear trickled down her face. Even her posters seemed dispirited.

Water dripped rapidly into the bath. She pushed open the bathroom door and watched a separate leak stream down the wall, nourishing the fungus. It didn't matter that it would saturate the floor below, no one lived there any more. There was a lesser breach in the kitchen over the cooker. She moved a pot until it was directly underneath, the thick drops striking hard.

Her body tensed and her teeth began to chatter. She went back into the living-room with a towel, lit the gas fire and undressed, drying her body vigorously, oblivious to the spluttering flames. She tilted her head to one side to dry her hair and stared at the fire as it died. Cursing, she rummaged through her bag, but there was no fifty pence piece.

Tess felt the breadth of her squalor, but she steadied herself and weighed up her options. To go into the rain again, begging for a coin would be ridiculous, so all she could do was go to bed once her hair was dry. Taking a few blankets, she sat on her heels in the armchair and wrapped them around her. Clutching them to her with one hand, she furiously towelled her hair with the other. Both friction and action combined made her tolerably warm and also breathless, so she rested a while.

The blankets fell open, exposing part of her left breast. She examined it, not for lumps, but for its substance and texture as a sexual object. She laughed, without feeling. This was the piece of protruding flesh that turned men's heads, that they loved to handle and kiss and admire, and, not for the first time, she wondered about its fascination. Her breasts were small, with thick nipples which she considered ugly, and she was convinced they had lost their firmness. No fear of her tits fascinating men! Not that she cared. They seemed to retreat from the cold and were suddenly covered in goose pimples. She looked at her belly which was still slim but its skin was somehow slack, and blemished, as she thought of it, with the wrinkles of an ancient.

She looked farther down at her bush, and closed the blankets about her and towelled her hair again. She felt only an emptiness and bitterly knew that in such a state, far from wanting pleasure, she only wanted to hurt herself. Perhaps that's what puritans meant when they called it self-abuse. Not that she was against giving herself pleasure and she thought about some of her more memorable explorations, which made her feel good and she stopped rubbing her hair and silently laughed. She had done it first while still at school, where the precocious Marian had alerted her to its possibilities, but it wasn't until she had come to live here, at the age of thirty-two, that she deliberately sat down one evening in this same armchair in her open dressing-gown before a warm fire, and began to explore her body, inch by inch, in a way no man had done and perhaps no man could know how.

That was very beautiful and not just because of the pleasure, but because it gave her back hope. It was so difficult to recapture a moment like that, and why it should be so she didn't know. She would try again, yes, but not now, the mood wasn't right, even if the thought had cheered her. Yes, it had, and she hugged herself in gratitude.

In bed she threshed her body and legs about until the friction warmed the sheets, but she still wasn't warm. A chill breeze, blocked on one side of the bed, made its way in somewhere else. Too lazy to get up again, she tried to stick it out, but in the end she jumped out of bed and found the oversize tee-shirts she was fond of and donned three before jumping back in, threshing about again.

It was no use, she would have to make the bed properly. So, getting out once more, she did a little dance as she carefully tucked in the sheets and blankets. Back in, she wriggled about for a while, then paused to gauge the effect. Not bad. She pulled the tee-shirts down her thighs. Better still. Content, she turned on a Schubert tape and played it until she could no longer hold off sleep.

*　*　*

Mungo lay awake beside Connie, who was snoring. She had most of the bed but that didn't matter. His arm ached badly and his hand tingled and this worried him, as he had heard someone in a pub saying that it was the sign of a heart attack. Or was it a stroke? The side of his head tingled as well, so maybe it was a stroke. That was queer because he had never felt better physically and his arm, he felt sure, was coming on well. The irony – to get yourself to the peak of fitness, and then die of a heart attack! Or a stroke. American suburbia was famous for it.

Then again, maybe the tingling in his scalp was due to the hard pillow and maybe he had lain on his arm. He had slept deeply before waking. Now he longed to know the time, but the luminous figures on the clock had faded long ago. It was probably two or three. The wind had risen and it was still raining, and the leak from a gutter was blown onto a roadworks drum in a tattoo.

He rubbed the side of his head briskly and the tingling faded. Then he put his left arm across his body and caressed it, slowly, from the shoulder to his fingertips. Lately he had discovered that as well as making his arm feel better, there was sensual pleasure in it too. He looked over at the shadowy figure of his wife. They had not had sex since before he gave up drinking. She was steamed up that night too, singing all the way home with a few of her girlfriends, their men a few paces behind shouting friendly abuse, but excluded all the same. The defences were down and the baby-sitter from next door was paid off quickly, and the singing continued *sotto voce* up the stairs as their clothes came off, and into bed until it was silenced by famished lips and tongues.

Shag it, he had an erection. Weary, he sighed and thought of welfare bureaucracy and it subsided. This never failed and as there was no point in tormenting himself, he used it every time. The kettle boils over if it's left too long on the flame but it couldn't be helped, and if Connie noticed when the sheets were washed she never protested. She turned and her arm fell haphazardly on his chest. He was about to gently remove it when she moaned. Her arm twitched a few times, and he left it there, sorry for her now. It couldn't be easy for her either, with no one that he knew of to touch her, to convince her that she wasn't a fleshless soul wandering around the city of the lost. He thought he knew how she must feel. As suddenly as before, she turned and moaned again. He hoped she was having a nice time.

A scream came from the children's bedroom and without thinking Mungo was on his feet. As he knelt by his bed, Aidan was fighting off some danger, and Mungo knew what it was. Ethna was sleeping peacefully so he switched on Aidan's torch, still unsure if he should wake him or let the nightmare take its course, in which case it might leave him be for a while. He watched his son struggle and sweat and suffered with him as he pulled him from the flames which he, Mungo, had set alight. One night of drunkenness, his cigarette had made his son's bed an inferno and had almost killed him and Ethna, too, if it hadn't been for Connie. They might all have died.

Aidan sat up suddenly, gasping, his arms flailing.

'Da, Da!' he shouted.

'I'm here, son, I'm here,' Mungo whispered urgently, holding him. 'I have you out. You're safe. As safe as could be.' Ethna was still asleep, and he rocked Aidan until he calmed.

'Was it the same dream?' Aidan nodded. 'Gawd – it's a tough one, isn't it?' The boy nodded again. 'You haven't had it for a while, though, have you?' Aidan shook his head. 'I'd say you'll have it less and less, until you won't have it at all. Maybe this is the last one,' he added optimistically.

Aidan was silent for a while. 'I was in a church.'

'A church?'

He nodded, this time vigorously.

'You never had a church in your dream before, had you. Was it a big church?'

Aidan reflected.

'No. It was small. And there was no altar.'

No altar? How could he know it was a church if it had no altar, Mungo wondered, but didn't ask as he knew there was more to be told. But Aidan said nothing and there was silence, apart from a bluster of rain against the window. Mungo gently laid him back and tucked in the bedclothes.

'Will I leave the torch on?' There was no reply, but Mungo stayed, on his knees beside the bed. Then Aidan mumbled, and alert again, Mungo leaned over to listen.

'A bush ...' Aidan's heavy eyelids opened and he looked at his father.

'Yes? A bush?'

'There's a bush in the middle of the church.'

'Is it a nice bush?'

'Very nice.' Aidan seemed to drift back to sleep again, and Mungo let him be, but he rallied, as if he had a need to tell his father. 'A bush ...'

'The bush ... the bush is important, isn't it?

'I take a leaf off the bush, and then ...' Aidan whimpered and sat up in bed again, rubbing his eyes. Mungo sat up quickly beside him and held him close, almost weeping.

'What happens then, my precious boy?' Aidan buried his face in Mungo's belly.

'The bush goes up in a big fire,' he said in a rush. Mungo stroked his head and rocked him.

'And do you run?'

'Oh Da, Da ...' Aidan was crying now. 'Oh yes Da, I'm runnin', an' the bush is runnin' after me.'

That was it. That was enough, it was too much for one small boy to endure. It was too much for a man. Does the bush catch and consume him? The question tormented Mungo, but he didn't dare ask.

'You save me, Da.'

'Do I?' Mungo choked.

'You're very strong and brave.'

Aidan had calmed. Mungo was adrift, but by some intuition, he realized what was happening and accepted a healing peace. They were being men together, or that mythic, heroic part of man which slays the dragon that the boy dreams of and to which the man has long bade his wistful farewell.

Aidan was asleep. Mungo laid him back and tucked in the covers again. He gazed at the peaceful face turned on its side, wondering if he had been the same when he was nine years old. That was all of twenty-six years ago and he had only the vaguest image of himself at that age. He must have been happy, being useful about the small farm, trudging to school, playing hurling in the long summer evenings. His childhood was a pleasant journey until hormones ambushed his brain at eleven or twelve; and then his father died, steering his motorbike into a telegraph pole. What age was he then? Sixteen.

He went over to Ethna – the happy, impish, stubborn, lovely, bad-tempered, charming, whining, tell-tale beat of his heart. Her fist was closed at her mouth, curling open her upper lip, making her snore lightly. He had nearly killed her, too. He had nearly killed them all, including himself. Connie was right.

The bed lamp was on when he returned to bed and Connie was awake, looking at him. Suddenly he felt the cold on his back and shivered.

'Well?'

'Well what?' He got into bed.

'Aidan had another nightmare.'

'Yes. But he's fine now.'

'The same one?'

'No. Well, yes, but a different version. He was able to tell it to me in detail. It was that clear. Maybe they're ending.'

She asked him to describe it for her, and he did. He would have done so anyway but was pleased at the soft, unguarded tone of her voice. It was as if there had never been a rift. They talked for some time. Then she said: 'He needs you a lot at the minute,' and she turned over, put out the light and went back to sleep.

At the minute ... The northern phrases of her childhood came back sometimes. He couldn't sleep until he realized she had spoken to him for Aidan's sake. He admired her for that, and he pulled the blankets over his shoulder to settle down, content. He had a place after all. But sleep would not come.

Connie took a deep breath, and her body relaxed. He felt her heat. It was doubtful if his own body gave off such warmth for her, though maybe it did. That they were still together, warming each other in the same bed was a kind of love, he supposed; one which had no spontaneity and no expression except the care of their children, which was no small thing. Then again, maybe he was clutching at straws, and maybe it was better to admit there would never be any love between them again.

He needed an interest. Something frivolous. Jogging was all very well, but he did it to make him fit. He needed something without purpose. As every day passed, their children were becoming individuals, separate from their parents and would soon be away in the world. There would be nothing left then for him and Connie but to ignore each other in the silence of their marriage bed.

- *Four* -

Tess managed to get out of bed. Pulling her tee-shirts down around her knees so that she crouched, she stumbled into the kitchen. It was almost eleven and the morning was fine, and while the water had left its tracks down the wall, it had dried. She filled the kettle and struck a match for the gas but there was no gas. Damn. Pouting, she absently scratched under her breast. How was she going to face the day without a pot of tea? She poured out some flakes and milk, and ate, only half awake, standing on the floor and unaware of the cold. Finished, she put the plate and spoon into the sink, not bothering to rinse them. She rubbed her caked eyes. There was a smell of dampness, so she opened the window and the sharp air flowed in. Shrieking, she closed it again. That was enough fresh air for one day and, pulling a blanket around her, she curled up on the sofa. A raucous gull flew past the window. What if she fell ill, she wondered. Would anyone even know? She drew the blanket tight around her, but as soon as she was comfortable, she thought she heard a knock on the door.

She dressed quickly, and as she went downstairs, her shoes clattered on the bare wood, and echoed through the empty house. It had been the postman. There were bills, two for her ex-landlord, and a card from Marian.

She pulled herself slowly upstairs by the heavy oak banister, waving the card with her free hand. So there was still someone out there after all. Who else would it have been? Bless you Marian, she whispered. Bless you.

Back in the flat, she pulled the curtains in the front room and, wrapping the blankets around her again, sat into the armchair. The picture was of the U-Bahn network, with round colour pictures marking the termini. The only ones she recognized were the Olympic Stadium and Checkpoint Charlie. She read them aloud in a faulty German accent before reading Marian's few lines again:

'Tess you darling bitch, why haven't you answered my last two letters? I need you to tell me I still exist and that what I write to you isn't a figment of my imagination. My life is so real that I don't believe in it. In case you've lost my address it's at the top of the card, you blind wagon. Write, you lovely woman you, write! Love, Marian.'

She recalled the headlines about East German refugees, and how she had stayed on in Fairview for the television news at six o'clock, watching in fascination as the Berlin Wall came down. Marian was there, in the midst of history being made. Tess should have been excited, but she wasn't. What she had felt was more like resentment.

But now, with her card in front of her, she chose to forget all that. Dear Marian, who kept her alive in secret ways. She had encouraged her to leave Brian. She had found her this flat, however temporary it might be, through friends who were emigrating to Berlin. Above all, she continued her efforts to persuade her that life was there to be lived. It was true that she hadn't written, but what was there to write about? Sweet fuck-all. She roused herself and flicked through a German grammar which had gathered dust on her bookcase. Despite her best intentions, her meagre school German had been allowed to wither. Now she had all the time in the world to learn it properly, but knew that she never would.

She washed in cold water, ran a brush over her tangled hair and went to The Winding Stair. Pausing on the return, she browsed through the posters, vaguely hoping there might be something that would interest her that she could also afford.

Billie Holliday was singing 'Detour Ahead' and amongst the music, books, posters, photos and potted plants, she felt an ease soaking into her like a drug. A few browsers and couples drank coffee by the windows. Eileen climbed down a ladder and greeted her with a smile.

'Hi. How are you?'

'Death slightly warmed up. A coffee, Eileen. A large one.'

'It's like that, is it? How's the leak?'

'You might say I've running water, Eileen, though not all of it's on tap.' It was their joke.

Tess drank her coffee by one of the windows. It was a luxurious way of being part of the morning, looking over to the Ha'penny Bridge where streams of people crossed in both directions. The variety of the human form never failed to engross her, as did the traveller children, thrusting their plastic begging cups towards oncomers.

She felt like staying there all day, but needed to get some food in the supermarket. And what else? Some fifty pence pieces for the gas.

The street was icy cold and she paused to pull her scarf a little tighter. Her eyes settled on a man at the bridge, waiting with a dozen others to cross. Some didn't wait for the lights to change, but he did. The traffic kept blocking her view of him, but despite his heavy overcoat she could see he was freezing. There was something about him that was familiar. Then she openly stared. Yes, she thought, averting her head, it was him, the shy one.

Once in the supermarket she relaxed, except that she didn't know why she was in the supermarket. Bread. Milk, matches and some plaice. A piece of plaice please. She amused herself by thinking up variations: a prime piece of plaice please. Pardon? A particularly pleasing prime piece of plaice please. She spluttered, alarming an old lady, but when she got to the fish counter what she said was: 'Could I have that one over there – yes, that one, thanks.'

As she walked back along the quays, she found herself thinking of him. There was something she had to figure out. Somehow, that time they had nearly bumped into each other he had made her heart jump. Not today; today she had felt nothing except a desire to be as far away from him and his pale, haggard face as possible. And yet ... now that he was safely gone it was diverting to think of him. He was married – she had decided that immediately. Unemployed. Yes, he was unemployed. His main interest in life, now that he had tired of conjugal bliss, was soccer, and probably darts. Peripheral interests were: walking in freezing weather and following women. Perhaps she had something to write to Marian about after all.

It was another week before she was in The Winding Stair again. This time the tables on the first floor were full, so she went up to the second, browsing for a while before her cup of coffee. Kevin came pounding down from the third floor.

'You have a customer,' she called from behind a stack of books.

He stopped short, peered over his glasses and shook his balding head. 'Oh no, you again. I was afraid it might be.'

'Only for my business you'd have to close down, Kevin. You know that well.'

'At least one floor,' he laughed, going behind the counter to put on fresh coffee.

Van Morrison was singing 'Have I Told You Lately That I Love You?' She leafed through copies of the *National Geographic* and came across one which featured Berlin, East and West. As it was several years old and recent events had made the Wall redundant, she was gripped by the fascination of one looking through old photographs to see how much their subjects had changed. Kevin gave it to her for a pound and as she sat by a window, drinking her coffee, she wondered if Marian knew these streets. As she read, she imagined herself there, and remembered the place-names Marian had mentioned in her letters, which conjured up a life with possibilities. A respite. She sipped her coffee and looked out at the bridge.

Jesus. Here he was, coming over the bridge again. It was him, wasn't it? Yes, it was him, definitely. But this time he stopped in the middle and stared up-river. She saw that he was dropping his head on his shoulder, now left, now right. Intrigued, she turned on her seat to watch him. He moved a few steps to his left, keeping his eyes ahead. Then after a while he moved some steps to his right. Then finally, she was sure, he moved back to precisely his original spot. This was too much.

'Kevin,' she called, 'don't throw out my coffee.' Valerie shielded a customer's soup she was bringing to the second floor as Tess rushed past. Eileen glanced up.

'I'll be right back,' she called as she slammed the door behind her. She crossed through a break in the traffic, and strode up to him, out of breath. His head was resting on his right shoulder, and giving it a little jerk, he shifted his gaze from the river to her face. The wind on the river was cutting and he looked very cold.

'What are you doing that for?' she asked, more aggressively than she had intended. 'What's so damn fascinating?' she demanded, unable to stop herself from looking up-river. 'What's so damn fascinating that you come here everyday and look up there?' and she pointed, her arm rigid. He straightened and turned to her.

'Well ...' he faltered. 'It just struck me today, as a matter of fact. Do you see the domes of the Four Courts, and Adam and Eve's on the left side of the river as we look, but a bit closer?

'The church? Yes.'

'Then farther down on the Four Court's side there's another church with a dome, although you can't see it because of the bend in the river. All three domes being of lovely oxidized copper,' he said, 'and so the same pleasing colour.'

'So?'

'So they make a very interesting triangle, don't you think? And then farther again down the river on the left, there's the Guinness steam house, which also has a copper roof, now oxidized.'

'So?!'

'Ahm ... have you ever heard of the Golden Rectangle?'

'Yes of course,' she said, trying to remember what it was, and suspecting that he wasn't too sure either. She could sniff out a spoofer at a hundred paces.

'Ah. Well, I'm trying to figure out if the composition made up by these four buildings in relation to each other constitutes a Golden Rectangle. I'm handicapped by not having either a camera or an aerial photograph, of course.'

He was spoofing. He was definitely spoofing.

'And you come here everyday because of that?'

'I don't come everyday. The last time I even crossed here was a week ago.'

'But that's why you're here,' she stated, annoyed with herself.

'That's why I'm here. At this moment.'

'I don't believe you.'

'Oh.' He looked back up-river as if he were saddened by this, and she waited for a response, feeling the goose pimples all over her body as she stood there without a coat in the wind, knowing her coffee was rapidly going cold. Why was she doing this to him, and herself? Why couldn't she just leave him alone to figure out his golden mean or golden triangle or whatever the hell it was? He put his hand above his eyes as if to shield his view from the weak sun.

She was shivering now, looking at him intently and still combative despite her better judgment.

'Do you know something? I left a cup of coffee to interfere in your business,' she said, as if it was his fault.

He turned his head and smiled, but didn't otherwise move.

'God!' she exclaimed. 'I'm going to get a dose out of this. Are you coming for a cup of coffee or aren't you?'

He nodded. She could see he was half frozen, and in danger of catching a dose himself, and as she led him to The Winding Stair she couldn't help feeling that he was smug about the way things had turned out.

Upstairs, Tess sat him down at her table. He rubbed his

hands and she could see he was grateful to sit in the warmth. As she ordered two coffees – an extravagance but this was no time to count pennies – she watched him out of the corner of her eye. He was looking around appreciatively at the books and plants, posters and photographs, and the framed newspaper clippings which sang the praises of the place. Then he looked out onto the bridge and grinned. 'I knew it,' she fumed. 'I fucking knew it. God, I'm a right eejit,' she said aloud.

'Thou hast thyself said so.' Kevin was amused.

Her lunatic thawed as he sipped the coffee.

'What's your name?'

She didn't answer immediately but now that she was warm again and had a chance to study his face, she softened towards him.

'Tess. I mean Deirdre. My real name is Deirdre but most people call me Tess. My mother was a fan of Thomas Hardy.'

'Oh. Tess is short for Teresa, isn't it?'

'I suppose it is. I don't know really.'

'I thought for a moment you might have been called after Teresa of Avila?'

'The saint? Lord, no! No no no!' she laughed.

'Would you like to hear how I first saw Avila?'

'What? Oh I see. You've been to Spain.'

He nodded. He was easier to be with than she had expected, although his limp arm made her vaguely uneasy. Somehow she couldn't imagine this thin pale man under a hot Spanish sun, but she was curious.

'Were you there long?'

'Long?' He hesitated just too long for her to believe another word he said. 'Several years ... On and off. In the seventies, early eighties. ... My wife and children are still there. I've two children,' he said. 'A boy and girl.'

'You're separated.'

'And you?'

'Me?' She hadn't expected him to move tack so soon. She knew he was playing for time, that much was obvious. 'Yes, well, I'm separated too ... I've a little boy, Arthur. He lives with his father.'

'Where?'

'Where?' What a question! But she thought about it for a moment, partly because the word *Berlin* had been in her head all day. Berlin. Why Berlin? Why not Berlin? He was a total stranger, and if he could spoof about a family in Spain, then she could spoof about a family in Berlin. Two spoofers. It might even be fun, and she smiled.

'Neukölln,' she said with a hint of defiance. 'Tell me about Spain,' she added quickly.

'Avila ...' He sighed and smiled at the same time, ruffling the back of his hair. She could see he was gathering his wits to rise to the occasion. But it didn't matter if she didn't believe him; what mattered was that he would tell a story, no matter how unlikely it might be.

'Well,' he began, 'I was travelling through Spain – in January 1975 – and I couldn't believe my eyes. The Central Plateau was covered in snow. I was a passenger on a train from Vigo to Madrid, and we had met the snow somewhere west of Zamora.'

'Do you have to talk of snow on a day like this? And in Spain of all places!'

'It gets warmer,' he laughed. 'Anyway, I didn't think of myself as a tourist – though that's what I was – but as a traveller, ignorant of the climate and geography but discovering a new terrain and my own ignorance.'

She looked at him askance, and he cleared his throat. She was determined to avoid bullshit, and to his credit, it was obvious that he saw that. He actually cared.

'But that's jumping ahead. It was a long journey, especially as I was on a mail train, or *expreso*, which despite the description stopped at every village. I shared a compartment with a middle-aged man and wife, their adult daughter and two conscripts. There were many conscripts on the train, on the way to begin their military service, and a lot of them were drunk in the corridors, singing all night. Morbid songs. Their loneliness seemed to hang in the air, sealed in a train moving through the darkness, and even though I was very tired, it affected me. As well as that, the heat in the compartment was stifling and made it difficult to sleep, and then there were six feet and legs, and it was a delicate operation to move.'

He had been caught up in his story, but now he noticed that she was listening intently.

'At ... about two in the morning the women fell asleep, and when he was sure of this, their man took a bag from the luggage rack and produced *jamón serrano* – that's a leathery, rich ham – some bread and a *porrón* of wine. A *porrón* is a kind of jar with a spout and you raise it at arm's length and let the wine stream into your mouth. There was just a dim light from the corridor. I was hungry and thirsty and the soldiers must have been too because we all leaned slightly towards the man. He cut the ham slowly and passed the sandwiches around, and we ate. Then he took a long stream from the *porrón* and passed it to me. I hadn't the panache at first, and the wine streamed down my shirt, to their great amusement; but then I succeeded, and the *vino tinto* washed into my mouth. I produced what food I had, and a broken, inevitable conversation began.

I was English, of course. No, I was Irish. Ah. The Galicians were Celts, like the Irish. Red hair. The red-haired Celts of Galicia. A stone in Galicia which commemorates a voyage to Ireland three thousand years ago.

"*¿Es verdad?*"

"*Sí, es verdad.*"

The Celts, the older man said in the gloom, they have always wandered. His own sons were working in Germany; his brothers at one time had all emigrated to Cuba.

But the soldiers weren't interested in this. They wanted to know about Ireland's religious war and about the IRA, which the Spanish pronounce as 'era' – the same as *ira*, which means 'anger'. A religious war. It sounds medieval, doesn't it? And you try to explain that it isn't as simple as that; but it's too complicated in English, never mind in broken Spanish. We talked for another while about Ireland; about pubs and the

Church and all the clichés you can think of; but then I couldn't stand it any longer and escaped into the corridor, glad of the conscripts who were amiably drunk, and singing miles out of tune.

When I went back to the compartment, the others were asleep, and I had a few hours myself. It was bright when I woke. The others were still asleep and it took me a while to realize where I was.' Mungo laughed. 'I was as stiff as a board, and the compartment smelled of stale wine – or maybe I did. I went to the jakes and gave myself a cat's lick, and reasonably awake, I stopped by the carriage door to look at the snow, which lay on a plain that stretched to the horizon and reflected a weak sun. The sky was cloudless. As the train braked, I pulled down a window and felt the shock of the air. It was like taking a cold shower. Just then the carriage came alongside a herd of young, galloping, black bulls. You could see it was great fun as they bucked and snorted, kicking the snow into a spray. No doubt it was a regular game. As the train left them behind, I stayed at the window, smiling. And at the same time uneasy, somehow. After a few moments I stuck my head out, not back at the bulls but into the cold slipstream and saw, for the first time, on an incline which rose out of the plateau, the old white walls of Avila.'

He stopped, absorbed. In a way, he had been talking to himself. She said nothing, knowing he had never before seen the walls of Avila, but it was a fair bet he could see them now. Then he glanced at her.

'I closed the window and took a deep breath. Back in the compartment the young woman was snoring and for some reason I wondered if a man before me had ever seen her tonsils. The blind was still drawn but there was light enough. Had a man's tongue ever touched those tonsils? "Leave her alone," came a loud voice – my conscience, don't you know – as if I had my hand up her skirt. The mother's mouth had dropped open, but she wasn't snoring. Her bottom teeth were visible and discoloured, as if she chewed tobacco. Her husband's head rested against her shoulder, his jaw falling to one side and distorting his face.'

Mungo's lips had set in a narrow smile. He was obviously enjoying the discovery of this cruelty in himself; this safe cruelty at the expense of people who had never existed. Tess watched, fascinated.

'Then I noticed that the man's wallet protruded from inside his jacket pocket. The train had slowed as if already entering the station, and they would wake as it halted, but the temptation was overpowering.'

'To my surprise and relief it came out with ease. Twenty crisp notes, twenty thousand pesetas. Obviously this was a special trip to Madrid, possibly of importance to the young woman. Yet, having taken the money, I couldn't leave it back. Then I remembered I had Irish notes stashed at the bottom of my rucksack. The train would stop at any moment and I'd be caught, maybe beaten up by the conscripts disillusioned in their romantic idea of the Irish, but I couldn't stop now. I plunged my hand down through the books, maps, toilet bag, towels and underwear and found the embossed leather wallet, quickly counted the Irish notes and calculating the exchange, found that it amounted to a thousand pesetas more than I had stolen. What the hell. He would have a pleasant surprise when he went to the bank, and laugh about the crazy Irish for years to come. I hadn't the nerve to replace the wallet, but left it beside his open hand and was out of the compartment just as the train stopped.'

Mungo smiled. It seemed as if he thought it a natural conclusion to the story, but Tess wasn't satisfied.

'What then?'

'What then? Ah ... let me see. What happened then.'

'I presume you got off at Avila?'

'Of course. Yes, I remember now. I had a breakfast and stayed on in the café over several cups of black coffee. Two *Guardia* came in and stood at the bar, drinking coffee, but didn't pay me any heed. It was only when they had gone that I realized I had been waiting to be picked up, and if they didn't find me in Avila, then they'd be waiting for me in Madrid.'

'You were a dangerous criminal, of course.'

He grinned. 'By this time it was almost mid-morning, so I dodged down a side street and ended up in a chapel with a golden altar. It was dedicated to St Teresa and I got the fright of my life when I saw the embalmed body of a nun in a casket with glass on the side.'

'It's not still there, is it?' Tess interjected, alarmed.

'Well, I could have sworn it was herself, in person. But someone told me afterwards that the real Teresa is in a place called Alba, near Salamanca.'

'Oh. It's an effigy, then.'

'I suppose so. But it didn't stop me feeling a bit weird in its presence. It had a sort of authority, you know, lying there, as I thought, for four hundred years and not a wrinkle out of place. Oblivious to everything, and yet still there, being an influence on things. I can tell you, the twenty thousand pesetas were burning a hole in my pocket and I got out of there as quickly as, I suppose, respect would allow, and got the next train to Madrid.'

'And they were waiting for you?' Tess was grinning.

'The *Guardia*? No. No, I got away with it.'

They laughed together.

'How about you? You have to tell me about you.'

'Me?' Somehow she had forgotten he might ask that and now she was uncomfortable. He was waiting, his eyes questioning.

'What time is it?' She uncovered his watch and looked for herself. 'Twenty past two! My God, I have to run!'

He looked up at her in mute appeal as she donned her coat. She was in a quandary. She liked him and his tall tales, if she could keep him at arm's length, but she guessed that he would insidiously occupy her life.

'I have to run,' she repeated, biting her lip. 'I'm here at lunch hour some days. 'Bye.'

The time had flown. The God-awful time had flown!

- *Five* -

The Special-Branch cars sped along Fairview Road, their sirens wailing, the flashing beacons held on the roof by the second man. A marked squad car emerged from a side street, its tyres screeching, and followed them. Then, as if on cue, an ice-cream van cruised by, playing its barrel-organ jingle, 'A-Hunting We Will Go'. How those people sold ice-cream in this weather she could not tell.

She realized Arthur was looking up at her as they walked by the park and glanced down at him, flashing a nervous smile. He persisted. Was he reading her thoughts? He never looked at her like that; he always looked straight ahead, absorbed in himself.

'What's wrong, Arthur?' she asked, unable to keep the sharpness out of her voice, yet without the nerve to look at him. She could see from the side of her eye and that was enough.

'Why are you so quiet?' he demanded. 'You always talk to me on the way home.'

'Is that why you always look straight ahead and never say a word?' she countered. This was one opportunity she refused to miss. He considered her point and smiled, as if acknowledging its truth. Then he looked ahead as usual, though still smiling faintly.

What a strange child I've given life to, she marvelled. As always, the realization made her a little afraid, but she was very pleased too, that he had missed her talking to him, even if it was usually about nothing at all.

Arthur picked at his food. Usually he ate it in a functional, matter-of-fact way. Tess was tempted to hurry him, but she saw that he was getting through it, however slowly. Once or twice he glanced at her to see how she was reacting but she pretended not to notice. She tried chatting to him, to make up for her silence on the way home, but he just answered in monosyllables or with a shrug.

Later, he went to the living-room to watch the cartoons as usual. The evenings were bright for noticeably longer, so that Arthur knelt in a grey light before the television. Tess watched him from the doorway and gnawed her knuckles. She felt bad that he should be so alone. He should have a brother or sister, or at least she ought to be around to tell him stories and tuck him in at night. He shouldn't be kneeling alone in front of a machine, her forlorn child. Just then, a cartoon cat was squashed and Arthur laughed.

'Arthur!' she barked.

He turned, his eyes hard and unfamiliar, his face contorted in hatred. Her anger subsided as quickly as it had come, and she faltered, confused and afraid.

'Where is Annie? I haven't seen her ...'

He got to his feet and ran against her, his little fists pummelling her body. Surprised, she hardly felt the blows at first. Then she reacted, and struck him continuously, without a word, and conscious only of release. He battled with her, silently, blindly and without caring. She beat him until both were exhausted, and gasping, reaching for the armchair, she fell into it. His back was turned to her, his body jerked in sobs, but no sound came except his broken breath. She pitied him and reprimanded herself, despite the increasing pain in her shin and the ache in her ribs; but behind all that, violence had given her a craved-for satisfaction, and for the moment she refused to be appalled by this.

Arthur recovered and, without looking at her, sat in front of the television again; but when the cat was elongated as a result of its own greed, he did not laugh. She too watched the cartoon for a while, but vacantly. The advertisements replaced the cartoon, and still they watched in silence, like a couple dead to each other.

She roused herself to look after Brian's dinner, feeling awful. Peeling the potatoes, she began to cry. How could her own son do that? Was he going to turn out like his father after all? She bent in two as if suffering a spasm and wept. 'No, no,' she whispered, 'please, it can't be happening. Please, oh please, don't let it happen ... He never kicked me like that.' Then she couldn't hold back her sobbing any longer. When it was over, she steadied herself against the draining-board, and vacantly stood like that for a long time.

She sat by the cooker, watching the food cook. When Brian arrived, she hastily repaired her appearance in the mirror on the window and busied herself setting the table and draining the vegetables, her face momentarily bathed in a cloud of steam. Ironically, she hoped he was in a bad mood, in which case he would sulk and not notice anything unusual. Her timing was perfect. As he sat down, she served up the steaming peas and potatoes and the still-sizzling steak, overdone as he preferred.

She should have left then. He normally made his own tea and washed up. That was their understanding, but she wanted to make it up with Arthur and hadn't the courage to face him for the moment. The cartoons were still on but it would soon be six o'clock, the news would replace the children's programmes, and she would have to make some move. Or more likely, the drama would come to her, overwhelm her, leaving her without control, as ever. Taking an apple, she sat down at the table and ate it slowly, trying to think. Brian, continuing to chew his steak, looked at her curiously. He swallowed, removed a fibre of steak from his front teeth with a prong of his fork, and went on eating, his eyes on his food.

'What's wrong with you?'

'Nothing.' Her mouth was full of apple.

'There's something up. You're usually out of here like a bat out of hell.'

She ignored him, but his curiosity brought her thoughts into focus again. What she feared was Arthur's rebuff, but she'd have to risk it. Yet she sat where she was, gnawing the apple to its core.

'If it's money you want, you can forget it,' he said, finishing his meal and rummaging in his jacket pockets for a cigarette. He swore silently as he realized he had none, then looked about the kitchen. Tess glanced at him anxiously, and then she went cold as he pushed back the chair and went into the living-room. Her heart pumped as if it would explode. It was too late now. It was too late.

'Arthur, have you seen a packet of cigarettes anywhere?'

It seemed to Tess like a long time before Brian returned to the kitchen. She didn't look up, but she could feel him there. 'What happened to Arthur?'

No matter what she would say, it would come out like the cold assault of a child.

'What did you do to Arthur?' he shouted. He grabbed her by the jumper with both hands, hauling her to her feet to face him. He panted with rage.

'Well?' He shook her, and she turned her face away. 'When I ask you a question,' he shouted, 'you answer it. Do you hear me? Do you hear me?' Head bowed to one side, she didn't move. She knew that he wanted her to struggle, or answer back, or even whimper. Then, by some odd code he adhered to, he could strike her with a clear conscience. She knew this of old, and remained unresponsive. He let her go, and stood in front of her, frustrated but waiting for her to make a false move.

He would always remember her like this, she supposed. As she was now she would always live, so long as he did. Tess knew she was on the verge of hysteria, but she could hold this moment in suspension, until the episode had spun out its conclusion. Suddenly Brian had hauled Arthur before her, demanding of her what she had done to his son. A gale broke. She tried not to look at Arthur, who was crying. Of course he was crying. Of course he was. Oh Arthur. She was crying too. Brian was triumphant. It hadn't turned out like he had expected, but he was triumphant. She hadn't moved, or uttered a sound, but she was crying. Brian said something about stopping her seeing his son. A solicitor. Barring order. He was enjoying this overflow, this slopping-out.

He quietened. The venom was gone. She knew it, knew they were only words filling the silence. She looked at Arthur, his eyes swollen from crying and from her blows. Arthur broke free, ran to her and she hugged him. Then she lifted him into her arms. He was heavier than she had expected, but then she hadn't lifted him like this for a long time. Brian was sneering, but his ground had been cut from under him. Arthur clung to her neck.

'Charming. Charming. Well, ye love each other so much, ye can hold onto each other for the rest of the evening. I'm going for a drink.'

Then he was gone. After a few moments the outside door slammed and a blissful silence fell.

She dreamt about Arthur several times after that evening. In her dream she longed to see him, to bathe his healing bruises as if to wash away her brutality and the awful but undeniable feeling of power. He mocked her lack of goodness. She, who had thought herself superior to Brian, was no better than he was, and it galled.

Spring was seeping into the year, giving a definition to things. Tess awoke, thinking about Marian. She'd had some vague dream about her. She went to the toilet, sat on it for a while brooding, until she realized she was cold. There was a letter from Marian. Often, when she dreamt of someone, she heard from them the next day. Usually that seemed to give depth, or warmth, to the letter; but Marian's was brief and hurried, it didn't give anything of herself other than the few moments it took to write it. Her social life took up too much of her leisure to allow her to settle into herself. Her life was all surface. Tess put the letter into the biscuit tin in which she kept all correspondence. She resented Marian's carefree life and brooded over breakfast, sifting the letters in the tin beside her. A glance told her what was in each one. On her loneliest nights she read them until she probably knew them by heart.

It was Wednesday. Doleday. Her time had been changed from afternoon to morning, but she was still on time, only slightly resenting the fact that she could no longer go straight from the dole office to collect Arthur. Her stride was loose and relaxed as she came back along the quays.

She spotted Mungo in D'Olier Street as she stood on the traffic island on O'Connell Bridge. At first she wasn't sure, and then to her surprise she thought it might have been wishful thinking, though she hadn't thought of him in weeks, or not much; but no, it was him right enough. He was still a distance away, walking slowly past Bewley's, but there was no mistaking that walk of his, his left hand in the pocket of his heavy black coat. The lights turned green. She crossed and waited for him, surprised that she was pleased and, even more so, that her heart was thumping. To her relief, his face lit up when he saw her; better still, he blushed.

The awkwardness of their greetings somehow pleased Tess. They interrupted each other nervously, and Tess realized that this had not happened to her since she was a girl. Her dole money allowed her to suggest a coffee again in The Winding Stair, and when he mumbled that he didn't have money she could pat her bag, in which nestled her temporarily plump purse. To occupy her hands, she bought an apple from the fruit seller on Aston Quay.

He recovered once he had the coffee before him, an old blues song in the background, and he smiled. He had just come from another bookshop, Books Upstairs, when she had met him, and he joked about the link between stairs and books. She had forgotten, in her pleasure at seeing him, that he would ask her about herself, but he did.

'Are you married?'

'We've already established that, haven't we?' She shifted on her seat, clutching her cup. 'Yes. I mean, I was. You definitely are, aren't you? I know by the look of you.' She laughed as she said this, it was an attempt to lighten the conversation, but she realized before it was out of her mouth that it was aggressive, an accusation. He didn't, or pretended not to pick up on it.

'Yes, I am. Well, sort of. We've two children, and that keeps us together, I suppose.'

'I see.' He smiled.

'You're separated?'

'Well …' she faltered, 'he's in Berlin, so you could say that, yes.'

'Berlin?' He sat forward, his face bright with interest. 'Really?'

'I left my son with him,' she said, pushing her cup in a small circle. 'I suppose you think that makes me a bad mother. No proper maternal feelings and all that.'

'Don't push your guilt on me.' They glared at each other until he said, 'It's all I can do to handle my own. Tell me about Berlin. About you in Berlin, I mean.'

'Me in Berlin … ? What's your name again?'

'Mungo. And yours?'

'Tess. And I'm sorry Mungo. You're right.' She sighed and looked out the window. 'Me in Berlin?' She looked back at him and grinned. 'God I loved it. Why I came back, I'll never know. The cafés serving breakfast at four o'clock on a Sunday afternoon. It says it all, doesn't it?' She laughed at this scrap from one of Marian's letters, but only to buy her a moment to gather herself.

'But it's so full of people larger than life, you know. I had an Irish friend there called Marian. She saved my sanity when my husband was at his worst – she knew everyone, or so it seemed to me. I remember once she brought me to see this old lady in … what the hell was it called … Nollendorfstrasse! Yes, that's it. The street where Isherwood lived in the thirties.'

'Isherwood?'

'The English writer. You know, *Cabaret*, the film? "Money, Money, Money"?'

He nodded, doubtful but amused.

'Well, it was at night, hardly anyone in the streets, a car passing the intersection now and then, slowly, as if it was kerb crawling. Marian pressed the intercom and answered someone in German, I hadn't a clue, and the door buzzed and she pushed it and we were in. It was like a big adventure for me, the walls clad with marble, spotless and cold, and quiet as the grave. Then we were in one of these old cage-lifts and up we went, three or four floors, and the lights went out, and all we could see was the red glow of the time-switches. A maid, a young Turkish woman, let us in. There was this lovely smell of flowers and wood wax, and there were huge ceramic vases of flowers and plants and ferns, and the parquet floor squeaked and sent a shiver down your spine. There was no hall to speak of, and one room opened into another. In one, there was a tall young woman with her back to us. She had a pile of art books on her desk, I remember, and she was staring at a computer. She obviously made a mistake, because she swore in German, Spanish and English, quite fluently I think.'

'Spanish? Can you remember what she swore in Spanish?'

'Oh no. I just recognized the language. The maid knocked on a tall double door, of mahogany I'd say, and announced us to Frau Pohl. There she was, eighty-five years old, propped up in bed by silk pillows and cushions, a pair of headphones on.'

'Janey.'

'Yeah. It was a hot night, but she was sitting up in bed, dressed as if she was going to the opera, but Marian had told me that she hadn't left her bed in thirty years. Her dress was plain black silk, quite low-cut, and she wore a single pearl, which drew the eye to the clusters of freckles on her chest, as did the long black gloves to the freckles on her forearms. She was a thin bird of a woman, and her eyes were of a cornflower blue, very aware. A silver fox-fur was draped over her shoulders and her silver hair was clasped with a jet brooch.

'The maid caught her attention, and announced us again. Frau Pohl pointed to the headphones, and the maid removed them, and, I presume, announced us a third time. "Ah

Marian," Frau Pohl said in English, ignoring me, "how nice to see you again. Come here and kiss me." Marian smiled and kissed the woman on both cheeks.

'"Frau Pohl," Marian said, "I've brought a friend this evening, she's from Ireland and has come to live in Berlin." "Ah, another Irish," Frau Pohl said, turning her gaze on me. "Berlin has many, it seems." Her accent was strong, but her English caused her no effort. "Several thousand, I hear," Marian said.

"Do you go to concerts?" Frau Pohl asked me. When I said no, she looked at me, you know, as if she pitied me.

"But you are so young!" '

Tess broke off and looked for signs of reaction to the words 'young' and 'pity' but she could discern none. He was a little older than her, a piece of flotsam like herself and, in seeing him like that, it gave her a good feeling of affinity.

'She searched about the cushions until she found a pack of cards. "I think you must have a hard life in Ireland. I will look in the cards and see for myself."

Marian looked at me and I looked at Marian while Frau Pohl shuffled and cut the cards with surprising nimbleness, then scrutinized each one, her nose screwed up as she peered through her glasses, tut-tutting every so often. "Oh my poor child," she said then, and I thought she was foretelling something dire for me, but these cards looked into the past, it seemed. "You are married and have a son. He is eight years old, and naturally you are emotionally close to him, but ... "'

Despite the caricatured German accent, Tess was wary of revealing her troubles to what after all was a stranger, who she now realized she wanted. Then she shrugged, and smiled at him, resuming the character.

'"But, you and your husband ..." Frau Pohl looked up from the cards, then back, and said nothing for a while. "If a woman is unhappy for too long, she eats up everything around her, she sucks it dry until the life is bled white; but that is because she craves for life. When a man is unhappy, he is worse than a beast in a corner, he is eaten away by a wish to destroy, he empties himself of life and light, he sinks lower and lower, until he wants only that which is a perversion of what once made him happy. And the cards say that this is your husband, and the first one is you."'

Tess pushed her cup in semi-circles, and was quiet.

'Phew! And was she right?' Mungo asked after some time.

'Yes. All very black and white, of course.'

'Very. What did she say then?'

'I'll tell you another time. Do you like music?'

'Irish. And Spanish. Some jazz.'

'Do you know Schubert?'

'Naw. Heard of him, that's all.'

'I have a tape if you'd like to hear it.'

'You mean now?'

'Yes ...'

He looked at her, suddenly beware, and her heart pounded at her audacity. Well, is he a man or isn't he? What was all this supposed to lead up to anyway? Damn men. They blame you no matter what you do or say. And then, sweet Jesus, he smiled.

'We might as well improve my education – in case I ever bump into this Frau Pohl.'

She smiled back, repressing a sigh of relief. She must, above all, retain her veneer of composure, otherwise she was lost.

Self-conscious, she led him from The Winding Stair and along the quay. The traffic was deafening, so she just smiled to encourage him and reassure herself. When she closed the heavy door behind them, shutting out the din, she smiled again. He cleared his throat and looked about the bare but still imposing hall.

'A great city for stairs,' he remarked.

'Not as many as Berlin.'

The spring sun washed the hall for a moment, bathing them as they clattered up the bare stairs, before clouding over again. They said nothing, but Mungo betrayed his nervousness by missing his step, and Tess bit her lip. She had hoped he would be confident enough for them both.

Once inside the flat, she noticed he stretched out his hand to touch her, but lost his nerve and turned away. She took a deep breath.

'A nice place you have here,' he said, clearing his throat.

'It's okay,' she said quietly. She lit the gas heater. 'Sit down. I'll get the music and make us a cup of tea.'

In her bedroom, she looked in the mirror and stared at her image, running her fingers along the wrinkles under her eyes.

'I look old,' she whispered. 'But then, he's no great shakes either, so maybe it's okay.' As she slipped the tape into the machine, she wished she could feel a wild desire for him, that he might do something unexpected and wonderful, but all she could feel was her heart beating a little faster because some little bastard of a voice knew she was making a fool of herself. She pressed the button and the music was happy, optimistic, and totally alien to her emotions.

'Where's the jakes?' he called. She turned her head, but didn't answer immediately.

'Down the hall and up the steps,' she called back to him. She listened to the muffled sound of his stream into the bowl, and remembered that the toilet was in a mess, brown from accumulated urea, but at least there were no serious stains, so it wasn't too bad. He wasn't here because she was a good housekeeper. What was he here for? Her bed wasn't much better than the toilet, the spots from her last period were still on the sheets, and that was more significant than the state of the toilet, which flushed. She pulled the blankets off and turned the sheet toe to head, and replaced the blankets loosely almost in one movement. It was then she realized that her bedroom was cold. Damn. Was it going to happen? She didn't know, and didn't know if she cared, but she knew she couldn't wait much longer. She took a deep breath and joined him.

'I like the music,' he said.

'Is that all you like?'

He turned her around, slowly, which was pleasing, but she could feel the tremor in his hands. He looked into her eyes as if he was in great turmoil, or needing to know what she was up to, if she was playing with him or if this was real, and she hoped he wouldn't ask. He kissed her, and she put her tongue into his mouth, but he pulled away, waited a moment, and started again.

It seemed he only wanted her lips, and she went along with it, beginning to enjoy herself. Tentatively, his tongue began to explore her lips, and then her gums and teeth. Fuck! His tongue would jag on her cavities! She launched her own to grapple with his. He flicked rather than thrust in response. He was dictating, which she could accept, but his lack of subtlety irritated her. She wished he could do all this without thinking, as if he had really mastered the skill, if he couldn't be naïvely sincere. She forced her tongue into his mouth again and he allowed her to plunge deeply, before disengaging and turning away.

He kissed her cheek, and her ear, and then her neck which she exposed to him, and pleasure burned along her skin. He was by now unbuttoning her shirt, his tongue in the cleft of her breasts, lingering, for reasons best known to himself, on the one, two, three – fourth rib. She pushed him away, and staring at him in passionate hatred, led him to the bedroom. They were breathing heavily, his eyes fixed on her breasts, but it was her lower clothes that she removed first, and as if in a trance, he took off his jacket, jumper and shirt. Only when he leaned over to untie his shoes did she quickly finish undressing, and before he had the second sock removed, she was safely under the blankets, her belly hidden.

He sat on the other side of the bed to remove his trousers and underpants, so that, daring a glance, all she saw of him was his pale, bony back, a few hairs curling on his shoulders, before he turned and was under the blankets in one movement. Her eyes were almost closed. They must have seemed closed to him, but she saw that he was leaning on an elbow, his tongue nervously moistening the thin lines of his lips, as he watched her, unsure, she thought bitterly, of what to do next. Then, to her surprise, as she hadn't seen or sensed him move, she felt him kiss her, lightly, just as, she realized, she had wanted him to, and her lips parted.

He explored them tenderly, just where they become moist, as Brian had done in an inexplicable moment years before and had not done since. Irritation rose in her again, this time against Brian, but as Mungo's hands moved down her body, as his kiss became fuller, she felt herself beaten, and instead of anger, she was filled with mourning for what should have been, what should have filled that emptiness which had become so much a part of her she hadn't named it until now. His lips were covering her right nipple which was erect and she was crying silently, even as a wave of pleasure rippled through her. Then, inevitably, his fingers inched their way across her bush, having lingered on her belly as if it was a treasure, and she knew they would slip between her legs and find her very wet. Without thinking, she wrenched his fingers away.

'What?' he whispered in bewilderment. 'What? Did I hurt you?'

'I'm sorry,' she said, her voice muffled in the pillow.

'What?' he repeated. She could hear his rapid breathing, feel him get to his knees, and she wiped her eyes in the pillowcase and faced him. Her eyes involuntarily fell on his cock, which wasn't very big, or at any rate not nearly as big as Brian's, but it was full and hard all the same, and she wondered, with a *frisson* of fear, if in his frustration and bewilderment he would rape her.

'I can't,' she whispered. 'I'm sorry.' And then, as an afterthought she said: '... I've my period.'

When, in apprehension, she glanced down at his cock again, it was, as if by a miracle, soft and small and somehow pathetic, and it crossed her mind how powerful a word could be. She bit her lip. His chest was still heaving and his face flushed, but his eyes were blank, and she wondered if the memory of a similar rejection had made him crazy and prone to violence; but after some moments in which she truly feared him, he recovered and dressed at the foot of the bed. He turned then, eyes averted, looking for his jacket, and she stifled a shriek of laughter with her hand.

'Mungo ...' she said, struggling for control, noticing how he was still shaking.

'What?'

'Mungo ...' and she couldn't help smiling, though her pity had finally vanquished the laughter, 'Mungo, your trousers are on back to front.'

'Jesus,' he whispered, and she was in agony at humiliating him further, but then he saved them both by smiling. 'I think I came into the world back to front.' Then he set about putting it right.

'Mungo? Thanks.'

He said nothing until he was fully dressed and ready to go.

'For what?'

She shrugged and pursed her lips, glancing at him nervously. And then he left.

It had been so long, she had wanted it to be right first time, knowing that it never had been. Given the chance, he could have given her comfort, the attention her body craved. It was true she had relished the power she had over him for those few moments, its delight heightened by fear, but it had quickly soured, and she wept in rage at whatever had made her act against herself.

- *Six* -

Ethna went down with chicken-pox, and Mungo stayed by her bedside and told her stories until she slept. They revived forgotten memories. Some detail always surfaced in the telling, though in truth there were few adventures to recount. One day had blended imperceptibly into the next, for the most part, but Ethna didn't mind hearing a story over and again and spotted a new detail every time, which was perhaps why he resisted invention. He was afraid he would have been found out. So it was: the comic personalities of the cows; the dog's genius with the sheep; the silken *bainbh* born to the huge sow under the warm lamp; the stream alive with flitting trout; all which once seemed eternal and now seemed on an island of the past, a realm of wonder for his children. To bring them to see it now was like showing them a shadow. Only through memory did it take on flesh, and he realized that memory was only so enriched by the profound familiarity of seeing and experiencing the same animals and people and things day after day, in their own places, according to the season. It was, he thought, high time he brought the children to see their grandmother again.

He resumed his jogging. It was spring and he could lay off his heavy coat, but whenever he came across a jogger in the accepted apparel, he remembered his boots and jeans and heavy jumper, and slowed to a walk until the real jogger was well past. He preferred the empty acres of the Phoenix Park, away from the roads and where only the deer would stare at him, running like a countryman over a bog as he had done so often as a boy. His arm was strong again, weaker than the other but strong enough to pump it in a matching rhythm as he ran. He would soon have to face a medical referee to determine if he was still entitled to his disability benefit, but he put that out of his mind, enjoying the clean air and the fresh smells of spring. The phallic monument to Wellington provided a line for him to run towards and, judging from experience how much puff he had in hand, he sprinted towards it, running up the steps of the plinth two at a time until he reached it, and he gasped, hands on knees.

He sat down, uncomfortably sweaty, and calmed. It had been a month now since he'd seen her, perhaps more, and he had thought of her every day, sometimes only fleetingly, before he fell into sleep, or for a few moments when he woke, but sometimes, when he was alone, he would think of no one and nothing else for as long as he was left in peace. It was funny, how she was in the city, there along the quays below him, no more than a few minutes bus-ride away, and yet he hadn't seen her in a month. He hadn't gone into town for a while after the fiasco, but still, in a city where you met people you knew at every corner, she may as well have been on the far side of the earth.

He wondered if it had been a womanly ploy to make him lust for her, but dismissed the thought. There had been real hurt in her eyes, and it haunted him. He longed to heal that hurt, as if only by doing so would he gain his own peace. And it was obvious that she too was embarrassed by what had happened. This cheered him, as it brought them back on equal terms. Them. Us. We. Why did he think of them as a couple, two people who interacted in an intimate way? His momentary happiness drained away as he realized he had been harbouring a fantasy for a long time. He looked about him, trying to forget it, to maintain some dignity; but the more he tried to rid himself of her image, the more his involuntary being rebelled. That this should happen to him at his age was the worst humiliation, as if he were a youth again, ignorant of women.

He ran blindly down the steps and around the monument until he was wheezing, and he staggered to a halt. Here he was, literally running away from her. The green expanse of park land reminded him of Wexford and he was conscious again of the strong pull of the countryside. Connie wouldn't go, of course, but the children would love it and maybe Connie would like a few days to herself. Strange woman, Connie. She liked her own company, but she could sing her song, a glass in her hand. Those few hours of revelry, of forgetting everything, were further apart as the money grew tighter, and the only thing that bound them was putting the children before everything. How long was it now – months? With her barricades down she liked her sex, and he recalled that deep grunt of pleasure when he slid into her, if he was fortunate enough not to be too drunk himself, or unsure, or too tired, when she would turn away from him as if to say, it's always the same, the same old story.

She was washing out the fridge when he got home. The sunlight reflected off the back wall which he had painted white a few years before, and the back door was open so that a cheerful freshness enlivened the kitchen.

'Have a nice walk?' she asked without turning around.

'Yeah. I was up in the Park, as far as the Welly Monument.'

She sniffed. 'You stink of sweat.'

He sniffed under his arms. It was true.

'Sure sweat's a natural thing.'

'So's shit.'

She got off her knees, and cast him an ironic glance as she squeezed the cloth into the plastic basin.

'Right,' he said. 'I'll wash in a minute.' He was stalling and she knew it.

'You want something, don't you?' She had got fresh water and was down on her knees again, rinsing out the fridge.

'How's the cash-flow these days?'

'Ah. Tight as usual. Why?'

'I was thinking it was time we went down to Wexford.'

'You know I can't stand that mother of yours, and she can't stand me.'

'I know, I know. But she's the children's grandmother.'

'They've two grandparents in Donegal. When was the last time they went to see them?'

'They've been down twice in the last year, haven't they?'

'Oh yes, they have to come down, don't they? Otherwise they'd never see their grandchildren, never mind their daughter.'

'They have the free travel.'

'So has your mother. As well as a car.'

It was true, but this was getting nowhere.

'Why don't I bring the children to Wexford, seeing as ye women don't get on, and you can slip up to Letterkenny for a few days?'

She paused, and he knew he'd said the right thing. Even if she had been in Dublin for fifteen years, he had always noticed that a break amongst her own people charged her batteries, and in truth she hadn't been north for over a year.

'We don't have the money for both,' she said, and continued her work. He deemed it wise to withdraw, to let the thought settle, and he went to the bathroom to wash his stinking body.

Two weeks later, he handed her his disability money as usual. She sat at the kitchen table and counted it carefully, then produced money from a tin box.

'I suppose you want to go by train.' He did. 'There's enough here for my bus and a phone call to Letterkenny, a phonecall to Wexford, our bus fares in and out of town, train fares to and from Gorey and a few bob for comics and sweets for the children.'

'Great.'

'It's not great, but we can scrape it if we can count what we save by scrounging off our families for the weekend. And I need to get out of these four walls.'

'Me too.'

'Right. It's settled then.'

There were tears as Connie hugged her children at Busáras, but as they walked up the steep approach to Connolly Station, Aidan and Ethna bickered and had soon forgotten their mother. They were early, and Mungo settled them on the seaboard side of a non-smoking carriage, bribing them with crisps and a supply of comics which they would happily read a second or third time, or so he hoped.

He was looking forward to this trip. On the phone his mother had been cool at first, which he knew was her way of making her point at his prolonged neglect, but before his money ran out she had agreed to meet them in Gorey, having subtly ascertained that Connie would not be with them.

He glanced up-river as they passed over Butt Bridge, and he wondered what Tess was doing or thinking at that moment. How many weeks was it now? Almost six. He bridled at their separation, which seemed unnatural somehow. He looked about him, wondering if his face had betrayed his thoughts. He would have to shut her out, at least until he was alone in the big field at the back of the house, when he could risk shouting out her name and have it echo over several hills.

'What are you smiling for, Daddy?'

'Eh? Was I smiling?'

'Yeh.'

'Yeah Dad, you looked like you'd won the bleedin' Lottery,' Aidan joined in.

'That'll be the day. Lotteries don't bleed by the way.' They thought that was hilarious. 'Go on back now to your comics.'

'But why were you smiling, Daddy?' Ethna persisted. Trust Ethna.

'What, did you never see me smile before? Look, we're on holiday, aren't we? And you're happy when you go on holidays, aren't you? And it's a lovely day, and it will be even nicer in Knockmore. That's a good reason to smile, isn't it?'

Content, they went back to their comics, but he thought how sad it was that he couldn't tell his children, or anyone, not even the woman in question, that he was in love. At least and at last he had said it to himself. He would have to tell lies to hide it, even to Tess, and he knew how much it cost him to lie, or even to avoid the truth; how it made him say foolish things, make foolish gestures, act foolishly.

He dozed for a while, until they came to Killiney Bay, a curve of sea and land culminating in Wicklow Head, the glory of which he never tired.

'Look,' he said, 'isn't that lovely?' They looked.

'We saw it before, Dad,' Aidan said.

'What? Well you didn't see it today. Something really beautiful is beautiful in different ways every time you see it.'

'Really?' Aidan was impressed by this and they both checked it out again.

'It's nice,' Ethna said.

'Even if it didn't change everytime,' he said in an effort to be truthful, 'it's good to look at something nice more than once – many times!'

'Why?' Aidan asked.

'Why? Because ... it makes you feel good, that's why.'

They looked out again, and this time they watched the sea until it was blocked from view near Bray, and Mungo wondered if they had learned what beauty could be to them, and if they would remember this afternoon.

Below Greystones there was another favourite stretch, with the sea close to the tracks, the mountains in the middle distance to the west, with marshland and fresh water between. Today he was luckier than usual.

'Look!' he said, pointing. There were swans on the water, basking in the sun. The children were entranced, and now he was sure they were touched, and he felt wonderful and more at peace than he had been in a long time. His happiness lasted while they passed through the spring foliage which flanked the track below Wicklow, over the black, pure river beneath the bridge below Rathdrum, past the Arklow golf-course where the stones and banks of the river were discoloured by the copper sediment from the defunct mines at Avoca – even past the fertilizer factory, spewing out its sulphurous smoke, his happiness held.

Only when they passed Inch Creamery, a few miles from Gorey, was it displaced by a need to be prepared, in case his mother could read it on his face, or worse, read into it. He wasn't supposed to be happy with Connie, that was a guiding principle, so it would follow that something or someone other than Connie was making him happy.

Despite what had happened, despite their separation, despite his despair, he was happy. Or to be more precise, Tess had given him a depth of feeling he hadn't believed possible, and it was the knowledge of his capacity to feel so profoundly that made him happy. He wallowed in the warmth which flooded him, as if the pain of the last six weeks had never happened. The children had been miraculously quiet, reading, telling jokes and even talking to each other as companions, which was rare and to be noted. As the approach of Gorey was announced, Mungo pulled himself together, organizing the children and preparing their paltry luggage.

'Where's Granny?' Ethna demanded, looking worried. Mrs Kavanagh was not on the platform to greet them.

'She's probably in the car outside,' Aidan reassured her. Ethna would have forgotten, but that was where she usually waited. Mungo spotted the blue Ford and sent his children ahead. They ran to the car, but when they reached it and Mrs Kavanagh opened the door to greet them, he saw that as always they suddenly became shy, and Ethna looked back to him for reassurance. Mrs Kavanagh drew Aidan into the car to kiss him and he acquiesced, though he squirmed a little.

'Give Granny a kiss,' Mungo told Ethna, but Granny was still caressing Aidan's face, telling him what a lovely boy he was, and for a few awkward moments, Ethna was stranded. Then, to Aidan's relief, Mrs Kavanagh shifted her attention to Ethna.

'Oh aren't you lovely?' She exclaimed, drawing Ethna into the car as Aidan escaped into the back seat. Ethna was more comfortable with the attention, and pointedly looked down to her new dress, which wasn't new, but had been given to her by her maternal grandmother, was only worn on special occasions and was now almost too small for her.

'What a lovely dress!' she declared, thus gaining Ethna's favour. She glanced at Mungo by way of acknowledging his presence, but continued her caressing and praise of Ethna. Mungo wondered how long it had been since she had touched a human being.

'You've grown up into the sky,' she said in wonder, guiding Ethna into the back seat where Aidan was slumped, his hands in his pockets. Mungo sat in and kissed his mother lightly on her weakly proffered cheek.

'Well,' she said. 'You're welcome.'

'Do you want me to drive?' he asked as usual, knowing the answer.

'You can't drive with that arm of yours,' she said, starting, and chugging onto the junction with the Avenue.

'It's much better,' he said. 'I've been exercising it a lot.'

'Well you can give me a hand at home, so. There's enough for you to do, God knows.'

Being Friday, Gorey was heavily congested with traffic, and the conversation was for the moment dominated by Mrs Kavanagh's nervous difficulty in negotiating it. As they crossed the main street to head out the Hollyfort Road, Mungo recalled how he had begun to drink in Gorey during the long, hot summers of his teens after a hard day on the farm. Then the forays to Courtown Harbour with his mates from Monaseed and Carnew to dance with Dublin girls who knew more than he did, such as the layout of the locally notorious courting ground.

Mrs Kavanagh was by now giving a running commentary on the families who lived along the route: births, deaths and marriages; jobs, redundancies and emigration; exams, harvests and financial standing; affairs, solitudes and diseases, whether alcoholic or cancerous. To Mrs Kavanagh it was a drama, the stuff of life. To her adult son it seemed like a chronicle of local history, of a time not far removed, perhaps, but removed nonetheless, the personae like dimming photographs in his memory.

As they approached Hollyfort his interest quickened. He had known some of the people there as he grew up, and as they turned uphill towards Monaseed, past the Protestant church and graveyard where some old friends of the family were buried, it seemed as if he was slowly being restored to the fabric of the area.

Mrs Kavanagh changed gear to climb the steep hill to Knockmore. Her commentary had hardly stopped for breath. To the left was the village of Monaseed, where Mungo had gone to school and Mass, and he interrupted his mother to remind the children of this. They sat forward in interest.

'Monaseed,' he said, relishing his fatherly role of explication. 'The name comes from the Irish *Moin na Saighead* – Meadow of the Swords.'

'There's one now for you, Aidan,' Mrs Kavanagh said. 'Meadow of the Swords.'

'Me too!' Ethna protested.

'You too, Ethna,' Mungo laughed. 'There was a battle there in 1798.'

'A battle!' Aidan exclaimed.

'A battle!' Ethna copied.

'Yes, a battle. Well, a small one. Hollyfort – that comes from the Irish *Ráth an Chuilinn*. And then Kilanerin, that's another village farther back, that means *Coill an Iarainn* – The Wood of Iron.'

'What does Knockmore mean?' Aidan asked.

'Do you know something, Aidan, I never thought of that. Do you know, Mother?'

'Well now, I don't,' she said, concentrating on getting the car up the hill.

'Let me see. Knock – that comes from *cnoc*, which means?'

'Hill,' Aidan said.

'And more – that comes from *mór*, which means?'

'Big. So it means Big Hill,' Aidan smiled.

'Big Hill,' Ethna repeated.

In a few minutes they turned off the road and down a rough laneway to a farmhouse partially hidden by trees. An old dog struggled out to greet them. A sow, rooting in the grass near the edge of the yard, ignored them but a pet sheep, trotting in from a field, stopped dead, regarded the visitors with confidence, then came up to receive attention from the delighted children.

'You should bring them down more often,' Mrs Kavanagh observed with satisfaction. 'Young children need freedom, and pets, and all those things you took for granted when you were growing up.'

'They prefer computer games nowadays, Mother.'

'Nonsense. Children will always love the same, simple things. Come on,' she said. 'Let's get the kettle on. Ye must be starving.'

The farm, he saw, was vivid with life: the animals, always so unpredictable, the birdsong, the trees, the hens clucking in the yard. It was like being in a timewarp in the farm-house, a strong two-storey building where the only change in a generation was the phone and colour television. All the old furniture remained, the same lino on the kitchen, the Aga cooker which had seldom been out, the heavy kettle seemingly always on the boil. And the oleograph of the Sacred Heart, the red electric lamp burning beneath it like a coronary pulse. He had to swallow to get a grip on himself. Every detail conspired to drag him back to childhood, to being a child, even.

'Your old clothes and boots are under the stairs. There's enough for you to be doing,' his mother called.

'Right,' he called back. He needed to do something which would physically tax him, to do the things a child hadn't the strength to do. As he changed, he heard the children laughing outside. They were making fun of the sheep.

After a tea of fresh scones and butter, and some home-made apple tart, he cleared a drain the pigs had trampled and used two flagging stones, which were exactly where he had remembered them to be, to shore it up. He cleaned out the pig house and spread fresh straw. Once, his mother crossed the yard with an air of satisfaction. The children were some-where down the fields, with the dog and pet sheep. His arm hurt, but he didn't care. The more he worked, the more he could avoid thinking or daydreaming or remembering. It was almost a pure state, a technique for being in the present and free of guilt or yearning.

They sat down to dinner at six thirty and Mrs Kavanagh switched on the radio news out of habit, but it was low and in the background, her real interest being in the children. Her absorption in them made her look as if she was in her prime again as she ruled her seven children, but happier, more relaxed, delighting in Aidan and Ethna's rapturous account of their afternoon. Mungo smiled. It was as if they were living out the stories he had told them, which had been replaced in their imaginations by experience, an experience enriched by the stories. Once or twice Mrs Kavanagh glanced at Mungo as she laughed. Were they casual glances, he wondered, a shared indulgence of the innocence of children by two knowing adults? Somehow he doubted it.

After dinner the television was switched on to see a fav-ourite programme, a long-running soap which bored Mungo. The children watched it with apparent interest, but then they loved television. When it was over she rummaged in a drawer for a pack of cards and called them over to the table. 'You too,' she commanded Mungo.

Oh God, he hated cards, and he suddenly longed to be with Tess, to ask her to finish her Berlin story. A bland TV pro-gramme remained on as the games of 25 or Snap progressed to the obvious delight of the grandmother and her grandchil-dren. The son and father survived, feigning an occasional laugh, consoling himself that Tess existed, and had given him a glimpse of a risky but interesting vitality. It was good to know he was capable of feeling alive.

The card games lasted until Aidan suppressed a yawn and Ethna wilted, the fresh air and excitement combining with the hour to tire them. Mrs Kavanagh put them to bed and Mungo settled to watch a show which had been running for as long as he could remember. It could be very interesting or very boring, within the same hour and a half.

Mrs Kavanagh returned with the air of someone who had done a job she was mistress of, rubbing her hands and suppressing a smile.

'Well well, those children have grown into the sky – who's on 'The Late Late' ?' she asked in one breath.

'An American writer.'

'Ah, we'll make a cup of tea at the break,' and she instantly tuned in to the American who had spent much of his early life addicted to drugs and petty crime. At the break Mungo offered to make the tea but she refused, and returned with tea, scones, apple tart and a tumbler of whiskey for Mungo, having missed an excellent ensemble of unaccompanied women singers.

'Aidan has healed up well,' she said at the next break.

'Yes.'

'You'd never have believed it after the fire.'

'No. No you wouldn't.'

'They love it here, you know.'

'Yes, I know. And it's good for them.'

'That's right. It's good for them. And I can't carry on for much longer on my own.'

'Mother, what are you trying to say?' He remembered now that they'd had this conversation before.

'Well now, it's obvious isn't it? You've no job in Dublin, you're living hand to mouth there with two young children roaming the streets, who *love* being with their granny, and I'm not able for the farm any more. I was never able for it on my own, you know that well, and yourself and the children could have a wonderful time here, and we could all be happy.' She had worked herself into a state and was almost in tears.

'Connie doesn't like the country,' he said, though he was thinking of Tess.

'I could never see what you saw in her. You were never suited, you know, and I've a fair idea you know that now.'

'What makes you think that?'

'Ah now, I know. I'm not a fool. I know you think I am, but I'm not.'

'Are you saying ... ?' 'The Late Late Show' resumed, and they left the question hanging. I'm going to die, he thought, knowing I've lived an awful life, and he drank half the whiskey back. His heart pounded from the shock of the alcohol, but he didn't care.

'Will you have a drink?' he asked after a while.

'No no,' she said, keeping her eyes on the screen. 'But you help yourself.'

He didn't move, except to sip the whiskey, which he was now enjoying. The one thing I really went after in my life, he thought, was marriage to Connie. And I was right. She was the only happiness I've ever had, but now it's all gone wrong, it's over, and I've probably half my life to live. He clutched his glass tighter, and this time drank back a mouthful. There was another commercial break, and Mrs Kavanagh prepared herself for another speech.

'Well, as you well know, there were seven children reared in this house, though the Lord knows, I sometimes ask myself what I reared ye for.'

'For emigration, of course,' Mungo laughed.

'Oh you're very funny.'

'Well it's true. That's what happened. And,' he added cruelly, 'I'm thinking of going myself.' She paled for a moment, but then, deciding he was baiting her, recovered.

'There were seven children reared in this house, and there's room to spare. I could have a little flat and Connie could have the run of the rest of the house.' There, it was said, the die was cast. Then, to push home her point, 'I'm leaving the place to you anyway, so what's the point in wasting away above in Dublin when you could be leading a healthy life down here?'

'I thought the place was Tom's – he's the eldest, isn't he?'

'He's in Australia.'

'Have you heard from him?'

'Oh he never writes. Too much trouble. Sheila is the only one who writes. She's coming home with the children in the summer – she hopes.'

'Ah. Good.'

'It's funny how no one comes in the winter, when you need them most.'

'I do,' he said, aggrieved that he didn't count, as usual.

The programme returned with an Irish singer in a cowboy outfit, singing a sentimental song about a love far away.

'Wasn't that lovely,' Mrs Kavanagh said.

'I've heard worse,' Mungo said truthfully.

The next day proved as sunny and fresh, and they were out early feeding the pigs and hens, checking the sheep and the small herd of bullocks. Mungo was anxious to clear any work that his mother had been unable to do, but as a neighbour helped her out once a week there wasn't that much left over at this time of year. She hadn't kept cows since her husband had died, and the milk in her fridge was bought at the local shop. So were the vegetables, even the potatoes. That seemed to be common nowadays. At least Mrs Kavanagh still kept hens.

The sheep were all present and correct; the bullocks were content. He continued into a broad empty field leading down to the valley. On the far hill he could make out the spire of the Hillwell church; beyond that, the Wicklow mountains. Nearer, to his right were Annagh Hill and Croghan. *Cruachán*: stack or small mountain. Its full name: Croghan Kinsella. Just at this moment, as the clouds scudded across the sun, he stopped. If he stayed quite still and didn't think, perhaps he could hold onto it for a moment, this easiness where he and his surroundings were in harmony. It passed. He could still appreciate it, but that elusive relationship was gone. After such an experience it seemed foolish not to live here, but it only required a brief reflection to remember its bleakness in winter, and the isolation of the farm. His mother would continue to rule, of course. She was too set in her ways to change. He felt guilty because it was in his hands to transform her loneliness into a sense of continuity and fulfilment, but he knew the price was the destruction of what little autonomy he had. His siblings had removed themselves from such guilt, and could justify their long absences by distance and the responsibilities to families supported by good incomes. Except, perhaps, Tom. Sheila and Jimmy were married in England, with families. Ned, Lizzie and Matt were married in the States, with families. But Tom had been married twice, and divorced twice. Tom could never come home. He had a son by his first marriage, and two daughters by his second, but they were grown-up now. Tom was the outcast, the one who was never mentioned if possible, the one who had let the family down, who had thrown away his inheritance and all that he had been brought up to believe. His mother claimed that Tom had put his father in an early grave, although his marriage problems had surfaced after the accident. Having done that, he had not come home to the funeral. In fact he hadn't been home since his first divorce.

Mungo looked across the wide field, the biggest on a farm of fifty-two Irish acres. If he did in fact inherit it, it would cause him endless trouble as his siblings looked for their inheritance. The best thing would be to sell it, if he outlived his mother – which was not a foregone conclusion – and divide what was left after debts. And if for a moment he could fantasize that there would be no debts, no inheritance claims – what could he do? He would live in Dublin during the week, bring his family here at the weekends, or perhaps in winter come on his own, and little by little cover the farm with trees: oak, mostly, ash, beech, copper beech, birch, silver birch, and near the house, if it would grow here, a strawberry tree. He laughed out loud. Wouldn't that be wonderful? The colours in autumn would be fabulous. That would be his dream.

That evening, the children watched cartoons as Mrs Kavanagh made dinner, and Mungo retired to his room. He had shared it with two brothers, and now it was crammed with old drawers, their polish long faded. He lay down, staring at the ceiling, drifting through his thoughts of the afternoon. The Angelus struck on the television below, and his children called their grandmother. He closed his eyes, then rolled off the bed to go downstairs. At the door he hesitated before going over to the first drawer. It was full of loose photos, pamphlets, cuttings from the local paper which had lost their relevance many years before, and a collection of almanacs. The drawer beneath was stuck, and it took him a while to open, but he was patient. If he had one thing in abundance it was time, and he was rewarded. There were several old photo albums, mostly in black and white, and some of the earlier photos were tiny, their subjects, mostly gone to their rewards, barely recognizable. He was in some of them, mostly among the coloured ones, and there were some of his father, usually with his mother. Mungo looked very closely at one he didn't remember, a photo obviously taken in the mid-forties, possibly before they were married. They would have been much younger than Mungo was now. It was strange to think of them like that.

And then, in another album which seemed even older, he found a photo he had never seen before. It was of a soldier, dressed in khaki. Puzzled, Mungo looked at it closely. It was hard to say, but when he compared it with the forties photo of his parents it was obvious that the soldier was his father. Perhaps it was one of his father's brothers, who had also been in England during the war, but as Mungo stared at the photo he knew in his heart who it was, and that he had uncovered this secret after a silence of almost fifty years.

'Mother,' he asked quietly as she laid the table for dinner, 'Was Father in the British Army?'

'Shh!' Her eyes darted in fear in case the children had heard. She was very pale, and clutched a dinner plate on the table, unable to look at Mungo. Then she took a deep breath, and continued as if nothing had happened. The veil had been drawn over again.

He drank more whiskey and woke on Sunday with a hangover. After Mass, through which he dozed, Mrs Kavanagh brought them though south Wicklow, stopping off in a hotel in Avoca for lunch, which emphasized yet again Mungo's lack of money. On the way back they stopped at Hillwell church, where Mrs Kavanagh lit candles. Mungo did not have to guess the fervent wish which one of them represented.

'Make a wish to God,' she whispered to the children. 'I've lit a candle each for you.'

They closed their eyes and wished, the candlelight reflected on their faces. There was a tenpenny piece in Mungo's trouser pocket, and he dropped the coin into the donation box and lit a candle. He had one burning desire, and that was to see Tess.

'What did you wish, Daddy?' Ethna whispered.

'I wished that we'll all be happy.'

'That's what I wished too.'

'I asked God that we'll all see each other again soon,' Mrs Kavanagh said, looking directly at Mungo.

'What did you wish, Aidan?' This time Ethna's voice resounded around the church.

'Like Granny,' he said, but without conviction, Mungo thought. Like his father, he had a secret wish.

'Good boy,' Mrs Kavanagh said. 'We will see each other again soon, so.'

Outside, the children played an impromptu game of tig in the neat grounds.

'You'll see that Aidan's wish is met, won't you?' Mrs Kavanagh said quietly.

'As soon as we can afford it,' Mungo said.

'I have a few shillings set aside, I can send you the money.'

'No. No there's no need for that.'

'Humph. You and your empty pride. The very same as your father.' They sat into the car, but before she started, an idea occurred to her. 'Children, would you like to come down to Granny for your holidays?'

'Yeeaass!' they shouted in unison.

'They're big enough now, you know,' she said, looking over to Mungo.

'You mean on their own?'

'Please, Dad,' Aidan said. 'It'd be mega.'

'Please, Daddy,' Ethna imitated. 'It'd be mega.'

Mrs Kavanagh beamed.

'I'll have to ask your mother,' he said to the children.

The evening train was a beautiful sight. He was glad they had come. It had been necessary and the children had loved it and adored their grandmother. But Mungo had had to confront a problem which in Dublin he could put to the back of his mind. It was a cruel fate that had left his mother to cope alone, but there was nothing he could do about it. It was as if she had some lingering, incurable disease.

Crestfallen at their loss of freedom, the children were quiet, and succumbing to the soporific after-effects of the mountain air, they were asleep by Rathdrum. They had been lucky to get a seat. Most of the passengers were young people, returning, Mungo supposed, to college or work after a weekend at the family hearth. This was how it began, for those who were lucky enough not to have to go directly, still wet behind the ears, to another country, usually England. How many of them, he wondered, had their future planned; how many took it for granted they would go? Mungo had been lucky, or relatively so, coming to maturity at a time when such pressures were waning, and if he hadn't made the most of the freedom he hadn't realized was his, then the fault lay with himself. Mungo looked around him, wondering what it was like for them now, embarking on their lives. His head dropped. The weekend was catching up with him, too. His children slept peacefully. In a few years they would be on a train, travelling though a strange countryside, leaving himself and Connie behind. As he dozed, he wished them safe journey.

'Daddy, you're snoring!' Ethna was pulling his hair, which both Ethna and Aidan found amusing. Even more amusing was his bloodshot eyes, looking at them with vague recognition. He took a deep breath and smiled at them. They were passing Sandymount Strand, and so within a few minutes of arrival. The tide was out, and two horses were being exercised by the water-line. Nearer the railway, a man was digging for bait, or maybe shellfish, leaving a haphazard trail of upturned sand.

The children, it seemed, had forgotten the country already, but as they walked up the platform at Connolly Station they were more good-humoured and tolerant of each other than they had been for some time. And then, at the exit they spotted their mother and ran to her. She was the last person Mungo had expected to see. The children were excited, trying to tell her everything at once, and she was laughing. When was the last time he had seen her laughing, except in a pub with her girlfriends? She looked up at Mungo and smiled, and, warily, he smiled back.

'Ye had a good time, then?' She left the children and came to Mungo, taking him by surprise by kissing him on the mouth.

'Aye,' he said, seeing that Ethna, in particular, approved. 'These two had a ball.'

Connie put the children to bed that evening. Mungo heard them laughing and joking with her. Outside it was dark and cool. He went to the window and stared, idly aware of the flickering yellow street lamp. He realized it was raining softly. Connie had been nice to him – obviously her break had done her a lot of good; but having wanted a return of their closeness for so long, he felt deadened by its imminence. It was as though there should be a neutral interval, a mending, almost day by day, back to the time when they were easy with one another. To begin again as if nothing had been amiss was to begin without trust, and so it was false, but he knew he wouldn't say this, he knew he would go through the motions, and he wasn't sure whether this was because he wanted whatever comfort he could snatch, or if he was too cowardly to face unpleasantness, or whether in fact he didn't care.

Connie was standing behind him and he tensed slightly in case she should touch him.

'I'll make a cup of tea,' she said.

He stayed at the window as she busied herself making the tea, but he caught the aroma of fresh country bread as she sliced it, and when he heard the tea pour he finally gave in to the inevitable and sat at the table.

'You're very quiet,' she remarked. 'Is something bothering you?'

'Yeah,' he said, grateful for a plausible excuse. 'My mother wants us to move in with her. She said she's leaving the farm to me. She says she'll take a flat in the house and leave the rest to us. It's a big house, as you'll remember.'

Connie was silent for a while, sipping her tea. Then she asked him what he thought of the idea.

'I don't know. What do you think?'

'If your mother has a flat to herself and stays out of the way, maybe it's a good idea. The children obviously love it, it's your inheritance, and we're not getting anywhere here, are we?'

He shouldn't have mentioned the flat. He had walked himself into life imprisonment, and, yet again, he thought of Tess. Connie put her hand on his.

'Don't look so worried. We'll talk about it another time. There's a lot to consider after all. Alright?' He nodded. 'Come to bed,' she whispered, and the implication of her tone was unmistakable.

In bed Connie did not notice that his caresses were automatic, and it seemed that no matter where or how he touched her her pleasure increased, and she began to caress him feverishly in turn. He prayed that he wasn't about to make her pregnant, because despite himself he was fully erect. As he entered her she grunted and her face contorted, but a deep resentment welled up in Mungo as he thrust. He couldn't name its source, but it drove him to push deeper and harder in ever-increasing brutality, beyond when Connie climaxed in uncontrollable sobs, until he shouted out his own climax and they fell into the darkness together.

- Seven -

The repeated loudspeaker exhortation to get her key cut now bore in on Tess's reveries. She had been looking at the prices of paint, thinking it would be nice to decorate her flat. It would also be nice to have a spare key cut as a token to the gods who might send her someone special. Arthur said he preferred pale blue; Annie, in her superior way, declared she liked dark yellow.

'Come on,' Tess ordered the children, and led them across to the Car & Household Accessory shop. Annie was delighted, Arthur affected a disinterested air. She bought a packet of pot scrubs, five for Fairview, the rest for her flat. Then, to prod fate, she had a spare key cut, and bought each of the children a plastic game.

Although Mary Street was not pedestrianized, the Saturday shoppers spilled onto the road, oblivious to the crawling traffic. As Tess endured the crowds she focused on a man's back. He was carrying shopping bags and flanked by two children. The little girl fell behind and he half turned to wait for her. It was Mungo.

She turned away. It was bad enough to meet him again, but with children, that was worse, although she realized it was pleasurable to see him, and she resumed her course. He saw her and she swallowed, suddenly unsure, but he had the grace and wisdom to go pale. She smiled, and he smiled back, but she was relieved that he was ill at ease, knowing she was better at hiding such things.

'Hello,' she said. 'Long time no see.'

'How're you? Ah, these are ... this is Aidan, and this is Ethna. Say hello to Tess.' The children mumbled helloes, and Ethna moved as close as possible to her father.

'And this is my son Arthur, and his friend Annie.'

Arthur and Annie said nothing but looked at one another before assessing the other two.

'We're off our feet,' Mungo said. 'Would you like to join us in the park for a minute?'

The small park was a reclaimed graveyard, overshadowed by a deconsecrated church in which Wolfe Tone, Richard Brinsley Sheridan and Sean O'Casey had been baptized, and in which Wesley had once preached.

'What a relief!' Tess laughed as Mungo sat beside her. Arthur tried to scramble onto the slatted bench too. 'Go on now,' she said, 'Why don't yourself and Annie make friends with Ethna and Aidan?' He looked at her for an unnerving moment, and then at Ethna, who immediately clung to Mungo. 'I'm tired, Daddy,' she moaned. Mungo lifted her and stood in one movement, then swung her around several times.

'Tired? Tired? My Ethna is tired? That's impossible! That just can't be!' She squealed in delight, and by the time he left her down, she was mollified.

'Come on, Ethna, the adults want to talk,' Arthur said, taking her hand and leading her to a nearby bench. She glanced back at Mungo, but went willingly enough. Aidan had been standing back from the group in his usual way, but Annie had been watching him.

'Come on, Aidan,' she said, tipping him on the elbow and leading him reluctantly to the others.

'That's some young fella you have there,' Mungo said.

'Yes.' She smiled. 'I think he's taken a shine to Ethna.'

'Looks like it.'

'And you've two beautiful children,' she added. They watched the children, then she said, 'I'm glad we met.'

'Me too.'

'I wanted to apologize for what happened. It wasn't fair on you.'

'That's okay.'

'I felt really bad about it, and I'd no way of contacting you. Anyway, the harm was done.'

He didn't reply, and her confidence ebbed. Somewhere in the back of her mind she had imagined a future with him, however tentative, but now it seemed that would be beyond her.

'You never finished your story,' he said quietly, his face lightening.

'That's right, I didn't. Listen, there's a film I want to see. I was going to go on my own tomorrow night. Will you come? I don't know when I last saw a film.'

'I'd prefer to hear your story.' He turned to her and grinned, lazily.

'Oh come on. Please come.'

'I don't know if I can,' he said, serious again.

'If the shillings are short, don't worry. I know how it is, and I've a few spare pounds this week. I'm going over to my parents for dinner tomorrow evening, and you can ring me there. The last show doesn't start till twenty to nine. I'll wait for you till eight and not a minute more.' She handed him the number on a scrap of paper. He looked at it and put it in his breast pocket. Then he grinned again.

'What's the name of this film anyway?'

The Sheltering Sky.'

'Oh-huh?' He looked up at the sky which was mostly blue. 'I suppose it is.' He looked at his watch. 'My wife's uptown doing the shopping,' he said. 'I've to meet her in Abbey Street in a few minutes. The bus home.'

'Oh.'

He stood and called his children, then turned to her, patting his breast pocket. 'Thanks for this. I'll try and call around six tomorrow.'

'Good.' They smiled as the children arrived and exchanged good-byes. Tess followed with Annie and Arthur, watching Mungo walking down Jervis Street to Abbey Street with his children. 'It's in the Savoy,' she said to herself. She wanted an evening out with a man friend; it was something she hadn't enjoyed for a long, long time, and she wanted it very badly, caring not at all that he was married. She guessed that he was so in much the same way as she was, and he would call at six. What might lie beyond the cinema she refused to allow herself to consider.

In Fairview, she whistled, off-key.

'Stop that, Tess!' Arthur commanded. She laughed. God, it took so little to make a body happy, it was a mystery why people weren't happy all of the time. Even Brian, pottering about in the garden, was happy because it was Saturday and so he was free to go for a few pints. So little to look forward to, and yet it was enough.

Arthur expected a long story to complete a satisfying day with his mother and she rose to the occasion, glad that he had made continuous demands on her, as if drinking her in to satisfy a thirst. Being needed so was her central reality, her linchpin. Take it away, and she would fall to powder. She threw herself into the story, the actions, pauses, bulging eyes, an elastic face, acting for her life. Arthur loved it, as much for the complete attention as for the entertainment. When the story ended they smiled at each other, and she felt wonderful. As she elaborately tucked him in, he became serious.

'Tess, is that man your new husband?'

'Which man?' she asked too sternly. 'What do you mean, my new husband?' The little swine had to ruin it all, and now he was sulking, his head turned away and punishing her as only he knew how. 'I'm sorry. Which man do you mean?'

'How many men did we meet today?'

'Oh. You mean the man in the park with the little boy and girl! You liked the little girl, didn't you?'

'Don't be stupid.'

'Of course, he's not my new husband. How could he be? I

don't have a new husband, and I won't, ever.'

Arthur tried to suppress a smile. So that was it.

'Promise?'

'I promise.' She stroked the hair back from his forehead, and leaned over to kiss him. He smiled. 'I promise,' she whispered.

She tidied up and watched television, preoccupied by the boy's jealousy, chiding herself for having toyed with the idea of a friendship between him and Mungo's child in a cosy arrangement which would have suited her. Those few minutes in the park had been part of a special day, a very important part, and if Arthur came first, then she had needs too.

'I'm grumbling. I'm moaning. I'm giving out,' she declared aloud. 'Shit.'

Her eyes kept closing, the price of a day of close attention to Arthur, until she could no longer resist sleep. When she awoke the television was still on, some American cop opera. It was midnight, and Brian wasn't home. Or had he slipped in while she was asleep? Not wanting to go to bed before he came in, she went upstairs to check. His bed was untouched, so she watched the cop opera, but after a few minutes her chin was on her collarbone again. She turned off the television, pulled out the sofa-bed and was almost immediately asleep.

She woke to the overpowering fumes of Brian's alcoholic breath. He was trembling, staring at her as if in fear, his upper lip curled a hand's length from her face. As she woke, bewildered, her hand instinctively shielding her eyes from the light, he drew back a little, at first as if guilty, and then as if to study her better.

'What do you want?'

Breathing through his mouth, he looked dazed and didn't answer. She was afraid he was crazy enough to rape her, but managed to conceal her fear and when he pulled back the cover and squeezed her breast through the cotton of the tee-shirt, she had to use her full strength to prise his hand away.

'Don't touch me,' she whispered, as if she was in full control.

'Fuck you,' he said, breathing heavily now. He wasn't dazed

any more, but looked angry and intelligent. At the door he turned briefly and repeated, 'Fuck you.'

She held her breath as he stomped up the stairs and slammed his bedroom door behind him. There was still a chance that his frustration would turn inwards and propel him downstairs again, but gradually her fear subsided, though she lay awake, not really secure, for more than an hour.

As she woke, she heard Arthur talking to the cat in the kitchen. She dressed hurriedly and put up the sofa-bed, and on her way to the bathroom popped her head inside the kitchen door. Arthur was on his knees, stroking the cat, which lapped its milk from a red plastic bowl.

'Morning,' she said in a stage whisper, and smiled as he looked up. He smiled back, before concentrating on the cat again. She pissed and washed quickly, anxious to be with Arthur as soon as possible, to make him breakfast, to be motherly. He had already helped himself to corn flakes.

'Did you wash your hands after stroking that cat?'

He hesitated, then rubbed his hands along the front of his jersey.

'Come here,' she said briskly, wetting one end of a towel and soaping it. He dutifully rose from the table and held out his hands, and they got it over with. Toast popped up in the toaster. She took it out and put in two more slices. She supposed she ought to be grateful that he was so independent, and she was, most of the time, but not this morning. As the kettle boiled, she buttered the toast, and dripped honey on it, to the consistency he liked, and poured the weak tea just as he finished his flakes. Milk, lots. No sugar.

'Now, there's a good boy.'

If he'd had a brother or sister they'd be arguing or fighting by now, jealous of a scrap of favouritism, but Arthur ate and drank in silence, accepting the attention as his due. She looked at him as she waited for the tea to draw and wondered if it was indifference or whether he basked in her motherly care but hid it well. No matter, she felt deeply satisfied in being with him like this, having him to herself to enjoy and spoil.

He refused to invite Annie when they went to the park, and Tess felt a ludicrous pleasure, as if she had vanquished a rival. She could see that in his quiet, aware way, he was determined to make the most of their hours together. It was the simplest and happiest of times as he talked to her about school, where he shone with ease, about his friends, his favourite programmes, about nothing at all. He delighted in being pushed ever higher on the swing. He clutched his belly in helpless laughter at her exaggerated difficulty in running after his football, especially when she slipped and fell heavily on her rear, looking around at him with a clownish, hurt expression.

Brian was up when they returned home. He was unwashed and his eyes were bloodshot, but he seemed happy enough with his cup of tea, and was immersed in the sports pages of a tabloid.

'Hi Dad,' Arthur said, nestling into his father.

'Morning, son,' Brian mumbled and put an arm around Arthur's shoulder, but continued to read. There was a colour photo of a half-naked woman in a part of the paper which lay on the table. Tess noticed that Arthur looked at it for longer than she might have expected, and her face hardened as she set about making the Sunday dinner, even though by now Arthur had found the comic section.

'Turn on the news, Arthur, will you?' Brian asked him quietly. 'There's a good lad.' There was a brief silence as Arthur turned on the radio, then came the pips for one o'clock and the announcement of the main themes of the programme. Brian put down the paper and turned towards the radio. Arthur knew better than to compete with the news, so he sat into the table and read the comic, smiling from time to time. Tess busied herself with the dinner, which helped to cover her confusion.

She left an hour earlier than usual, unable to be in the same house as Brian any longer. Arthur didn't notice, or perhaps the morning had satisfied him. His interest in the picture of the half-naked woman had frightened her, and she kept blaming Brian for keeping porn videos. She wanted to throw a brick through a window, or slap someone across the face, someone who was helpless to strike back. It was fortunate for them both that Annie wasn't playing on the street and perhaps, also, that this Sunday Arthur would go to Brian's parents, not hers.

She reached Ringsend. The residents of her parents' street were ageing, so it was quiet, with only a few small children absorbed in a street game to suggest that it might renew itself. There were no front gardens here, the doors were flush with the pavement, and soon, because it was a spring day and the window was open, she faintly heard the resonant voice of Paul Robeson, her father's favourite singer.

Her father was a small but good-looking man with thinned, almost white hair and a neat moustache. He answered her knock and his face broke into a broad smile revealing strong, tobacco-stained teeth, and he embraced his daughter.

'Is that – ?' her mother called as she came out of the kitchen, from which came the smell of roast beef. 'Hello love,' she smiled. Unlike her father's, her mother's embrace was light. 'You're early,' she said in a mildly interrogative way.

'Yes. Brian was getting on my nerves.'

'Oh.' The subject embarrassed her parents, whose own marriage was one of unfailing companionship and mutual support. She saw that he didn't drink too much, and that he had a regular life, cunningly finding things to fill his day now that he had retired. Their greatest love was music and, like some Victorian couple, she had played the piano while he sang in a tenor voice that Tess had come to admire in recent years, having found it excruciating throughout her adolescence. For some reason, they didn't do that any more, at least not that she knew.

Her mother returned to the kitchen and her father poured her a whiskey. He liked drinking with Tess, and he smiled as he handed her the glass and they sat down together. Tess sipped the whiskey and sighed with pleasure as she relaxed into the armchair.

Her father asked her the ritual questions which masked his helpless love, questions to which the answers seldom varied: about her flat, lack of a job, her son. Since their separation,

Brian had been delicately left to her to mention and she never obliged beyond a brief, disparaging remark, despite the raised eyebrows which she knew were pleas to go back to him for the sake of their idea of marriage. But Arthur was their common cause, and it was a relief to tell of every detail she knew about his week since they had seen him. Her mother stood at the kitchen door, unconsciously wiping her hands on her apron, her eyes lively as Tess spoke of their darling grandson.

After dinner Tess washed up and her mother dried. This was their time together, although her mother always stopped short of intimacy, which, although she could not define it or give an example, Tess knew would satisfy her in some way. And yet chatting away like that was a way of being intimate.

The phone rang and Tess caught her breath, the dish sliding from her fingers back into the basin. Her mother was already away to answer it, a lightness in her step. Of course it was Don, ringing from Dallas. Slowly her heart calmed, and she finished the dishes. Her father was on the phone now.

'Yes, she's here,' he said, but Tess pretended not to notice until she was called. She was a little mad at her brother for giving her a fright like that, but she could never be really mad at Don. She loved his warmth and gentleness, his soft voice which she could never remember being raised against her in anger or accusation, so that whenever they spoke, whatever she said had always a backdrop of gratitude and love. Now, knowing he would understand, hand cupping the mouthpiece, she whispered that she was expecting a call, and then in a normal voice asked about Mac.

'He's fine. And thank you for asking, sis. You always do. Bye for now.'

She replaced the receiver, hesitated, then turned, smiling. At least there was someone who would understand. The television was already on, her mother looked around and she joined her mother on the sofa.

'Don seems in good form.'

'Yes,' her mother beamed. 'He's a good boy.'

Tess winced.

'He said he was getting a rise,' her father interjected.

'Oh?'

'The man has brains to burn. How he understands them computers I don't know – and "programmes" them, if you don't mind. Jazes, it bates the band.'

'He's brains to burn true enough,' her mother added.

They were right to be proud of him. They never said it, or even hinted, but she had given them nothing to be proud of. Except Arthur. They watched television. Now and then Tess looked around at the phone, as if by looking at it she could make it ring. At seven, her father looked at his watch for several moments, before looking meaningfully at his wife, who, after a moment's hesitation, rose to get ready for the pub, their ritual Sunday outing.

'Do you fancy a drink?' he asked Tess. She shook her head, unable to repress a smile. He always asked, intimating that it would do her good to get out, and she always declined.

'Maybe I'll have one here.'

'You do that daughter,' he said, and went to get ready himself. They were gone by seven twenty. Tess poured herself a whiskey to quell the tension, which seemed to sit in a ball beneath her heart.

She sipped it quickly, then took her bag to the bathroom and made up her face, slowly, deliberately, and gradually she calmed. The make-up was subtle, apart from the carmine lipstick, and she smiled inwardly as her mask fell into place, making her look as she had ten years before – alert, bright-eyed, with her life before her as a blank page, waiting for a hot man to inscribe it.

She shook with laughter, and returning to the living-room feeling strong and relaxed, she sipped her whiskey again, noting the ghost of her lipstick on her glass.

As she grew drunk, and the telephone remained silent, her sips became more frequent and her irritation mounted. For once, for once in her life ... The last show was scheduled for eight thirty-five. If he rang now, she tried to convince herself, if he rang within the next ten minutes, they could still make it.

They'd miss the ads and the trailers, they wouldn't have time to buy chocolate or popcorn, but they'd make the feature. As the minutes passed she made more concessions. They'd missed the film. So what. They could go for a drink. Maybe he was looking after the children or something. He could step out to a phone, apologize, arrange to meet again, and to her horror, she realized she would be grateful for that small gesture.

It was nine thirty and her third glass of the evening was empty. She raised it to her face and watched the traces of lipstick near the rim. The tip of her tongue stole between her lips, and stayed there for a while, before moving slowly, round and around. Then, as far as she could manage without strain, she extended her tongue until its tip could wipe the glass clean.

Tears trickled onto her cheeks, leaving a ragged trail of mascara. The house was completely silent. She poured herself another whiskey, this time half filling the glass, and drank back so much its fumes flooded back through her nostrils and made her cough. Her heart pounded, scaring her into being more careful. As she drank a glass of water at the sink, it calmed, and she cried some more. Taking a fistful of paper towel, she wiped her lips and eyes, haphazardly, the vague intention being to remove her useless make-up, but instead she smeared it across her face in a mess of red and black.

In the living-room, Tess lay on the settee and stared at the piano for a long time before rousing herself to check the music sheets. It had been so long since she played, but now she ached to play, if there was a piece within her range. There was nothing except tunes from musicals, some faded Moore's Melodies, which, like the songs from the century's turn, were family heirlooms of a kind; but none of this was what she was looking for. She took a cautious sip of whiskey. Schubert. That's what she wanted. Schubert's 'Wanderer' Fantasy. So what if she couldn't play it all; she'd play the slow bits, the adagio, wasn't that what it was called? It didn't matter what it was called, she had heard it often enough on her old cassette-player, and now, taking another drink and turning out all the lights except for one over the piano, she sat in to play.

She fumbled the keys at first, but eventually she mastered the tune in her brain, repeating it several times until it flowed. It was necessary to *dada da*, because one of the keys was dead and she was forced to sing the note.

Leaning into the piano, her faint shadow playing about the wall above, she forgot everything but the music. She paused only to drink, or to laugh with abandon.

But suddenly she stopped – mentally if not physically sober. It was past ten and, being Sunday, the pubs had served their last drinks and her parents would soon be home. She closed the lid, turned out the lamp and went into the bathroom, scrutinizing her grotesquely daubed face with detachment before cleaning it.

As she walked unsteadily along the quays, the wail of a siren rose above the hum of the city, and she wondered if it was the police, or an ambulance, or the fire brigade. Someone, somewhere was in trouble. Real trouble. At another time this might have assured her that her life wasn't so bad after all, that she could pick herself up and make something of it, but not now. All she wanted to do was sleep, for days on end. No, that wasn't it. She wanted to give in.

- Eight -

Mungo walked past the queues waiting for buses by the walls of Trinity College. He liked to look at people, especially at women in all their marvellous variety, and bus queues were full of wonder. A light rain was falling. In his coat pocket he clutched an appointment card for a medical referee who would decide his fitness for work. Mungo knew he would be declared fit, and knew also that there was no work – at least not regular, paid and taxed work; so that meant a move down from the luxury of getting a cheque through the letterbox to joining a queue at the dole office.

The façade of the building was ugly; inside it was drab and functional. The information clerk directed him along a narrow corridor which led to a waiting area. To his surprise this was bright and comfortable, decorated with a few pertinent posters. This queue was at least seated. Below a certain income, Mungo reflected, a man or woman was condemned to queues: for buses, which might not come; for money; for medical care; for charity. The world was divided into those who queued, and those who kept appointments and drove cars, the lot of one being resignation and the other, purpose. There were magazines on a low table, but Mungo noticed that no one was reading. Perhaps it was the early hour, or because it was Monday morning. He shifted in his seat. Everyone, he noticed, was very tense. Perhaps he should be tense as well, but he was by far the fittest person in the room, so there was no doubt in his mind that he would be declared fit to work. They were mostly men; a few women, mostly partners of the men. All, it seemed to Mungo, with the possible exception of a pale youth, were obviously sick, or handicapped by injury or illness.

Mungo's resignation turned to pity as he glanced around the room. A husband and wife spoke in low, worried voices to each other. He was thin, painfully so, and his skin was grey. A middle-aged nurse entered and called a name. A woman on a stick rose awkwardly from her seat, and the nurse hurried to support her. Mungo watched their slow progress until they disappeared behind a door, the nurse declaring her name again for the benefit of the doctor. The man beside the vacant seat coughed. His face was red, laden with fat beneath a slack skin. His lips were moving and for a moment Mungo thought he was praying, but then realized he was rehearsing what he would say.

Mungo got himself a magazine from the table and flicked through it. It was a month since he had his last certificate, and his arm had improved dramatically since then because of Tess. He closed the magazine. What had Tess to do with it and where had that thought sprung from? He had worked very hard at building up the strength in his arm and he had done that because ... of Tess. He put the ridiculous notion out of his mind and tried to imagine his interview, although maybe that wasn't the right word. There would only be one view. He tried to work out the sums of entitlement he had talked about with Connie, and if his family would be worse off, but he couldn't grapple with this. Very often the professionals didn't know for sure.

His turn came and he sat before a man of late middle-age who seemed upset about something. Perhaps he had sciatica, or gout. Perhaps he hated his job. Mungo wanted this over with as soon as possible.

'I was at my doctor a month ago – '

'Yes, I know.' The doctor looked up from Mungo's records, but Mungo was determined, although he didn't want his anger to show.

'I've been working really hard on it since, and it's responded very well.' Mungo knew that 'responded' was a good medical term since Aidan's time in hospital. 'Especially in the last week or so. You could say I'm fit in other words.'

The doctor, who had been reading throughout Mungo's speech, looked up again, and stared at him.

'I could, but then again I might not. Take off your shirt.'

Mungo burned, but did as he was told, glancing at the nurse who had busied herself at a separate desk. After a brief examination, Mungo dressed, and the doctor ignored him as he wrote his report.

'Well? Am I fit for work?'

'You'll hear in a week or two.'

Mungo shook his head in disbelief, but said nothing, unsure if he was expected to leave or not. He stood. The nurse rose and asked him how he had travelled into town. By bus, he said, and he received a voucher which he could cash in the front office for his return bus fare, and with it, a mildly satisfying theft from the tormenting State, as he had walked in, and he would walk home.

Outside, he took a deep breath, and caressed his ill-got gains in an otherwise empty pocket. He had, perhaps, enough for two cups of tea and a shared bun, and, thinking this, he gave up denying that Tess had been at the back of his mind, that there was a possibility of meeting her in The Winding Stair, and that that was why he found himself walking there.

He spent a pleasant hour in the book-café, watching the crowds cross the Ha'penny Bridge, listening to the music and sipping tea long after it had gone cold. He had not bought a slice of fruit cake, in case she came after all. Then depression set in as he realized the futility of his vigil and he left, knowing that all he had to do was walk down the quay and knock on her door. But instead he walked home down Great and Little Strand Streets, Arran Street, Chancery Street, past the old, crumbling distillery into Smithfield. All the way, he was rehearsing the story he would spin for Tess when they next met. Half-way up Smithfield he noticed debris where the travellers' caravans had been. At first he thought that they had dumped rubbish before moving on, but there was something about it that was odd. He went across to see for himself. All that was left of the caravan was a rectangular heap of ashes, an axle, and an aluminium chimney.

At home, Connie listened to his account of the morning in silence, but when he said he'd told the doctor he thought he was fit, she looked at him in exactly the same way as the doctor had.

'Are you a clown or what are you?' she asked, the humiliation of their predicament now compounded. She put her head in her hands. 'Oh what am I married to? Did no one ever tell you to keep your mouth shut in a situation like that? What am I saying? Didn't I make myself hoarse telling you that last night?' She looked up at him, her eyes bright with tears.

'Did no one ever tell you that sometimes you have to do the wrong thing for the right reasons?' he retorted.

'What reasons?' she shouted, knocking over a chair, as she ran upstairs to the bedroom. He heard the springs groan under her sudden weight, and then the sobs.

What reasons? It was a good question which he couldn't really answer, except that it had given him strength of a kind. It was a decision, and he needed to make a decision. He poured himself a cup of water from the tap, afraid that his one decision would have to suffice for some time.

A short time later a decision was made for him. He was fit for work and should report to his local labour exchange. His arm felt weak again, but he didn't dare mention this to Connie and suffered his fears alone as he walked through Stoneybatter and up to the Navan Road.

As it turned out, the woman at the new applicants hatch was courteous and efficient, tracking down stamps he had forgotten about on her computer, and adding them to the total, which would boost his income, if only for a few months. He completed the form and waited for the woman to come back. Already there was a queue behind him. He could sense the restlessness, the moving from foot to foot. To his left, a large, middle-aged policeman manned the staff door, bored but at ease. The woman returned, satisfied with the details, and he signed on. He wouldn't get money until the following week. If he had difficulty, he should go to the supplementary welfare officer at his local Health Centre, who would tide him over. The clerk smiled. As he left, he glanced at the long queues he would be part of in a week's time. There was a murmur from them like distant traffic.

At the bus stop he looked back at the dole office, which was built away from the road itself, behind a fence, maybe for security reasons, but it seemed as if it was in a field. He realized he was waiting for a bus, though he was within easy walking distance of home. A bus was coming at speed down the dual carriageway, and he checked if he still had change. He went upstairs, elated. Several people were smoking, although smoking was banned on buses, but a window was open and the air was fresh so Mungo didn't mind. He was going to see her. What had got into him? He was going to see her, and the prospect made him feel alive.

He knocked loudly three times. No reply. He knocked again and was on the point of leaving when she opened the door, hair dishevelled and in her dressing-gown.

'O God – you!' she said. 'I thought you were the postman.'

His heart sank. He had been in dreamland. Now he was yanked back into the real world.

'Some parcel,' she said.

'If you don't want to see me I'll go.'

She stood back and opened the door. 'It's just that I'm in a state. I'm not even dressed,' she said, mounting the stairs ahead of him.

'Don't mind me,' he said. She stopped and looked back at him for a moment, but said nothing. This was awful, but here he was going ahead with it, like an idiot. What would they say to each other, for Christ's sake, sipping tea across the table from one another? He thought of his story, but the problem was the lead into it. Jesus.

'What happened you last Sunday?' They had reached the flat.

'Last Sunday?'

'Yes. Last Sunday night. You can think of a good excuse while I'm dressing.'

She disappeared into her bedroom. What could he say? One day was the same as the next to him, and he couldn't remember what happened the day before, never mind the previous Sunday, though now that he thought of it she had mentioned something about a film, something to do with the sky. He couldn't have gone, and he was sure he didn't agree to go, but how in the name of Christ could he have forgotten?

'So how are you anyway?' she asked him as she emerged from the bedroom. She seemed relaxed, very pleasant, as if her clothes had transformed her. He was relieved.

'Fine. As a matter of fact, I've just been declared fit for work.'

'Is that so?' She grinned. 'Do you know anything about repairing a leaking roof?'

'A leaking roof? Where's the problem?'

'Do you really know something about it?'

'We can have a look, anyway. It might be simple, and it might not.'

She showed him the tracks the water had left in her bathroom and kitchen. Though she had cleaned it away, a light fungus was growing again. He looked out her kitchen window and saw that there was a lean-to roof beneath it. Tess, he realized, was now serious, weighing up whether he could in fact help her or whether he was playing her along. He wondered about this himself, and tried to ignore the question of his arm, whether it would let him down in a dangerous situation on a roof.

'Well, let's see what it's like outside.' He leaned out, twisting his head upwards. The gutter was a good distance up, so there was no question of standing on the sill to reach it. On the other hand, the lean-to roof would most likely support a ladder. 'You don't have a periscope handy, do you?' he asked, closing the window. She grinned again.

'Mission impossible?'

'Well yeah – without a ladder, rope, hammer, roofing nails, probably a few slates and some flashing.'

'Oh. I have a ladder.'

She found the ladder in one of the vacant rooms. There was also a length of rope heaped in a corner. It was frayed in parts and probably unreliable, but he decided to try the ladder. He could see she was serious now and willing to believe he might be able to do it, and remembering he had a toolbox at home, long idle, he was beginning to believe it himself. They left their footprints in the dust of the room.

The ladder reached to just above the gutter, which was enough to let him clamber onto the roof, and the rope was long enough to lash the ladder to the gas pipe which ran below her window, which, hopefully, would stop it sliding down the lean-to.

One of several problems was that the bathroom was on one side and the kitchen on the other of the roof. Still, it was a narrow roof. He got out on the sill, and dropped gingerly onto the lean-to.

'Careful!' she implored. He licked his lips. He lashed the ladder to the gas pipe and climbed to the gutter, remembering that he had no head for heights. The things a woman could make a man do! The ladder gave a little, and he heard Tess asking him again to be careful, but the rope tautened and held. When he got to the roof there was no perceptible damage, but he guessed the flashing was at fault. He leaned across, guessing where it might be, and, sure enough, it had raised a little, enough to allow a stream of water into her kitchen. It was probably the same on the other side. A few nails and sealer. That's all it needed, or so he hoped. The slates although probably old were in perfect condition. He was enjoying himself, and he looked into the clear blue sky and, with great satisfaction, took a deep breath.

He descended, untied the rope, and between them they got the ladder back in. Then she helped pull him inside. His arm was aching madly.

'Well?'

'If I can come back tomorrow with a few tools I think I can fix it. No promises, mind.'

She smiled and thanked him, put a kettle on the gas and told him to light the heater in the living-room. He warmed himself, surprised that he'd been so cold, and looked around the room. The clear light revealed the tattered details. Over the fine mantelpiece was a plastic sun, its jolly rays dancing around its circumference. He sat into the armchair, its springs protruding under the leatherette, and waited. He could hear no sound from the kitchen, and for a moment he imagined he was alone in the house. She was standing in front of the kettle, waiting for it to boil; or staring out the window, brooding; or putting off the moment when she would have to face him again. After a few minutes she pushed the door open with her foot, two cups on her left forefinger, a pot of tea in her right hand, a plastic bottle of milk held between her left arm and her breast.

'Do you take sugar?'

'No.'

'Good.' She smiled quickly and he was relieved to see she was nervous. 'I don't have any ...'

'About Sunday night ... My wife's parents were visiting.'

'That's okay.' She sipped her tea, eyes lowered. She had lovely eyes. He thought of a desert animal, eyelids spreading over the eye under the blast of the sun. The light made her seem peaceful, her skin pale and softened by departing youth. She looked up, blushed slightly at his gaze, which he quickly averted, before looking back at her again. His throat was dry. The side of her mouth quivered.

'How're your children?'

'Well.' He shrugged. 'The same as ever. And your boy?'

'Oh he's fine.' She lowered her eyes again, then looked up and smiled. Her eyes shone, and he noticed that her hand was open on the sofa, towards him. His heart pounded. He reached out and took her hand, gently, then turned it over and caressed it. Her breasts were lifting and falling. The smile was gone, completely, but her lips were slightly open. He reached forward, brushing them with his own, forgetting everything else. It was awkward like that, but he kissed her face, her closed eyes, before returning to her mouth. They moved closer, arms around each other, his fingers tracing her backbone through her jumper. The tip of his tongue touched hers, the merest touch, the cool breath from her nostrils blowing against his light stubble. He put his hand under her jumper but she pushed it away.

'No,' she whispered, 'let's go inside.'

Once in the bedroom they abandoned themselves to a deep kiss, standing fully clothed, their tongues bathing now in one mouth, now in the other's. Gasping, she bared her neck to him. Shaken, he traced it with his fingertips, then holding her nape, he covered her neck with lingering kisses so that the lightest pink bloomed and faded as he moved across it. She pushed him away then, to undress, and she watched him follow suit. He supposed his face too was flushed with desire. He knew his body had moved into an automatic mode he had forgotten, his muscles jerking, yet in a primitive control, which gained him a different kind of movement, blood pummelling his head. As she straightened, naked, the fullness of her bush and the way her breasts bounced made him catch his breath, and she smiled nervously, turning slightly before pulling back the covers and, for a moment, as her right knee supported her as she climbed into bed, her stretched body seemed perfect, her buttocks curving fluidly into supple, graceful legs. He lay in sideways, pulling the bedclothes over them and falling in towards her, and they kissed urgently. He rolled over her, to her other side, so his good hand could caress her, and then found that he could rest his weak hand beneath her thighs, so that both his hands were exploring her, the weak one softly and slowly, the strong one quick and firm, until it slipped into her mound, moving lightly across her soft flesh.

This was something new to him and her moans surprised him at first, then encouraged him to be more daring until it seemed he had acquired a natural way to her, and his pleasure became commensurate with hers. More rapidly than he would have guessed, she was lost to him and, it seemed, to herself, aware only of the deep roll of sensation his fluent hands were feeding her. He lifted his cheek from her breast, and saw her ecstatic face, her teeth bared, her skin flushed, a sheen of sweat on her forehead. When his cock struck her thigh he faltered in his rhythm, aware of himself again, and his caresses became mechanical. She opened her eyes, whispering, 'Please, Mungo, please,' and tried to pull him on top of her, but his stiffness was gone and he felt stranded. He closed his eyes tight, beginning again, the pad of his finger tentatively circling her hidden bud until her sighs, then groans, drew him out of himself once more. He worked patiently. Her hips were bucking now, she wanted it harder and harder, and when he slipped his finger to the knuckle into her, she cried out, her arms over her head in complete abandon. His muscles were aching but to stop now would be cruel, and he drove his fingers faster and faster until she shouted and arched her back, pushing his hands violently away and closing her legs as she huddled into herself foetally. She was shaking, as if she had a chill, her legs jerking in spasm and her lips curled grotesquely as she gasped for breath. He was sweating profusely, hardly believing what had happened, his groin congested, his forearms aching, his heart in his mouth, witnessing this little death. He didn't dare touch her in case he would intrude on her oblivion. Then suddenly, it seemed, she was calm, and he felt she was ready for him. He felt so tender towards her, moved her hair to one side and kissed the back of her neck, softly. She smiled, languorously turned and took him in her arms, running her fingers through his hair, holding him close. His groin still ached, but he felt no desire, thinking that for the first time he had achieved a selflessness in love. He could even smile at his impotence.

When he opened his eyes, she was grinning at him.

'Old sleepy head. I must have worn you out.'

'Eh?' Had he been sleeping? He had only closed his eyes for a few seconds. 'You look refreshed yourself.'

'Oh yes.' Her fingernail played around his nipple. 'And what about you?' she asked coyly.

'Me? I'm fine.'

'Are you sure?'

'Very.' It wasn't something he would confide to a man, but in the time they had left he was content to forego his own bucking and curses, happy to be with her now like this. It seemed to please her very much.

'Tell me,' she said, running a finger along his cheekbone, 'Whatever happened to you after you got to Madrid.'

'Madrid?'

'Yes, Madrid. You dodged the police by the skin of your teeth, remember? When you robbed the family when they were asleep?'

'I didn't rob them. I gave them something to wonder about.'

'You robbed them, poor things.'

He grinned.

'I didn't stay very long in Madrid. Too big and too busy. I liked the Metro though. It was old and it brought me to all sorts of ordinary, dull places. I like that, somehow. Of course I went to the Prado, to see the Goyas.

'I got the train that night from Chamartin to Barcelona. It was a nightmare, with so many packed onto it. There were hundreds of North Africans. When I got to my compartment there was a row going on between some North Africans and Spanish over a seat, and someone had called a Civil Guard, who was losing patience. I tried to ignore the argument, which in any case I could barely understand, looked at the seat number, saw that it matched my ticket, and proceeded to settle in. There was uproar. The other passengers looked at me anxiously, and it began to dawn on me that something might be wrong and I was at the centre of it. I looked up to see the Guard staring at me as he fended off the angry Africans. Then he stretched out his hand. "*Billete*." No please or thank you – just *billete*. The train jerked, and was moving smoothly out of the station as he examined the fine details of my ticket, then matched it to the number above my head. "*Muy bien,*" he said abruptly, handing me back my ticket and closing the door almost in one movement. My fellow passengers heaved a collective sigh of relief.'

'They were shut of the rabble.'

'Exactly. One was a very proper, thin woman in her fifties or so, but lower middle class, or else she would have been on a more expensive train. She was obviously still recovering from the prospect of sharing the compartment with a Moroccan – her lips were trembling. When she had composed herself she spat it out: "¡*Moros sucios!*" Filthy Moors ...

'The Spaniards looked at each other as the Moroccans began to clap their hands in a slow but then faster and faster rhythm outside the compartment door. My heart was beating like a steam hammer, whether because of the rhythm or the infectious fear in the compartment, I couldn't say. Your hatred of people you don't know is a more pure hatred, I suppose, because it feeds on the fear that they're capable of things you can only faintly imagine.'

Mungo paused for a moment and reflected. Tess raised herself expectantly on her elbow.

'But they were courteous and generous people. The older woman said that the *Moros* would rob them as they slept. She really feared them.'

'Ho ho! Little did she know who was in their midst!' Tess said.

'Naw. I'd no more Irish notes.'

'But your pockets were burning with hot pesetas, all the same.'

'Which of us is blameless? But I still felt that their hatred of the Moroccans should have been a hatred of me too, which doesn't make sense, but I felt it all the same. After a while I fell asleep. It was stuffy in the compartment, with six bodies packed together. When I woke the lights were out. The soldier was in the corridor, smoking. It was four a.m. I needed to piss, I needed air and I needed a drink, so I got my water-bottle, strapped it to my belt, carefully stepped over legs and got outside quietly. The cold in the corridor was a shock. I hesitated, wondering whether to talk to the conscript, but he seemed deep in thought and unaware of my presence so I let him be. The corridor was full of men, most of them smoking, staring out into the darkness. The end of the carriage, at the toilets, was almost impassable, with Moroccans seated on the floor, their heads resting on their knees, packed together for mutual support and warmth. A few were dressed in the *burnous*, their hoods up, the others in European clothes with woollen caps. In the middle of them were two young women and a woman of late middle-age, all of them in black, and asleep. The toilet door was jammed open by the pressure of bodies, so I had no choice but to stretch my legs over a couple of sleeping men and piss in full view of whoever might wake or pass. No one did, that I noticed. When I got back out the older woman caught my attention as she stirred. They had blankets – richly coloured, I seem to remember, with a lovely blue pattern – but this, I thought, was no way for a woman of her age to travel such a long distance. It's no way for anyone to travel, with the temperature so low, in a strange country. I turned and saw a man watching me. He was dressed in a *burnous*, but he seemed more suave and relaxed than his companions. We looked steadily at each other for a few moments, and then he nodded at the woman.

"That's the woman the row was about last night," he said, in English. Surprised, I looked at the woman again.

"What do you mean?"

"You were rather late taking your seat. Her sons were arguing that she should have it while it was vacant."

"I see. Well tell her she can have it now. I didn't realize what was happening."

"I don't think that's a good idea. If you like, I'll tell her sons in the morning, but it won't make you very popular with *los españoles*. In any event, it's your seat."

'Perhaps it was the rocking of the train, or maybe she felt me watching her, but the woman opened her eyes just then, and they met mine. They were the sad, strong eyes of a woman who has seen everything, and she outgazed me,

"Tell her she can have it now."

The Moroccan laughed. "Do you enjoy riots at four a.m.?"

"We can tell them she's been ill."

'The Moroccan shook his head, amused, but nevertheless lightly touched the shoulder of one of the woman's sons, who was immediately alert, and said something to him. The woman caught my attention again, with her gaze and the faint trace of a smile, and I didn't need to understand Arabic to know what the response would be. They had all obviously been dozing rather than sleeping and they were appraising me now. My friend smiled and said that the son thanked me but that his mother was comfortable where she was. I bowed, which is all one can do before dignity.'

"My name is Ahmed. Would you like some tea? Mint tea?" He pulled a flask from his bag, which was leather, and I wondered if he smiled in his sleep too. I smiled myself, and nodded. There was no question of sleep now, anyway, and I had never tasted mint tea. I told him my name in turn, and as we drank the delicious tea you'd think we had been friends for years. He asked me about Ireland, of course, but he didn't go boom boom, and of course I asked him about Morocco. He was from the Atlas Mountains. I had thought it was all desert, but Morocco has everything. Sea, sun and snow.'

'Mungo,' Tess whispered. 'Mungo, you'll have to go now.'

'Eh?' She had yanked him from a village in the Atlas Mountains to a bed in Dublin. 'Oh, getting a bit boring there, was I?'

'No, but I've to collect Arthur.'

'Oh yes. That must mean it's time to collect my two.'

'It must. Will you come again soon?'

'Well, I've to fix your roof, haven't I?'

She grinned and quickly got out of bed and dressed. He watched her, lazy and feeling good.

'Come on,' she said, clasping her bra.

He walked to the school, early for once, so he took his time. He thought about the progress of the train story, how it seemed so natural to tell it to her. How would he finish it?

Children were streaming out of the school gates now, but no sign of his own. Mungo always stayed a little away from the gates, leaning back against a gable wall, partly out of laziness, partly out of discretion. He wasn't sure if Aidan was at an age when he would be embarrassed to be met by his father at the school gate. Then Ethna skipped out and ran up to him, leaning in to but not hugging him. Maybe she was self-conscious too. Aidan took a while, coming out, Mungo was pleased to see, with a friend and stopping to talk to him.

'Tell Aidan to hurry up,' Ethna demanded.

'Oh he won't be long,' Mungo said. Ethna leaned in to him again. He was prepared to wait as long as Aidan needed. The boys seemed impressively composed, as if discussing a topic in an adult way. Everything appeared so calm this afternoon. Mungo was glad to be alive. Aidan's friend went in the other direction, and without greeting, apart from a light tip on Aidan's shoulder, they walked slowly home.

Connie was in a good mood as well. Perhaps it was the fine weather. Or maybe it was because her mother had been nice to her on the phone, and was sending them a loan to tide them over the week. He had forgotten about the need for that. No wonder she thought he was a useless dreamer. Her cheerfulness irritated him. The radio blared, she sang out of time, forgetting the words as she drained the potatoes, engulfed in steam. He used to enjoy her at a time like this, but now it seemed that his happiness required her to be surly and hateful. She made him feel bad and he resented her, yet somehow he managed to conceal his state of mind and indulged Aidan and Ethna, who once they had their homework done never let him be, as if they sensed his tolerance and were eager to make the best of it. In a way it was to his advantage, as he didn't have to face Connie; but then she looked on with approval and in all likelihood would look back on this evening as an example of when they were all happy together.

When the children were in bed, they watched television. Connie made them tea and she talked about the neighbours and things of little consequence to Mungo, but he feigned interest, asking questions and leading her away from anything serious. He was afraid, above all, that she would talk about living in Wexford. As a programme ended Connie gathered up the cups and plates and brought them to the kitchen. He could hear her rinse them and then there was silence. Perhaps she was looking at the back of his head which he knew was visible over the sofa. Maybe, he thought with a twinge of panic, she suspects what happened. Had she found a woman's stray hair, could she smell the trace of a woman on his body, or on his clothes? He stiffened as her arms came about his neck and she kissed the top of his head.

'I'm going to bed,' she said.

'Okay. I'll be up soon,' he heard himself say in an even voice. She left, and he stared at the television without taking anything in. Why now? Jesus Christ, why now? He had been desolate for so long, and now two women wanted him. There was so much hurt involved with Connie, on both sides, yet she, it seemed, had forgiven him, still thought of him as her husband, however flawed. Maybe she was more mature. He had always believed in one man, one woman, but now he had discovered magic, and he wanted it. He knew Connie was waiting for him, but he stayed watching a stupid programme. All he had to do was go upstairs and fuck her, and everything would be fine, but he couldn't bring himself to do it. He stayed more than an hour, until the National Anthem played and the colour card came on the screen.

The bedlamp was still on when he went up, and she was lying away from his side, her eyes closed, but he knew she wasn't asleep. Connie was a proud woman and would only wait so long. He stripped quickly and got into bed, noting she had her usual nightie on, and switched off the lamp. His guess was that while she had waited for him, she was naked, but now, in the silence of her head she was calling him all the foul names a woman can think of for a man. He was tense until he knew she was asleep, and he could think over an extraordinary, sensual day.

It was one or two in the morning and he was wide awake. Connie moaned and turned, and he waited anxiously while her breath returned to an even rhythm. He looked towards her in the darkness, this complex woman, who he knew so well, and yet she had become a stranger to him. Even if he had hurt her tonight, and he knew he had, his resentment was now displaced by sympathy, or tenderness, or both. She had a point of view, conflicting emotions, bewilderment, just as he had, and for a moment he was tempted to wake her, though he knew it was ludicrous, and take her in his arms, but even as he wanted this, he knew he would go to Tess in the morning and make love to her.

Tears. At two in the morning. He held them back, swallowing hard, and even as he did so, yawned. He had a piss and carefully got back into bed. Connie grunted as the mattress took his weight, but did not wake.

When he got back from leaving the children to school, Connie was out. They had barely spoken at breakfast and he knew she was avoiding him now. Unreasonably, this irritated him, but what else could he expect, and he knew he would have been irritated no matter what she did or said. He found his toolbox, selected a hammer and screwdriver, wrapped them in a cloth and put them in a plastic bag. His heart and the back of his head were pounding, as if he was about to commit a murder, and, yes, he was killing off something, he knew that, however dimly.

He walked to Capel Street and bought a tube of sealer and some roofing nails. The nearer he got to Tess's place, the more remote Connie and his problems with her seemed.

Tess was in the same dressing-gown, dishevelled and mildly surprised, but this time she smiled.

'I've come to fix your roof,' he said, holding up the bag.

'I see.' She said nothing as they went upstairs, but turned a few times to glance at him. 'I'll get dressed,' she said, closing the door behind them.

By the time she was dressed, he had the ladder on the lean-to, and was lashing it to the gas pipe that ran along the wall. She leaned out the window and held onto the ladder in a token gesture. She had to stretch out so far that if the ladder slipped she would be forced to let go.

He was confident until he climbed onto the roof, but once there he was scared. Splayed onto the slates, he didn't dare move.

'Are you okay?' Tess called.

'Yeah. Yeah, I'm fine ...' He was going to have to move. The only problem was that he didn't know how. If a slate came away he was in trouble. He edged his way up by using the sidewall of the adjoining house as a reliable edge, and one foot on the top of the ladder as a lever. The ladder gave a fraction, but held. It was then he realized he needed crawling boards. He didn't have far to go, and in fact could reach it, but he needed that extra few inches to work, and those inches caused him much sweat. He felt underneath the raised flashing and found what he hoped was an undamaged slate nailed to a batten. He pressed the flashing down and drove home the nails. He hesitated, waiting for some disaster, then sealed it. Now he had to get down, move the ladder to the other side and repeat the process. What should have taken a few minutes took almost an hour.

'If I'd had crawling boards,' he said as they got the ladder in the window, 'it could have been done in no time. But it should be okay now.' He wasn't sure about that, but she was pleased and that was enough for now.

It was good to feel useful again, to have his labour and risk acknowledged. She made tea, and he forgot his weariness.

She asked him to tell her about the farm and his childhood there. He was surprised by that, and very slowly he told her the simple memories he had of growing up on a hillside farm. He was telling her about how he had discovered his father had been a Desert Rat when she kissed his neck. Arms around each other, they went into her bedroom and made unhurried love. Instead of feeling driven, he felt light, at ease, able to let his pleasure flow through him like a warm stream. They could stop, kiss, caress, as if it was all part of the rhythm they had struck, before continuing. He could hardly believe it was happening, yet beneath him was a woman who he seemed to understand; everything he did with her, said to her, was right. A burden had lifted from him and had gone far away, as if it had never weighed on his body, or kept his feet too heavily on the ground.

Afterwards, as they lay together, still sweaty and dazed, this thought was still with him and he was grateful. He opened his eyes, and brushed away hair which had fallen over her face. A faint smile acknowledged him. She looked ... purified, light, at peace. He looked at her greedily, wanting to remember every-thing, then wondered if he would look the same to her. He had felt like that until he began to think of it. He closed his eyes again, sinking back into a blessed darkness.

'Mungo?'

'Yeah?'

'Mungo, what ever happened that man in Morocco?'

'Morocco?' He was immediately alert, his brain searching for the thread. 'Oh you mean the man on the train.'

'The train? Yes, he was talking about Morocco, but he was on the train. He went to Barcelona, with you.'

'That's right. Well, there was no point in trying to sleep, so we talked till dawn. There was a fog, but here and there it had lifted and you could see we were on a plain – a plateau, I think you'd say about these parts.'

He was playing for time, delving into an empty bag, but then, as the train slowed, he remembered what had happened and wondered how he could ever have forgotten.

'Ahmed yawned. There was no sign of a town, but the train slowed, and then stopped, it seemed, in the middle of nowhere. Ahmed pulled down the window and looked out. He was silent for a moment and then he started laughing. "See for yourself," he said. I looked out and for a moment I was puzzled. There was no station, only a short platform. Bey-ond that, nothing, except a small tree, little more than a sap-ling, about a hundred metres away. Then Ahmed tapped me on the shoulder. "Excuse me Mungo," he said with a mischievous grin, "but I need to crap, and that tree over there is as good a place as any, don't you think?"'

Tess laughed, and cuddled in closer to him.

'Now the tree was no thicker than my arm, and of course I thought he was joking, but he wasn't. He got off the train, winked, walked to the tree, went behind it and disappeared.'

'What? You chancer!' She exclaimed, slapping him on his bare shoulder.

'It's true, I tell you! He disappeared – all you could see was this skinny tree. And I wasn't the only one to notice. You could hear people shouting and people were pulling down windows because they didn't believe their eyes, shouting about this guy who had evaporated into thin air. Some even got off the train, but they didn't go to the tree. They argued in groups, waving their arms all over the place, and shouting. I looked out the window again. People were leaning out of windows or getting off all along the train. On the platform, an official in uniform had sacks of mail on a trolley, but he too had stopped to look at the tree. Everyone was waiting and I think the driver was waiting too. The arguments stopped, replaced by a tremendous silence. I began to wonder if he had fallen into a hole behind the tree, but then, as if the breadth of the tree could in fact have hidden him, Ahmed stepped from behind it, zipping up the jeans which he wore beneath his *burnous*. Oddly enough, there still wasn't a sound as he came back to the train, but he was grinning from ear to ear. A path opened up in a group to let him pass, and as he boarded, the train jerked and moved off. The men below it seemed in no hurry to board, as if they knew it would take some time to pick up speed, and they all stared at Ahmed as they got on; but, oblivious, he continued to gaze at the tree with a tranquil smile. When we were cruising, he turned to me, still smiling.

"How did you do that, Ahmed?" I asked it very quietly.

"When you have little shelter, you must make the most of it," he replied, and that was all he would say.'

'Hmm!'

He threw back his head and laughed, and she *hmmed* again.

'And what about you? You left off your memoirs of Berlin some time ago, didn't you?'

'They'll have to wait for another time,' she said.

'Next time?'

'Alright. Next time. We'd better go now. We've children to collect, remember?'

'Yes, so we have.'

- Nine -

Tess laughed as she cleared Arthur's room. This had been happening for some days now. She looked out to the back garden. Her laughter reminded her that she knew it wouldn't last, but also of her amazement that it had happened at all. She didn't quite know the woman she had turned out to be and it was scary. It was as if she had been speaking a language without knowing the meaning of its words.

It had been too much, three mornings in a row. Suddenly Mungo had taken over her life, so she had applied the brakes, asked him not to see her for a few days. Maybe she was also afraid they would get used to each other too soon, and never having known such exquisite passion she wanted to keep it on edge. Yes, that too. So much to work out! She dragged herself from the window, humming as she tidied Arthur's books. At the back of her mind she knew she would probably never work anything out. An instinct against being taken over might well protect her, but as likely as not she would let the affair take its inbuilt course.

Her only problem was how to continue the Berlin story. He had pressed her and she had dodged it, smothering him in sincere yet manipulative kisses, but he wouldn't be put off another time. She laughed again. That was another reason she had banned him for a couple of days. As if their relationship depended on these crazy lies. Maybe it did, and in thinking this she sat on the bed and brooded. It was all they had to keep them talking to each other. The rest was sex. Or at least it made the sex work, it made them happy with each other, and in themselves. She recalled his face, happy, confident, strong, as he spun his tale, and she loved that in him. He would have seen the same transformation in her, she supposed.

Arthur was happy these days. He still came out of school in the same way, bumping his bag ahead of him with his knees, self-possessed, like a little man. He had picked up on her happiness, and it gave her a surge of joy, as if anything was possible. Now, when they stopped off at the park before continuing home, she played with him, kicking his plastic ball, laughing and screeching, not caring, for the first time, what anyone might think.

'O Lord, I'm far from fit,' she gasped as Arthur scurried off for the ball yet again.

He dribbled past, his co-ordination surprising her, and he laughed in triumph. He was growing up more quickly than she had imagined. Tired but happy, they walked home, closer, she thought, than they ever had been. At home, and over his meal, he played the fool. At first it was funny and then it was tiresome, but she indulged him until she saw he was losing control; so she hugged him till he was calm again.

'Hush my pet. That's enough for today,' she whispered. He still wore his foolish smile, but he settled, and went to the living-room to watch the cartoons. Tess stood by the sink, gazing out the window across the garden. It seemed warm and comforting, and she drifted into a childhood memory of the deep shade of monkey-puzzle trees within which peacocks stood, silent and motionless, their glorious tails at full display.

Brian looked at her curiously as she served him his dinner, but for once she didn't mind. She was imperturbable this evening, daring not to worry whether or not it could last. He said nothing, but she could see he knew she was happy, had guessed one of the reasons and resented her for it; but he ate in silence and that was fine by her.

There was a stretch in the evenings, so on her way home she strayed from her usual route and dallied on the Matt Talbot Bridge to gaze out towards the sea before going on to Books Upstairs in College Green to browse. This was a treat she hadn't given herself in a long time, for no reason. Even touching the books made her feel good. How long was it since she had bought a new book? Not for a long time, and that would have to change.

She left, going up Dame Street. She crossed by the Central Bank through Temple Bar and onto the Ha'penny Bridge, and stood there looking west, the smoke from the Guinness steam house blending into a violet and cobalt dusk, and fancied that darkness rose from the river and moved slowly along its walls towards her. Walking along the quays, she realized she loved Dublin as never before.

There was a card from Marian on the hall floor.

'Dear Bitch! What's with this MAN? And he tells you stories?? Sounds weird. Especially as you didn't mention anything about the other. Didn't think there was that kind of weirdo in Dublin (this place is full of them, whooppee!) but I suppose Dublin is like anywhere else, nowadays. Have to run. Writeandtellmeall Right? Love, Marian.'

Marian's handwriting was large and expansive but grew smaller as it went down the card until it was tiny and squeezed in at the end. Tess grinned. It was a good evening for writing a long letter especially as she could now report a great deal about 'the other', and she went upstairs eagerly, already composing the chronicle of her recent life.

She didn't notice anything at first, in the near darkness, but when she switched on the lamp her heart jumped and she screeched. Her letters, mostly from Marian, were strewn across the floor, out of their envelopes. She realized immediately that the intruder had gone through them all, perhaps had read each one. The old sofa was upturned, as if he – she supposed it was a he – thought there might be something hidden there. Her books had been thrown from their shelves.

Trembling, she forced herself to look in the bedroom and gasped at what she saw. The bedclothes were in a heap on the floor, the mattress and pillows upended like a sinking boat at the edge of the base. Her cassette-machine was open, yet it was still there, where she had left it. Her tapes had been looked through, but they were all there. The door and drawer of the wardrobe were open, her clothes and underclothes scattered about the floor.

In a daze, she went into the kitchen. The table was turned over, her cup was smashed, her pots were thrown about the floor. The window was open. Was that how he got in? But how did he get on the roof? She closed the window, and checked the bathroom. It was untouched, but it seemed unfamiliar, and she stood by the bathroom door for some time, shaking, feeling nauseous and violated. Then she started as she heard a noise on the roof.

'You bastard,' she whispered. 'You bastard you're up there tormenting me.' She checked her purse, and without touching anything, she went to the Lady Gregory on Jervis Street. Over her neat whiskey, she tried to decide what to do, but for a while her mind wouldn't function. Then, as the alcohol calmed her, she realized she couldn't stay in her flat overnight. There was nothing for it but to go back to Fairview.

She sensed a man sitting beside her, and then she heard a gentle voice ask if she was alright.

'Fuck off,' she hissed. How was it that a woman couldn't have a drink alone in peace. Then she looked at him, his hands raised, his shoulders shrugged and his bearded face open and half apologetic, half amused.

'I'm sorry,' she said quietly. 'I didn't mean that, it's just that I got a fright this evening. That's why I'm on this stuff,' she said, raising her glass.

'Were you attacked?' She looked at him closely. He seemed genuine, his question asked quietly, concerned but not melodramatic.

'No, but I feel as if I was. Someone got into my flat and threw everything around the place.'

'Did you call the Guards?'

'No. Oddly enough, nothing was taken.'

'You had no money in the house?'

'No. Not a penny.' She smiled. A thief wouldn't feed whatever habit he had on her income. And for now, it was good to talk to another, sympathetic human being, foolish as it might prove to be.

He offered her a drink and she refused, not wanting to be indebted to him in any way, but later she accepted. As well as needing his company just now she was enjoying it. He was a businessman separated from his wife. This evening he had come for a drink after a long day selling office stationery, but usually he came for the Irish music on Saturday nights. His tie was loose, his shirt open at the neck where his chest hair sprouted. He was very hairy and she wondered if she liked that or not.

About ten o'clock she caught herself slurring her words. If she didn't stop now she would do something foolish, like bringing him back and fucking him, because she needed to be with someone. There was no way around it: that was the only way a woman could be with a man. As he talked, watching his eyes go dusky from drink, she felt like blubbering. Why did it have to be that way between a man and a woman, like some unbreakable rule? She felt tender towards him. He was gentle and kind, and she would have liked nothing better than to talk with him half the night.

'I have to go,' she said interrupting him. He could let her go or ask to leave her home and for a moment she felt exquisitely alive as if the direction of her life depended on the next few seconds. He looked at her as if in a daze.

'I'll leave you home,' he said, without very much conviction, or so she thought.

'No, it's okay. It's been nice meeting you,' and then suddenly she was under the cold night sky, running. She did not look back until she was at her door, fumbling with her key. Once inside, she leaned back against the closed door, her heart beating painfully, her breath rasping, and she cried. She could not face her silent, violated rooms, and yet she had no choice. There was no choice. There was no question of going to Fairview now, and there was no friend to whom her presence would not be a burden and embarrassment. Apart from Marian, all her friends were married, with problems of their own. The women she knew, knew her as Brian's wife, and that was how she fitted into the scheme of things. All her pent-up self-pity for her loneliness, for the unfair difficulties she had to face, broke forth in sobs and tears. It was no way to live, she couldn't go on like this, and in frustration she turned and kicked the door. She limped upstairs, sure she had broken her big toe.

She paused at the door, taking in the room in the harsh light. Feebly closing the door behind her, she went to the toilet and sat on the bowl long after she had pissed, before pulling on her knickers again and washing her hands, rubbing them together until the soap had dried to a wax. She looked in the mirror and saw that while in the morning she had been young, now she was old.

There was no choice. She righted the mattress, made the bed, turned out the light and undressed. There was no sound, only the measured drip of the cistern; but in bed she lay awake, waiting for a footstep or a squeaking door hinge. The silence was a deep black pool, the drip from the cistern making noiseless ripples. A *dubh linn*. Dublin. She smiled. Dublin was a black pool. Despite her squalor, despite her fear, and despite her lack of Irish she could make a translingual pun at a time like this. She turned on her side, her body unwinding, no longer afraid of the intruder, or who it might be.

Tired though she was, sleep would not come. What she needed was a friendly body lying beside her and for the first time in several hours she thought of Mungo again. Her hand, that for a moment was his, crept under her tee-shirt, skimming her belly before making its way by a circuitous route to her heart, where it settled. Then, to her irritation, she couldn't help but think of Brian again. She could never see him doing this, touching himself, discovering that he could feel pleasure in more places that the great *One*. Fuck him; she was upset again. She supposed he wanked in front of his dirty videos; that had always been how she explained how he did without women. But now she wasn't so sure. He was too afraid of himself to do even that; afraid, no doubt, that he'd go blind. Then she remembered there was a brothel in Fairview, how she'd seen men, mostly of middle-age and obviously married, enter and leave in the broad light of day. Calm as you like, as if they had conducted a business deal, which, when she thought of it, was perfectly true. What were they like, the women who worked there, the men who came to them? Women like herself, men like Brian.

She woke early and the morning was fine. Rubbing her eyes and yawning, she surveyed the living-room. To her surprise she was calm, and she dressed and breakfasted as if nothing had happened, bringing a mug of coffee with her as she knelt on the floor to sort through the scattered letters. It was an opportunity to arrange them according to the stamp dates and when she had done this, she organized the rest of the room before she sat back into the armchair and read through Marian's letters in chronological order. In one, she read slowly Marian's throwaway description of a brothel. From the street you could see the men inside, waiting. They just stepped in through a bead curtain, in broad daylight. Had they no fear of being seen? She sat back on her heels, fascinated. She gathered the letters back into their box and put them away.

By eleven, the rooms were casually tidy, as he had seen them. It was important that she keep the break-in to herself. Time was short, and there was none to spare for distraction, and besides, she did not want pity or concern to complicate whatever relationship they had.

Having checked her own appearance – clean, but casual, with no make-up – she made sure the bedclothes were passable. There would be no concessions beyond those of normal courtesy and hygiene. Then she settled to wait and time passed slowly. As the minutes accumulated, the boundaries she had laid down for Mungo began to trouble her, as if she was being punished for being presumptuous. It was important to her to remain in control, but oddly enough, unless he was present, she was powerless and adrift. So she would set no preconditions; she would leave herself open to whatever might happen, if only he would come.

At midday she decided he wasn't arriving, and felt let down. In some way she needed him to counterbalance the violation of the night before to give her back what the intruder had taken from her. She needed him to assert herself by telling her story. Yes, that was it, and without him there was no one she could tell it to. She flung a cushion onto the floor. Where the hell was he, the very morning she needed him? And with a snort, she said aloud: 'Snuggled up in bed with his wife, I suppose.' Bitterly, she tried to put him out of her mind, and think of her life in Berlin. The next time she saw him, she would lay it on thick about Sascha, that much was certain. Sascha? But that was Marian's man! No matter. It would secretly even the score with the bitch. The cow. The slut. She laughed.

He was tall and muscular and virile. Moreover, he was well-off and educated, with a degree in … electronics. He was an electronics engineer and made pots of money. What a lover! He knew without asking where his hands should go, at what pace, at what pressure at precisely the right time. And there was never any question of drooping, no matter how much wine – no, champagne! – they had drunk, on a balcony overlooking the small-hour lights of Berlin. She laughed. That would teach him for not turning up when she needed him!

She turned lazily on the sofa. Such men did exist, that was the sad thing about her life. One of them, at least. This indulgence in regret was not like her, but was all the more enjoyable for that. Oh Berlin! It represented everything a woman like Tess should have as of right.

Instead, she lived alone in a squalid flat which some bastard knew he could break into any time he liked. She went to the bathroom to wash away the tears, but as she looked at her heavy face in the mirror, she realized the tears had not come. There was no release, but she washed her face anyway, and left for The Winding Stair. It was busy and she had to take her coffee and bun to the top floor to get a seat, but she was glad of the crowd, to be anonymous and busy and involved in life somehow.

Looking out over the Liffey, she saw that the Ha'penny Bridge was thronged with a lunch-time crowd, going in both directions, and was a little amused to see that Mungo wasn't there after all, striking some odd pose, as she half expected him to be, knowing perhaps that she would come here, and that such a performance would be a way of getting back into her good books. Perhaps she might even have left her coffee and have run out to the bridge, to demand what on earth he was up to. She smiled into her coffee cup.

But no, he wasn't there. It was only fantasy to hope he might have been, as some solace at the end. The real harsh world prevailed, with nothing to soften its blows. To think that twenty-four hours before she was a happy, deluded woman. But she hated when she was self-indulgent like this. She had, after all, her son, who she would see in a short time, and maybe, despite everything, they could be happy again for a few hours.

Arthur expected to be brought to the park, which was fine by her, as it was a lovely day. With abandon she perfected the art of letting him seem like a football wizard beside her, and he took on his role with glee. On the way home he spoke about his day, his friends and enemies, the fight he had been in, in a way she never remembered hearing before. This was what she had missed, and her loneliness was no longer total. In a moment that teetered on folly, she almost told him about the break-in, about her need for someone to talk to, before she remembered that he was a child. A bright child, mature beyond his years, but nevertheless a child. For now, his opening out to her, as if she was his best friend, was enough, more than she had come to expect. Perhaps solace would never come in the way she might hope for, but nonetheless it would come in unexpected ways, and the trick was to be open enough to recognize it. She acknowledged this, and yet she longed to be giddily happy with all her hopes fulfilled, as a girl might have the right to wish.

As she made Brian's meal she toyed with the idea of talking to him, perhaps in some roundabout way. Small talk. What she really wanted to know was if he was involved with a woman, or women, but that was a dangerous subject in several ways. In the end, she kept her silence, which now constituted normality within those walls.

As she prepared to leave, Arthur was watching the cartoons, but he was restless, and more than once he turned to her with a quizzical smile. She sat on her hunkers to say good-bye, and stroking his hair, she tenderly placed her forehead against his.

'Are you going to come home to stay, Tess?' he asked, so quietly that it could have been a thought of her own. She was shocked for a while, yet did not move her head from his, but kept it there, her one contact with reality.

'No, my love,' she whispered. 'I can't. Your dad and I aren't friends any more. We can't talk to each other, and if we do, we shout, and that's very bad for you. For us all. It's better this way. It's better to be happy for a few hours every day than to be miserable all day. Isn't it?'

'Yes, I suppose so.'

They were both clinging to this moment of togetherness for all they were worth, but suddenly it was over, and she kissed him quickly and was gone.

She crossed the Liffey and went to Trinity, plagued by the thought that she had left Arthur high and dry. All she could hope for was that he knew she loved him, and that in his precocious wisdom he would know that she had no choice but to live apart from his father.

Students were sprawled on the verges of the playing fields, talking and laughing. Several athletes were pounding out their laps. She lay on the grass for a while. After all, there was no hurry, and it was pleasant to lie in the waning sun amidst the indolence of youth. A few athletes ran past, one of them a woman, and she watched them hungrily. There were few things more beautiful than the human body responding to the will with ease. They were running at an even pace, but suddenly, halfway around the track, their strides lengthened into a long, powerful rhythm which fascinated Tess. The woman was good, she noted with satisfaction. She couldn't catch the leader, but she held her own with the third man and at one point she passed him before fading. During the sprint, their bodies seemed to consist of powerful legs, their torsos and arms superfluous appendages; but then it was over, and they jogged like ordinary mortals. Tess wished she could have been like the woman who passed her now, able to release a power in herself, to overcome her pain and catapult herself into a different way of being.

She watched the athletes complete a second lap. There was no sprint this time, so she decided to leave before she became bored with them. The roar of traffic in College Green always took her by surprise after the tranquillity of Trinity, just a few steps away. She stopped off in Books Upstairs again, browsing among the new titles, revelling in the touch of books, unresentful of the fact that she couldn't afford to buy them.

By taking her time in this way, it was almost nine when she got home. There was a note from Mungo saying he wouldn't be able to see her for a while, as his daughter was sick. For a gut-wrenching moment she misread it, probably because she had half expected it, and thought he had written that he wouldn't be able to see her again, but to her relief she saw that his absence would be temporary. That was an elastic word, but it probably meant the duration of a childhood illness – a week? Ten days? She would have to kick her heels for however long it took, having no choice, as there was nothing else in her life but her need to tell this man her story. At least he had the grace to add he was looking forward to seeing her.

* * *

Easter caught her by surprise, and the children's holidays meant they couldn't see each other for much longer than they had assumed. She had to stay in Fairview to mind Arthur during the day, but she slipped back every other day, when Arthur was with his grandparents, hoping there might be a note, hoping, even, that they might meet by happy accident.

It was two weeks before he arrived, two weeks of beautiful weather during which she went to Stephen's Green every day for a few hours, reading a book on feminism which she had picked up in the library. It was interesting, in that it highlighted many of the things which were wrong in her life, and many of the wrongs perpetuated against her as a woman, but it was interesting in a way that a book on dieting is interesting. All of it was perfectly true, but meaningless unless she acted on it. At least she had put down a healthy tan, plus the inevitable freckles to which she was resigned, between the Green and Fairview Park, where she played football with Arthur, which, she acknowledged with amusement, had made her fit after a fashion.

For a week she had stayed in until noon, hoping against hope for the ring on the bell which remained silent, when she began to think that the note was a ploy to let her down easy. For most of this time she was calm and could read or listen to Schubert and Schumann, or sometimes, Paul Robeson and Jessie Norman, but occasionally the frustration of the enforced wait burst through, and on one bad morning before her period came, she cried.

The weather broke. When the bell finally rang, Mungo was looking suitably apologetic. Despite herself, all she could think of was that she had him the way she wanted him. After the exchange of pleasantries and a light kiss on the cheek, she led him upstairs and made tea. He had called the day before.

'But you know that's my dole morning,' she said, irritated.

'Sorry. I forgot.'

So they had missed a precious day, and now he was looking at her with unmistakable lust. Well, he could wait, and if she couldn't tell her story, if he didn't give her the opening she needed, or encourage her, the wait would be indefinite.

'How have you been?' he asked mildly.

'Okay. How's your little girl?'

'She's back at school, but she made the most of it while she was sick. Little girls like to boss their daddies around, you know, and no easier time to do it than when they're sick.'

She laughed at that. Drops of rain were making their way down the window panes, just like they did in Berlin that November. Ask me, for Christ's sake, she thought. If she stayed silent, he'd be forced to cast about for an opening, and Berlin was the most obvious one surely. Or had he forgotten? She looked at him, but just as quickly looked away again and went to the window. A floorboard creaked as he followed and stood behind her.

'Was I away too long?'

'Yes.'

He put his hands on her waist, lightly; but as quickly she removed them. They were silent for a while. The rain was coming down in waves of fine mist, and the traffic had thickened along the quays.

'Maybe you'd like me to go.'

She turned, her eyes glistening and she resented him very much, but said nothing. If that was all he had to say, then maybe she would prefer him to go. She looked out at the rain again and the awkward silence was there again, but she was past caring.

'I was looking forward to hearing more about your time in Berlin,' he said then, and immediately the tension drained away, and without turning, she smiled.

'This weather reminds me of it,' she said very softly. She could tell he had relaxed. 'It rained all of the November I was there, and I used to stand at a window just like this, watching it dribble down the panes.'

She turned and directed him to the sofa where they both sat. This was what she had been waiting for, this feeling of being drugged and confident. Drugged with confidence.

'Brian and I had just separated, and if it was hell with him, it wasn't heaven being alone with a small boy who wondered every day if his father was coming home. Brian, to give him his due – or he was obliged to under German law, I'm not sure – he gave me money for Arthur through a solicitor, so while I was having a hard time, at least I had the means to survive. It was pretty lonely, mind you. I heard as much Turkish as I did German, always on the street or across a courtyard. The Turkish women sometimes talked from window to window. I don't know what I'd have done without Marian, my Irish friend. I think I told you about her before.'

'Yes. She brought you to Frau Pohl's.'

'That's right.' She was pleased, and could see that he was pleased with himself for remembering. 'She used to drag me out, sometimes with Arthur, and at other times, later on, she'd baby-sit. The first time, she insisted that I go to a dinner party. I was terrified, I had hardly any German, none really, and ...' she glanced at Mungo '... that's where Sascha and I ...' Suddenly she was nervous. Something had flickered in Mungo at Sascha's name; she wasn't sure what. But there was no turning back. 'Marian had brought Sascha along a few times to my apartment and it seems he liked me and asked Marian to make sure I went to his party. So I went.' Her confidence returned when she said that. She had every right to go, whether Mungo was happy about it or not, and if he wasn't, he could lump it. 'It was quite a place: a long pale blue room with a low ceiling and with nothing on the walls. Nothing. A few shelves, that's all, and in the far end of the room there was a big bed, covered in furs, would you believe. I ...' she grinned '... I got to know that bed very well.' Mungo smiled too. He's taking it very well, she thought, although – and she thought this with relish – there's a lot more he's going to have to take.

'There were six people seated at a table which was fully dressed with a saffron cloth, and candelabra and tureens – the works. Lots of wine, of course. They all spoke good English and for a while they were polite and spoke it for my benefit, even among themselves, but then of course, after a few glasses of wine, the conversation which was quite highbrow and a bit self-conscious, I thought, got more animated. It was then that Sascha began to hold my hand under the tablecloth and look meaningfully into my eyes. He was tall and broad and very solid, several years younger than me, and of course I was knocking back the wine, and his soft but very masculine voice was getting under my skin, so he didn't have to work very hard on me. When I first saw the room, the very idea of a bed in full view of the dining-table shocked me, and I didn't know what to think – whether perhaps I was in for an orgy or what. Maybe that's why I drank so much. Anyway, by the time he got around to holding my hand I was ready for anything, and I really did think he was going to make love to me in full view of everyone on that bed. Just goes to show how naïve-in-reverse you can be. But I was fully prepared to let him, even join him.' She paused for effect. 'For the first time in my life, I was as hot as a brick in an oven.'

She was pleased to see that Mungo's eyes widened.

'He waited until everyone had gone, about two in the morning, I suppose, but he had stoked me all night, a light kiss on the neck, his hand on my waist, a burning look that said everything I had ever wanted to hear.' She stopped and looked at him disingenuously. 'Do you mind me telling you this?'

'Ah, no ... no. It's very interesting. Go on.'

She could tell his mouth was dry, but what she hadn't bargained for was that her own body was betraying her, her palms were sweating and her heart was beating faster. If she wasn't mistaken she was very moist and her blood seemed to be lying just beneath her skin in languorous pools. There was nothing for it now but to continue, to play it out to the inevitable end.

'He ... When he closed the door on the last guest, he hesitated for a long time ... anyway it seemed like a long time ... looking at me. Then he changed the music, to something beautiful, I think it was a Schumann waltz, and he took me in his arms and danced me around that apartment, that heavenly-blue apartment until I felt like passing away. No faltering, no stepping on toes, just two bodies in harmony. And then he kissed me.'

Tess stared at Mungo, who stared back. They were both trembling. She closed her eyes, and cupped her breasts in her hands. 'His hands seemed to be all over my body, everywhere at once,' and Tess's hands began to move rhythmically across her belly, over her mount, around her neck, 'at the perfect pressure and pace,' and now her breath was laboured, 'until I was shaking. And then, kissing me on the back of the neck, kissing me like a god, he turned me around,' and Tess twisted on the sofa, groaning, her skirt riding up her leg, 'and I just knew, I knew I should lean across the table,' and Tess half stood and leaned on the arm of the sofa, 'so ... so he could lift my skirt ...'

Mungo stood and lifted her skirt. 'Like this?' he asked, his voice uneven.

'Yes, like that ...' she whispered, 'and he took down my pants and ...' as Mungo followed suit '... and caressed me softly down there ...'

As Mungo's fingers moved with surprising ease under the hood of her mount, her eyes began to go back into her skull. His free hands roamed her body, and when his finger missed its mark, she manoeuvred it back again, and her pleasure swelled, wave upon wave. 'Harder,' she groaned, 'harder.'

'Wait,' he said, his voice shaking and far away, 'I have a condom.'

That's what Sascha said, and if he said it, it was fine by her. She wasn't waiting, she was in a state of flux, and she didn't care: she had achieved what she had always dreamed of doing, she was making passionate love to a tall handsome German in a strange apartment in Berlin, and as Sascha filled her from behind she let herself go upon a great surfing wave, until she and her god were spent.

- *Ten* -

The weather remained broken and Mungo stayed indoors, haunted by the memory reflected in the rain as it trickled down the window. To have lived to find himself in that furnace of passion and abandon was a revelation of what life could after all hold. It would never happen quite like that again, if only because he now knew it existed. Perhaps it could happen in another way, shock him to the core, change him all over again; but he refused to hope for that; it was asking too much.

If it would happen with anyone it would be with Tess. Yet if he had known her ten or fifteen or even five years before, it would not have happened. They each had to go through their seemingly barren lives to reach the point where they could be like that. And, he consoled himself, even if he could have waited unattached and free it still would not have happened: they both had to go through marriage, children, the death of love.

How alive, he wondered, had their loves been, even in the beginning? He had perhaps not been very much alive himself. He was twenty-four when he met Connie, she a year younger. He had spotted her as she danced with a big countryman twice her age in the Irish Club in Parnell Square. It was quite possible that she had cast her eye on him first. In any event, it was soon clear that they fancied each other, and after two weeks, having overcome a token resistance, she convinced him he had seduced her. After a night of energetic tussle, there was no turning back. It was still like that: energetic, blind, craving for oblivion, and what came between was accidental and a means to an end. And then, long spells when they were strangers to each other. He had noticed it first after Aidan was born. The pattern had begun to establish itself then, he realized, and not after Aidan's accident. Perhaps if things had not gone so smoothly in the beginning, it might have been different. They might have been able to gauge their real need of one another, got to know each other, or parted. It was his fault. He had drifted on the ebb tide. He had felt it was time for marriage, and Connie was there. No doubt her reasoning had been the same. He liked her body, he still did. It was the main reason he still had sex with her, however rarely; and now he liked the comfort of his home, the backdrop of security for his children. And when the children were gone, he would settle for his own comfort. Was that it?

He longed for a cigarette or a drink. All this reflection was too painful to take neat. And yet he welcomed it; what had been blurred for years was now as clear as a formula. He wondered if Connie had seen this a long time ago, but had just given in and retreated to her bed, television and the Sunday night drink with the girls. Maybe she kept going for the sake of the children. She was a good woman, and he felt a sympathy with her. He couldn't be easy to live with, but something beyond being tied to him had died in her. Perhaps it was only the flush of youth which had given the impression that it had ever lived. He wished for things to be different, to roll back the years and build a bridge between them with what he was aware of now. But he knew it was too late, and it was impossible to change someone anyway. And yet ... and yet ... He was different with Tess, a different man to the one he had always known himself to be. The question was: did he want to take the leap into that way of being himself? Would Tess have him, once she became stronger, as he believed was happening, even if this was because of him? Could he give up being a father to his children, which had given his life any meaning it might have had until now? Perhaps on this point he could come to an arrangement, like Tess had with her son, but Connie was a proud woman in spite of everything and he felt sure she would use the children as a stick to punish him.

And yet, what did he know of Tess? Only what he knew through the tall tales she had told, and the tall tales he had told her. How strange.

The rain had cleared without him noticing, and now a band of blue sky lay between the rooftops and the lightened cloud. Connie came, laden with shopping, and proceeded to put it away. Somehow, she had avoided getting wet, though she had no umbrella.

'You realize the children get their holidays tomorrow,' she said.

'Thanks for reminding me.'

'Have you spoken with your mother about them going down?'

'No, not yet.' His heart sank. He would be expected to go too, along with Connie, to be a family, as a dry run before settling there.

'Tell her I'll go down later in the month,' Connie said, as if she had steeled herself.

'Alright.'

'I got a letter from Mammy this morning. Daddy isn't well, so I thought maybe I'd go up for a few weeks.'

'What happened him?'

'Took a weak turn. I don't suppose it's serious but you never know.'

'No. I'll ring Mother today, then.'

Connie went into the kitchen. So the die was cast and he was trapped. The possibility of an alternative life was falling away. Was he relieved? Yes, a part of him was, that lead in his bones and blood; but mostly he felt defeat, as if the events of his life had conspired against him for so long that he needed an anger and energy he could not find to throw them off. Yet, he found that it hurt him, and in that were the seeds of an anger that might one day liberate him. It was now very clammy and he needed to get out in the open.

'I'm going to take a walk as far as the GPO to ring, alright?' he called.

'The GPO?' Connie called back.

'Well, it looks like clearing. Anyway, I need some air.'

He walked by way of the cobblestones of Smithfield Market. Peace at last. Dressed in tee-shirt, jeans and runners, he exulted in his freedom in the hot sunshine that had broken through, so that for a time he found it easy to keep his predicament at bay. Halfway down, he saw that a broken mains near Queen Street had become a fountain, unnoticed, it seemed, by anyone except himself. He walked up to it, enchanted by the sparkling drops of water caught by the sun, as if each drop was a teeming world intensely alive for a moment before falling back into the gushing universe. Enjoying the cool air and the boyish novelty, he was tempted to walk through it; but no, he thought, let it be what it is. He walked away, but then he heard a Volkswagen van slowing, and he turned to see the driver and his woman companion grinning as they rolled up the windows and drove very slowly over the fountain. Now it was something else, but no matter, and Mungo grinned too. The van circled and this time a side of the van was simultaneously washed and cooled. They came a third time, laughing and conscious of Mungo observing them, and washed the other side of their van. They circled again, but this time they stopped, looking at Mungo and laughing. The driver nodded towards Mungo and then to the fountain, and Mungo looked from the couple to the fountain again, and on impulse he leaped to their suggestion and ran through the fountain, which almost knocked him out of his stride, and despite his run, drenched him. He turned to face the other two, grinning and breathless, and noticed that the young woman had stopped laughing, though her mouth was open, as if she was impressed or moved by what he had done. Then she decided to do the same and without hesitation got out of the van and flung herself through the fountain, stumbling as she passed through it but at the last moment staying upright. She turned in triumph to face her companion, and taken by surprise, it was a few moments before he took up her unspoken challenge and imitated her with a whoop. He jumped through it with such vigour that he ran on, and in those few seconds the woman turned and looked straight into Mungo's eyes. He saw at a glance that her breasts showed through her drenched shirt, and that she in her turn looked frankly at how his clothes clung to his body. But then the moment was gone and in the instant her companion turned, she turned to him. His lips twisted into a leer, and then he advanced towards her, and though her back was turned to Mungo he could see her shoulders rising and falling, and she spread her feet slightly, as if to brace herself – her jeans, Mungo noticed, clinging to her; and when her companion reached her, they kissed passionately.

Mungo turned away and hurried, walking as fast as he could, until he reached the fruit and vegetable markets where, although it was mid-afternoon, the fork lifts were still busy. Along Mary's Lane, past the aroma of The Pastry Bakery, it suddenly came to him: there were obligations he had to fulfil; there was a space to be cleared, and then in turn, and *then*, he would be free. That's what he wanted to say to Tess. That was her position too, with her son. They were both in the same boat, and he hurried along Capel Street to the quays, bursting to tell her.

Even as he pressed her bell, he knew she was gone to collect Arthur. His clothes were almost dry, though his runners still squelched, and he realized that he had attracted glances, but he didn't care any more what people might think, and took off his runners and went barefoot, airing them as he walked.

In the GPO, the phone rang for a minute or so before his mother replied. He persisted because he knew she'd be about the yard somewhere, and also because the GPO was a long way to walk to without an answer. He felt neutral, somehow beyond what was inevitably unfolding.

'Well.'

'The children are off school now. We were thinking of going down at the weekend.'

'You could have told me.'

'Well ...'

'And what about you?'

'I'll put them on the train—'

'What? and leave me—'

'I'm rising you. I'll be with them.'

'You never grew up, Mungo, you know that.' He knew it well, she'd been telling him for twenty years. 'And what about Connie?'

'Connie's father's not well. She'll be down in a few weeks – we're staying a few weeks, if that's all right.' There was a brief silence. Mungo knew that it was a moment of something more than satisfaction for her, which now that the die was cast he felt generous enough to concede.

'What do you mean – a few weeks? You'll stay for the children's holidays at least.' It was both plea and command.

'We'll see.'

'Tell Connie she'll have the run of the house.'

It had cost her a lot to say that, but she was nothing if not a realist.

'Fine, I'll tell her that.'

'Friday afternoon?'

'Friday evening. There's a few things to be seen to.'

Like, he thought, his eyes closed – like seeing Tess for maybe the last time.

Somehow he got through the rest of the day, caught up in the children's excitement and the practical details of organizing the holiday. It took him a long time to sleep. There was so much to do, according to Connie's schedule, that he would have no chance to see Tess. He would have to write to her, and he only vaguely knew her address. In fact there was no getting around it: he knew where she lived, but he had no idea of her house number. He didn't care about himself any more, only for Tess, who he had no choice but to abandon, when, he remembered with longing, her story was only half told. His too, but he would have to find a way for her to tell hers; he owed her that. And his story? It was stalled somewhere on the rail tracks between Zaragoza and Barcelona. Soon he would see the Mediterranean again and they would arrive in – what was the name of the station? Perhaps he could find it in the library in Gorey, but the name was only a detail, and he wouldn't know what it was, never mind being able to tell it, without her in front of him, listening to every detail, making sure it was true. His lips opened to tenderly kiss her ghost.

'You look wrecked,' Connie said at the breakfast table, after the children had bounced away. Already they were arguing in the yard.

'Didn't sleep very well.' He looked at her directly. 'I'm not looking forward to this.'

'To Wexford? Well,' she said rising to clear the dishes, 'neither am I.' She paused for effect. 'But your mother has made the effort and so should we.'

He smiled. 'You've really got your sights on the farm, haven't you?'

'Haven't you?' She hadn't taken offence. They were very matter-of-fact.

'No. I don't want it at all. If my mother died in the morning – and she'll live for the next forty years, by the way – or if she signed it over to us, my family would have their hand out for their share, and who would blame them? And the value of land on paper is always more than it's likely to produce in a lifetime.'

'We can sell this house, you know. We don't lack capital.'

'Capital?' He stared at her as she cleared the table, realizing that she was a business woman who would come to life if she got half a chance. Whereas he was a dreamer who would never do anything, his only value to her being as a means to an end, and an indulgent if wayward father to her children. He could see she was animated by her long-term scheme. No doubt she was seething with ideas. No doubt she could make the farm pay its way, and debts would be cleared, treated as a challenge. Of course he knew the basics, even if he had tried to forget.

She would use his knowledge until she was proficient herself. The children and their inheritance: that was the justification. He could only admire her.

'Here,' she said. 'Check this list and make sure I've thought of everything.'

'Wellingtons,' he said, glancing through it.

'What?'

'Wellingtons. I'm okay, there's boots down there for me, but the children need wellingtons.'

'Well now, aren't you great?' she said, seeing how pleased he was.

'There's been a lot of rain of late. They'll be up to their shins in muck.' He was grinning now.

'How would I cope without you,' she said, taking money from her purse and handing it to him. 'Sure you're great altogether.'

'It's what marriage is all about.'

'Don't start me.' She scribbled a note. 'Here, you can never remember what size they take. And don't be all day. I need some help.'

With one bound he was free. The phrase came back to him as he closed the door behind him. From some comic he had read as a child, no doubt, like *Dash it, old chap!* and *Achtung!* and *Schweinhund!* and *Himmel!* and *For he's a jolly good fellow!* and *Tallyho!* He could have used them all at various moments over the last twenty-four hours.

The fountain in Smithfield had been stemmed. He avoided the markets by opting for Chancery Street and cutting down by Ormond Square onto the quays. Small children were playing on the swings and slides in Ormond Square, their playground bordered by cherry trees whose blossoms had long since blown over the surrounding houses in the spring winds. The children's voices filled the square. Mothers sat with babies in prams, chatting, sunning themselves.

For once, Mungo welcomed the heavy traffic on the quays. By the following day he would miss it, but for now his only prayer was that Tess would be in. It was still early, she might not even be up. He rang the bell. Forty-two. That was her number. Forty-two, forty-two. He rang again. Forty-two.

She opened the door in a tee-shirt and skirt, obviously just out of bed, but she smiled and gave him her cheek to kiss.

'You're lucky,' she said. 'I wasn't going to answer but I looked out the window and saw you.'

'Thanks,' he said quietly.

'You look very subdued. Are you okay?'

'Let's go up.'

She looked at him but said nothing and led him upstairs. He could see she was preparing herself for the worst, and he wondered what in fact he would tell her. For the first time he noticed hair on her legs, and once more, maybe for the last time, he drank in the curves of her body through her light clothing. She seemed so vulnerable, balanced between youth and the attrition of age, and he wanted to say something stupid like, 'I'll love you anyway, even if you lose your figure.'

'Tea?'

'Please.' He closed the door behind him as she disappeared into the kitchen, grateful, he supposed, for the respite in which she could steel herself and save her dignity, if nothing else.

They drank in silence, each looking at the other, desire hemmed in by caution.

'You don't want to see me any more, do you?'

The question hung in the air.

'I won't be able to see you for a few weeks. That's why I came yesterday, and this morning, to tell you. And even then, if you still want to see me, there will be intervals of weeks.'

That was it. He had said what he had to say, in more or less the way he wanted to say it. By some magic her presence lent him a fluency, he who in other company rarely spoke more than a few words at a time.

'May I ask why?' There was no recrimination or drama, only a hint of loss. His estimation of her went up another notch; but now that he had to answer her inevitable question, he feared that he would descend in hers.

'I've let myself ... be persuaded by two women, my mother and my wife, that as I'm not gainfully employed here, I should help out on the farm in Wexford, which I am led to expect will be passed on to me. My children love it there ... and their grandmother adores them ... and so I tell myself I'm doing it for them.'

'You don't love it there.'

'No.'

Their eyes met and he reached out and lightly touched her cheek. She closed her eyes and pressed her cheek against his hand, and it seemed to him that she was taking the last delicate ounce of their time together, when she could have done otherwise without blame.

'The things we do for our children,' she whispered. 'Our one constant love.'

His hand moved across her face, and she dragged her lips against his fingers, then pushed back her head, exposing her neck to his kisses. He was powerless to hurry, even if he had wanted to, but he didn't care about the clock. This was their time together, which lapsed under its own rules.

After they had made love, they lay together for some time. Then she sniffed.

'We stink. You better wash if you're going back to your wife, not to mention your mother.' He laughed, but it was a pained laugh.

'What time is it?'

She leaned across him to check the clock.

'Twenty past one. I'll have to go soon. I've to collect Arthur from Brian's parents. Shunt him over to my parents. They all want a piece of him. Then he'll be with me for the summer.' She grinned. 'Maybe we could go down to Wexford!' He lifted himself onto his elbow, suddenly alert. 'Silly! I can't afford a holiday in Wexford or anywhere else.'

'Oh. What a pity.'

'Come on, get up.'

'Yeah. Suppose we better.'

She didn't move and he felt her watch him as he dressed

and wondered if she took pleasure from it, or if she merely saw that he too had lost his youthful sleekness. It embarrassed him a little to be observed like this, but he wasn't slow to do the same to her. Fair enough. He had his trousers on, and he pulled his shirt over his head. There was nothing further to see, or so he thought.

'I can't say whether I'll be here when you come back, Mungo.' He turned. 'There's no knowing what might happen between now and then.'

'I know.'

She turned away to dress, and certain this was the last time he would see her like this, he stared at her, trying to burn the details of her body into his memory.

'You've given me back my appetite for sex,' she said, still turned away. 'I don't think I'd be able to last without it now.'

He didn't reply. How could she say a thing like that, when she was still hot from his body? She was still dressing, slowly, her back turned to him, tense and silent. He was shaking, unable to handle this. Then the anger came and he made to leave, not caring if he ever saw her again. Furious, he turned at the door to say what he thought of her – but her back was still turned to him. So be it. He left, leaving the doors open behind him, slamming the front door closed.

He bought the wellingtons in Henry Street without any hesitation and strode home, throwing them on the table.

'Oh you're back!' Connie called from upstairs, her voice laden with sarcasm.

'Look,' he shouted up the stairs. 'I've got the wellingtons and I'm going to fucking Wexford. Is there anything else I can do for you, like drowning myself or something like that?'

He fumed, waiting for the retort which didn't come. Ethna came in from the street and he glared at her, but she was oblivious and danced up to him.

'Hallo Daddy,' she sang, and he relented.

'Hello pet,' he said, holding her. Content, she danced away again.

'There's still some hot water for a shower if you want one,'

Connie called. He caught her conciliatory tone and assented, remembering, as that bitch had put it, that he stank. Connie was standing at the door of the children's bedroom, a bundle of Ethna's pants in her hand.

'What's got into you?' she asked quietly.

'I'm going to Wexford,' he said with perfect truth, 'but I don't have to like it, do I?' and he closed the bathroom door for a respite. As he washed his hair, the water ran cold.

On the train, the children had settled by Bray. Once again, he had made sure they looked up from their comics to see the curve of Killiney Bay as the train slowed on the single track beneath the overhanging rock at the edge of the cliff. Below, there were families dotted about the beach, a few swimmers by the shore, a few small boats easing their way through the tranquil water. Again, Aidan and Ethna were silent while the view lasted, then returned to their comics without comment. Mungo wondered if it affected them at all.

It affected him. It calmed him, and he saw that he had been foolish. If he was deserting her, which he was, then she had every right to feel like that, to say it, to wound him with it, even. He'd write to her from Gorey. That was all he could do now. That the loss was not inevitable, that it was his choice in the end, made it very painful.

'Did we bring paper and envelopes to write to Mammy?' he asked Aidan.

'I have them in my bag.'

'Did we remember stamps?' Aidan made a face. 'Never mind, we'll stop off in Gorey and get some.'

Mungo, he thought, necessity is making you devious.

Thinking back over the day, he realized that his anger had surprised Connie. It was the first time he had shown anger since Aidan's accident and it had stopped her in her tracks. She had even kissed him good-bye at the station, for Christ's sake – to the amused approval of the children – and had deferred to him all afternoon. Could it be that she approved? He thought about that for a moment and dismissed it. She was humouring him, afraid he might upset the apple-cart.

They were now below Greystones, travelling at speed between the long stretch of narrow beach to the east, and the moorland and mountains to the west. The anger, the assertion had felt good, had given him back a feeling of his strength, of his right to say what he needed and what was detrimental to those needs. He would say it – he would make it plain, and if Connie really wanted that Godforsaken land, she would have to meet him halfway or lose everything. By Arklow, he was looking forward to the summer. Perhaps it would be a season of discovery.

In Gorey, he took the wheel.

'But I'm not insured,' his mother protested.

'Well, we'll have to get insured.' And he drove to the post office.

'Why are we stopping?' she demanded.

'Because we need stamps to write to Mammy, don't we children?'

'Yes,' they chorused.

'But I have stamps at home!'

'Oh we can't sponge off Granny! We have to get our own, don't we?' This time only Ethna agreed. Aidan was looking at his grandmother, who was looking at Mungo as if she sensed he was crazy.

'Can I come? I want to come!' Ethna shouted.

'No no, stay there with Granny. I won't be a minute.'

He bought a dozen stamps and a mail letter in the post office.

Dear Tess, I acted like a small boy, as you will have noticed. Naturally you've a right to look somewhere else – why wouldn't you. If you're still around, I would be very glad to see you the next time I'm in Dublin. I want to hear the rest of your story and I'd like you to hear mine – we can't finish until that happens can we? I miss you. Mungo.'

'There you are,' he said, turning to the children as he sat into the car. 'Three stamps for you, Ethna, and three for you, Aidan – that should be enough, shouldn't it?'

Mrs Kavanagh fretted about the insurance and his bad driving until they reached home. Bowing to the inevitable, she arranged the insurance the following day.

They settled into a routine, and Mungo revelled in clearing the backlog of work. In the evenings he walked to neighbours' houses to renew old acquaintances. Some of them called during the day. He ventured farther afield in the car, bringing his mother if she let herself be persuaded, but always taking the children so they would know the haunts of his own childhood and youth. To his gratification, they loved this. At night he was so tired he fell asleep immediately, knowing he was leaving no space to think.

His mother checked everything he did, but it didn't bother him. He knew she wasn't going to change now. How Connie would take it was another matter. Yet as he watched her, unknown to her, checking on him, he saw her vitality was ebbing, and for a stomach-turning instant he imagined a shadow walking beside her; that her energy was flowing, little by little, into this shadow. It was the first time he realized she was mortal, yet she was still vigorous enough to drive herself to Mass every morning.

The postman came with letters for the children from Connie. In Aidan's there was a note for Mungo. Her father was recovering well, and she would be down soon, would ring from Dublin. Love, Connie.

She came few days later, and to his surprise and admiration, she settled well. His mother too, seemed to have thought matters out, and their relationship worked from the beginning, despite the antagonism which had not always been disguised since Mungo had introduced them. Both women had been wary even before that, he remembered.

Now, it seemed, they were in league against him. He was amused, until he overheard them talking about him one morning, when his mother thought he had gone to check the sheep. They were washing and drying the dishes.

'You like it here, don't you Connie?'

'Aye, it's great, Granny. The children adore it.'

'Well, the city is no place to rear children.'

'No, it isn't really ...'

'You know I've left the place to Mungo in my will.'

'No ... no, I didn't know that ...'

'Well I have. And if ye were to come, to live – not just a holiday – to live, then I'd sign it over, on the spot.'

'God ... that's very good of you.'

'Well Connie, I'm getting old. Maybe I am old. Anyhow, I can't really manage any more, and it's lovely around here. You'd have the run of the place, Connie, there's no question about that. The house is big enough, God knows, and I could have a little flat to myself. So what do you think?'

'It sounds wonderful. It really does.'

'Well would you talk to that son of mine. Sometimes I think he's away in the clouds. Anyhow, he doesn't listen to his mother.'

'Ach, he loves it here as much as the rest of us, Granny. He just likes to be coaxed into doing what he wants. Sure all men are the same.'

'You'll see to it then?'

'Don't worry. I'll talk to him.'

'It'd be a great weight off my mind, I can tell you.'

Mungo left to count the sheep, bringing the dog who, without a word from him, rounded them up into a corner. He couldn't remember if it was easier to count them like this, bunched together, or scattered, but he counted them three times and came to the same tally. The air was heavy and it hurt his eyes to look at the clouds, so laden with rain that they almost glowed. Halfway up the hill it came, and he took shelter under the big oak in the middle of the field. Within seconds the rain covered the hills and valleys in great squalls which fascinated him. The stream would flood; a good time for fishing.

So all men were the same? Somehow he didn't think so. There was a time when he had thought all women were the same. Now he knew it wasn't true. Tess was very different to Connie, and although they shared traits, Connie was different to his mother. He could say with a degree of certainty that he was different from the man he had been, and that neither Connie nor his mother had noticed, or if they had, they had put it down to male pride. Pride had nothing to do with it. For one thing, the man they thought he was did not follow strange women. He laughed out loud, relishing the freedom to do so, surrounded by rain and the large field.

The rain lasted several days, and while the children played in the outhouses and the hay barn, they were about the house a lot and there was tension between the women, which Ethna finally broke by cutting her hand. Aidan looked on guiltily while Connie tried to stem the blood and Ethna screamed, but Mungo said nothing. The cut required two stitches and Ethna settled into being the focus of attention, her mother and grandmother outdoing each other to spoil her. When the weather cleared, Mungo brought Aidan to see the stream at the bottom of the big grass field, telling him on the way that the big oak, alone on a mound in the centre, was a fairy tree. All such trees were fairy trees, he said. Aidan was cynical, laughing at his father. He was too old to believe in fairy tales. Mungo tried to tell him that this was a different matter; this was a part of the land he was standing on, and which, perhaps, he would one day own. But Aidan wasn't fooled, leaving Mungo unaccountably sad. He cheered again when Aidan responded to stories about how Mungo and his brothers and sisters had played in and fished the clear stream; and they crossed the footstick, though the stream was only a few inches deep now that the flood had subsided, and explored the scrub where Mungo had set snares. This fascinated his son: the tracks, the burrows, the droppings, they were all still there, as Mungo remembered them.

Later, they rolled over the heavy bales of hay to air them. Mungo explained that when he was a boy, hay was cut with a mower in rows, its scent filling the air like perfume; then as it browned in the sun it was turned with either a hay fork or machine, before being gathered into cocks. Now most farmers seemed to favour silage; at least here, the hay was still made, in whatever way. There was much he had to tell the children. There was even more he had to remember and learn.

In Gorey, he bought a card which showed scenes from the town.

'Dear Tess, my train has broken down outside Barcelona, stuck there until I see you, which I hope will be soon. I miss you. Mungo.'

He had to go to Dublin soon. There was at least one excuse: to check the house. Maybe Connie would want to hand it over to an estate agent. He didn't want that to happen. Despite the disasters and unhappiness, he loved that house. It was his base and springboard. His children were conceived there, and there had been happy times, which seemed now to outweigh the unhappy ones. He supposed that for Connie, Aidan's accident was synonymous with it.

But the days passed, and neither broached the subject.

The following Saturday morning he was checking the sheep when he heard Aidan shouting, panic-stricken, and running towards him as fast as he could. Granny had fainted, he was shouting, Mammy said he was to come quick! Mungo ran up the hill, and Aidan turned and ran ahead.

His mother was dead. She had collapsed at the foot of the stairs and Connie had done all she knew to revive her, a doctor and a priest were on their way; but she was dead. Mungo stared at her, unable to believe it. The children were crying, afraid, knowing something beyond their ken had happened.

'Here, help me get her up to the bed.' Connie said. Then she remembered the children. 'Hush,' she whispered, hugging them to her. 'Hush, hush, it's alright.' They quietened. 'Go on outside for a wee while.' They obeyed, unsure, looking over their shoulders, and with difficulty the two adults carried the body upstairs and laid it on the bed. As Mungo looked on, Connie got some towels from the hotpress and placed them underneath.

'Close her mouth,' she whispered. He pressed the pale chin upwards, and, almost as an afterthought, closed her eyes.

'Is she really dead?'

'Yes.'

He stood back to look at her in a way he had never looked at her in life, and now that she was gone, and although he could not articulate a single word, his head flooded with what he had always wanted to say, but could not. So few meaningful words had ever passed between them, and now it was too late.

'She looks very dignified, doesn't she?'

'As she always did,' Connie said, and to his astonishment, he saw that she was silently crying.

The priest came first, and anointed her. Then the doctor, who officially pronounced her dead. So it was real after all. Mungo was dazed, and yet somehow he got through the motions, being polite, getting what was necessary done, not least a list, beginning with the undertaker, of who to contact.

When the doctor had gone, they called the children in again. There were smudges around their eyes, and Connie told them that their granny had gone to heaven. After a pause, Aidan said: 'You mean she's dead.'

'We mean both,' Connie said. 'Whichever way you understand.'

'She's dead,' Aidan said to Ethna, who nodded, wide-eyed, in agreement.

There were so many things to do. Somehow, over the next few days, they were all seen to, and arrangements fell into place. He marvelled at how efficient Connie was, and wondered how he would have coped without her.

His siblings were like strangers, uncomfortable in their childhood home. Connie ran everything, falling into the role of woman of the house. Mungo saw at once that it was noticed and resented, though nothing was said.

It was a big funeral. The family stood in the pews at the front and waited while the congregation filed up to shake their hands, and murmur 'I'm sorry for your trouble' like a healing mantra. It gave Mungo strength. People knew that he was the son who had come home to help out his mother, and there was a silent assumption that he would take over the farm and be their neighbour; so they paused that fraction longer with him, pressed his hand tighter. That mute language of the multitude had singled him out, and after a short time there was no mistaking it. As he realized what was happening, Mungo became acutely embarrassed. The neighbours had taken for granted what his family did not know for certain, and neither did he, if it came to it.

After the burial the house was full of family, and neighbours, and faces that Mungo barely knew. Connie, with the help of neighbours and Mungo's sisters and sisters-in-law, saw that everyone was fed. The men of the family looked after the drinks. Division of labour. There was a great deal of laughter. It was as if nothing had happened, apart from a gathering of old friends, swapping familiar phrases. Something a Yankee brother said stuck in his mind: he knew a guy who blew his nose in one hundred dollar bills.

Knowing what lay ahead, Mungo was nervous as the last neighbours left. He had been too busy to drink more than a cup of tea all day, but now he poured himself a large whiskey and drank half it back, neat. The family sat into a long table and devoured ham and chicken sandwiches and tea. It was Jim who broached the subject on everyone's mind.

'It looks like you're getting the place, Mungo.' Everyone stopped talking and looked at Mungo.

'I don't know, Jim. No one'll know till we see the will.' From the corner of his eye he saw Connie stare at him. 'And that won't be read for a while. In the meantime, Mother has only been in her grave a few hours.' He said this on an unexpected wave of grief, and everyone fell silent for a while, eyes lowered. Ethna came around the table, crying.

'I want my Granny,' she implored Mungo, who held her close. Aidan, Mungo saw, was pale and quiet.

'Poor Mammy,' Cathleen sobbed. There was silence again, until Mary spoke. 'You're the one who lives here, Mungo, so it's only right that you get the place. But we all have families too,' she added. The implication was not lost on anyone.

'Any idea how much the place is worth?' Jim asked.

'I haven't a clue, Jim. But I'll let ye all know as soon as I know myself.'

What had to be said was now said, and everyone relaxed, breaking into small groups of conversation.

They were staying in bed-and-breakfasts around the area and there was a prolonged series of good-byes the next day. Mungo sat into his evening meal with relief. Both of them had fallen into an exhausted sleep the night before, but now that they had the house to themselves Connie brought up her pre-occupation.

'We will get the place, won't we?'

'Ah ... yeah.'

'We have to know soon,' she said, her voice rising, 'the children'll be going back to school.'

'Relax, relax, who else would she leave it to? She schemed for years to get us down here. And we were here,' he said, as another wave of grief surprised him. 'She died at peace. What more could any of us ask?'

'You're right,' she said, assured.

'Listen, I should go to Dublin soon, to check on the house.'

'Oh yes.' She paused. 'You know, I'd almost forgotten the house. It seems like years since we were there.'

'Yeah. A lot has happened.'

'You should put it up for sale while you're there.'

'For sale?' His heart went cold. 'Ah, no.'

'Why not? We can't eat bricks and mortar.'

'Not till after the will is read, anyway,' he countered, kicking to touch. 'I'm going to count the sheep – I didn't get a chance this morning.'

He counted the sheep which were down by the river, then made his way back up the hill and sat under the oak. It was good there was some grit of uncertainty surrounding the will. He grinned, enjoying his malice. When you want something badly, you shouldn't get it too easily – otherwise you get arrogant. Slowly, slowly. Then he was serious again, remembering his own uncertainties about what he wanted so badly. At least he was going to Dublin. If he could send her a note the following morning from Gorey, it would arrive the day after, and she would have two days' notice. He'd ask to meet her in the evening, that way there was a possibility he could stay with her overnight ... if she would have him. The evening light took on a warm, amber glow. Sunset, he thought idly, without turning.

He would be in debt for many years, something Connie didn't seem to appreciate. If he had any sense he would sell the place and divide the proceeds amongst his family, and for a moment it was the solution; but the real solution, he knew, was to stick it out until Aidan and Ethna had grown, and then leave and strike out on his own to whatever destiny, even if, as he supposed, there would be no Tess any more.

Tess. Dear Tess. She would never fit in here like Connie did, so naturally. She was alien to all he was supposed to be, to all he had been brought up to be; but in a way that was marvellous, through her he had discovered that he was someone else, that something hitherto unknown to him which he couldn't describe which resonated with something in her. The only word he could think of to describe it was abandon: the desire to be lost, cut off. And it came to him again, this time more clearly: he would fulfil his obligations, and then set out on that adventure in which he would lose himself, cut free from the language and baggage of the past. And then? Who could tell, and he felt a joy that he could not bear without jumping to his feet and laughing. He strode back up the hill, vaguely aware of the strangeness of the light and then on impulse he turned, his mouth falling open.

The oak was ablaze with light. If he blinked, he could imagine it in flames, as he had once seen, he knew not where, a lone tree on fire. Now he could see it without blinking. He dared not blink; until, all too soon, the sun had gone down.

- *Eleven* -

So, she had thrown the dice. He had not made a sound, but he was gone sure enough, and now the muffled thud of the hall door was like a blow to her heart. Angry because he had not answered, because they had not clashed in a row, because he had not acknowledged her feelings, if only to rubbish them – she trembled as she finished dressing.

She went to the front window and looked out at the Liffey and the passing traffic. How quickly a body came to rely on another in order to know itself. Although not so quickly – it was over the past several months that he had become her only friend. Now he was gone, and she was alone – but, she swore, she wouldn't be alone for long. She ran to the bathroom and examined herself in the pocked, half-length mirror. With a little war paint, she could turn any man's head. She pulled up her tee-shirt and stared at her stretch marks. Her weak point, and she hated it, railed against the injustice of it. Mungo didn't care about them and she had learned to relax with him because of this. It was a lie, of course, but you needed lies to get along, sometimes. Still, with a little care and distraction they could be concealed, at least until her fish was hooked.

Three o'clock. Three o'clock. Why three o'clock? Why three o'clock?! Yes ... They had arranged that she would collect Arthur at three o'clock, but she didn't know why. Yes she did. So that she could stay a while, there would be no rush, it wasn't often they had time together. They were nice people, with little sign of their genes in Brian. There had been, which was why she married him, but he had turned into something else. Turned by life, and by what life had done to her, perhaps. It would be nice to talk for a while. She marvelled at how two conservative people could be so tolerant of her leaving their son.

They could talk for a while, then she could have Arthur in Ringsend a decent time before dinner at six. It was all worked out, all arranged to fit other people's schedules and habits. That was why and if she didn't move she'd be late. The angry part of her wanted to be late, if only by ten minutes, or a quarter of an hour, maybe. Somehow it would be a blow against other people's habits and schedules which ruled her life, and against Mungo, and not least, against herself, of course. She wanted that, because she hated herself for letting herself be judged null and void. She pinched herself hard, trying to feel something acute, but it was no use, it could not reach beyond that black, still sea of recrimination. If she butted her head through the pane of glass, perhaps, cut her forehead, let some real blood flow. No. She was not melodramatic. If she was going to hurt herself it would be subtle and concealed from judgmental eyes.

The storm passed, and she did not shake any more, but neither did she leave to meet Arthur and his grandparents until her quarter of an hour had elapsed, which she spent trying not to think. Then something clicked, and the Tess who acquiesced in everything took over. She was about to leave but then realized she could not go the way she was, that she should wash and put on a bra and bright summer dress she had picked up in a charity shop, and having done this, she stuffed a cardigan into a shoulder bag for the evening.

It was a cloudless day and she walked up Capel Street, across through the markets and up Church Street on her way to Phibsboro, glad she had put on the dress, even if she could have done without the bra, and wishing she had sun-glasses.

The markets gave her a lift as she sensed several men glancing at her as she passed.

There was a private door, but she preferred going in by the shop. It was a small newsagents and grocery, the front room of their house in effect, but fourteen hours a day there were always a few customers. Now there was only one, an old woman who loudly proclaimed she was dying of the heat and for whom Susan was preparing an ice-cream.

'Ah there you are Tess – I'll be with you in a minute.'

'Hello Susan.' The old woman looked her up and down.

'Isn't the heat fierce.'

'It is.' The woman looked her up and down again.

''Course it's alright for ye young wans', she said darkly as she limped out of the shop.

'It's a while since I was called a young wan, Susan!'

As the customers came and went, they chatted, talked about how Arthur had been during his stay with them. Susan was a small grey-haired woman with a kind face and a warm voice. She'd had a breast removed, and sometimes Tess thought she saw that experience flicker across her eyes. They laughed a lot, as usual, and for a while Tess forgot what had happened earlier in the day, as if it had happened in the distant past.

More customers came, and Tess went out to the large patio and garden to find Arthur and Tom, who was supervising as Arthur watered the dozens of potted plants and flowers and shrubs with a plastic watering-can. Tess watched as Arthur stopped before each pot to receive instructions about how much water these particular flowers liked, and asked its name, before watering it.

Tom was bald and wore whiskers to compensate. In the shop he was straight and business-like; he would joke with the regulars, but always kept his distance in the end. Here, in his garden with his grandson, he was a frail, gentle teacher imparting knowledge. It moved Tess very much and she was grateful that Arthur had such a man to look to.

'Hello Tom.' They turned, Arthur still watering. 'Hello Arthur.'

'Ah Tess!'

She kissed Arthur and then Tom, then sat with Tom on the bench and chatted with him. When Arthur had finished, Tom brought them on a tour of the garden, going over the names of each plant and flower with Arthur, who remembered many of them. It was a happy interlude, and Tess was reluctant to leave, assuring Tom and Susan that she would see them soon, knowing it was true only because she would bring Arthur back several times over the summer, and that otherwise, despite the serenity her visits gave her, she would not come.

They took a 22 to D'Olier Street and walked to Ringsend. Arthur was full of talk, and it seemed he was going to be a gardener when he grew up, a prospect which pleased Tess. Walking over the canal bridge, they fell to their own thoughts. Could Susan or Tom have guessed, she wondered, that an hour or two before they welcomed her as their daughter-in-law, she was in a sweaty embrace, writhing and groaning with a stranger? Could she herself have guessed that, minutes after their happy repose, she and that stranger, her only friend, would savage each other, with a few words and silence as weapons? *Ding-dong-dell, pussy's in hell.* And now she could repent at leisure when her parents went to the pub later on, and Arthur was in bed, all heavy-eyed after his gardening.

After dinner her father persuaded Arthur to learn a tune on the tin whistle. He had a few whistles, along with his mouth organ, his button accordion and fiddle. As far as she knew, her mother hadn't played the piano for a long time, which would explain the dud notes. An instrument could lose its potential to be played by not being played, or so she believed, thinking that pianos and humans were not all that different when it came down to it. Her father had Arthur play one or two simple Irish tunes on his own, then: 'Do you know this one, Arthur?' Arthur followed the tune, 'The Yellow Bittern', intently, as her father ran through it once, and then, encouraged, he joined in a duet.

Tess went to the bathroom and sat on the bowl, listening to Arthur's faltering notes breaking the smooth flow of her father's. He needed all this attention, this accumulation of love from his grandparents. It would deepen him as a man, make him more rooted and able to give, and she was pleased and glad for him, and for the men who were fulfilling their role; but she was outside it all, as if her role was all but over, becoming less and less, leaving her in the end with nothing but memories of him, and wanting, if she let herself be cursed, to relive them over and over.

She would have none of that.

The following morning she left Arthur with his grandparents for his holiday with them. His grandmother had discovered to her great pleasure that he liked her Schumann records and promised to get the piano tuned and to teach him. Tess was pleased too, not least because it would get her mother interested in playing music again.

She thought about Mungo all day and all the following days, and after she had received his card she physically missed him as time passed and took to relieving herself in the early hours of the morning to stop her tossing and turning and crying into her pillow, only to drift into a troubled sleep where she would see him loitering under the shade of an old tree, watching but never touching her.

She broke the days by spending an hour in The Winding Stair before going to see Arthur. A card came from Mungo to say his mother had died. Just that. She had no way to offer him sympathy or anything else.

One evening she surprised herself by going to see Tom and Susan. There were some very hot days, and she took Arthur and two of his friends to the beach in Howth. Tess settled on a place near the low dunes by the track as another DART train pulled in. The boys immediately stripped to their bathing trunks and ran to the water with their ball. The tide was out a good distance, and Tess watched them anxiously as they ran across the dappled sand, but then realized there were many children splashing happily about in the shallow water. Trawlers put-putted out of the harbour, by the island to the open sea. Tess stripped to her bathing costume, but instead of reading as she intended, lay on a towel and covered her eyes with her book. Then she sat up. She had, after all, come here to forget herself on a beautiful summer's day. There were very few young adults on the beach, which surprised her. Mostly there were parents and grandparents, keeping an eye on small children. But then she saw a handsome couple, obviously in love, walk very slowly across the beach. He, though not tall or muscular, was trim and well-shaped. She was beautiful, her black hair cut at the nape, her one-piece costume displaying her flowing buttocks in a way which seemed just right. Tess envied her her serenity, which she knew was the secret of her beauty.

A red inflatable whined across the water, making tight, foaming turns. They were obviously on manoeuvres; maybe it was a rescue team. Then Tess watched, amused, as four cyclists rode slowly in a line across the hard sand near the water. What struck her were the colours of the bicycles – red, yellow, green and orange – and how they rode wheel to wheel, as if carefully practising balance.

A few weeks after they had parted, she could bear it no more. All she had to show for her suffering were a handful of postcards, with messages so brief they might have been in code. They were, to an extent, but knowing this only added to her frustration. Her predicament, she knew, was in no small part due to obsession. There was nothing and no one – no adult – to replace him or at least put him in perspective. She went to the bathroom mirror again, and doubtfully examined her freckled and tanned but tired face from different angles. What had Mungo seen in a face like that, she wondered. She grinned, but the effect was grotesque. There was no way she could face a bar full of strangers like that. It was hopeless. At thirty-four her hour had passed. Mungo had been an aberration. He had been attracted to her because she was a lost soul like himself. It had, she conceded, turned out well for a while, but only because of the stories. If she attracted another lost soul and gave in to him because of loneliness, as she knew she would, it would be a disaster. She showered, washed and dried her hair, read a few chapters of a book and went to bed.

It was noon when she woke, and it took a few hours for her head to clear. The weather had broken and a light rain fell persistently. Cooped-up, Arthur would be bored stiff on a day like this. She went to Ringsend and brought him into town to see a children's film, her mother insisting on giving her the money.

Arthur loved the film. He laughed and laughed, but she fell into a drowse. Later, they ate in a fast food place. She felt queasy as she watched him slurp down the vanilla milkshake on top of his burger and match-stick chips, but he loved all this, and that was what mattered. Then he startled her by humming a melody from Schumann's *Kinderszenen*. He faltered, then grinned, pleased at her full attention.

'That's great,' she said, forgetting the garish surroundings and the numbing piped music, 'go on.' She couldn't name the particular piece, but there it was in her head, note perfect.

'I forget the rest,' he said. He twiddled with the milkshake straw. 'Granny's teaching it to me on the piano.'

'Did she get it tuned?'

'Yes!' he laughed.

'That's wonderful, Arthur,' she said, and felt an unreasonable joy. Later, when she brought him home, he demonstrated the notes he could play, and she felt another stab of happiness.

'Thank you, mom,' she said, putting an arm around her mother and squeezing her to her. Her mother blushed, her pleasure ill-concealed. Tess looked up the name of the piece. It was *Hasche-Mann*, Blind Man's Buff.

It began to rain as she walked home. This time, she welcomed it as it turned into a downpour, and she made no attempt to hurry, relishing her drenching, how it made her light summer clothes cling to her, how her tears, released again, burned out of her eyes and were washed away by the rain. Tears of happiness, of pain, of loneliness, of guilt assuaged, relieved, postponed. The evening cleared as she crossed the Ha'penny Bridge and she felt light and alive, as if her blood had congealed but was now flowing and throbbing through her veins again.

She had a hot shower and dried her hair as she walked naked about the flat. It was beautifully warm, and the rain had cleared that terrible heaviness that had been in the air. In a fanciful moment she imagined she was in a tropical paradise, where one did such things as walking about as nature intended. She giggled, grateful for her levity.

On impulse, she checked her purse. There was still some money left from Arthur's outing, enough for a few drinks, and doleday not far off. That was settled then; she was going to get herself a man. She blushed, as if someone had overheard her unbidden thoughts; then she repeated them. She was going to get herself a man, young, with a flat belly and a neat arse and soft eyes and nice hands and ... and ... and how's yer father! She laughed, nervous and delighted at once. The idea of landing a young man in her net was ridiculous, but it was thrilling, too. With a little luck, she'd find one who was attracted to the older, experienced woman. Why not?

She pulled in her stomach, making her inhumanly thin, then, unable to hold it any longer, she puffed. Your guts for garters ... The phrase came to her: *I'll have your guts for garters!*

Had she any garters? No. Of course not, but extending one to examine it, she knew her tanned legs, with their sun-bleached hair, would do nicely thank you. Brown and bare, all the way up.

The make-up went on, unhurriedly, with great care but with a light touch. Make-up was one skill at least that she hadn't lost, and she was enjoying the transformation of her face, an art she could take pride in. The faintest blusher, and then the lip-stick and the lightest mascara and it was done. One final touch, the dab of tissue on the lips ... and the metamorphosis was complete. Whoever he was, he hadn't a chance.

Grabbing her bag, she jauntily made to leave the flat, but instead she checked herself in the mirror one last time and froze in doubt. There was no way she could launch herself on the street like this, with her brazen shoulders and tarted face. It was all too obvious that her bright, backless frock was too young for her. Heart pounding, she stopped to consider. It was useless, she was fooling herself. Her breasts seemed ugly without the shaping bra, and her hairy legs, bleached or not, made her look like a sweating horse. Fuck it – fuck it. A fantasy had kept her vital and happy for an hour – but that was it, sister! That was it, and what more could she expect. The tears welled, but she fought them back, not wanting her careful work to end in smudge. So. So she still wanted to go out. Yes, and she would. Yes. But not like this. No. Not like this. A coat? Too warm. A jacket? Yes, a jacket, and she had a neat jacket that came to her waist. It had cost her fifty pence in a charity shop, but it was good quality stuff. Doubtfully, she put it on in front of the bathroom mirror, turned around, examined it from both sides. It covered her shoulders and back at least, and yes, her breasts weren't so blatant – not that they were big or anything, she thought, trying to reassure herself, though she'd often worried about their smallness. She took off the jacket and sniffed it. It was okay, but she would have to get out the iron again.

She had been on her way to The Jasmine, a snazzy pub, but that was out of the question now. It was a crazy idea, hit upon only because the svelte young men there had their trousers stuffed with their fathers' money, would buy her drinks and bring her to a night club. She hadn't been to a night club since before she was married.

Shit! She had almost ironed a hole in her jacket while she lamented a lost night on the tiles. It was okay, though. And there was nothing wrong with Grogan's. Especially since she'd heard, or rather overheard, that art students haunted it now, and she hadn't been in there for a long time. Or anywhere else. The art student she conjured was lean and hungry-looking, a few inches taller than herself, with two days black and even stubble. No. No, he was clean-shaven, and his facial bones were strong, but subtle. He was quiet, but was used to the sight of an imperfect naked woman in the life drawing classes as well as a few beds here and there. He could appreciate her, she had no doubt about it.

She put on her jacket and, as an afterthought, a silk scarf that she had also bought in a charity shop, and walked to Grogan's, apprehensive but with a steady, determined stride, open to what the night might bring but wishing to God she had a gin and tonic in her stomach. She stood outside Grogan's, lost her nerve, and kept walking until she reached Grafton Street, where at least she could lose herself in the crowd. She walked towards Stephen's Green and then back down again, pausing at the clothes shop windows, longing to touch the expensive fabrics, to feel the luxury of them on her body. She imagined how she would look in them, and decided which would suit her and which would not. On impulse she went for a drink in Davy Byrnes.

Self-conscious, she waited nervously for her drink, not daring to glance at the customers at the bar, and seated in small groups. It seemed so easy for them and so difficult for her. She sat alone at a table and felt shabby, although she knew no one had paid her the slightest attention. It was all she could do not to gulp back her drink. She would drink it slowly, and then go. She thought of the shops on Grafton Street again. What beautiful clothes! One day, she swore, if she had to rob for it, one day she would walk into a fashion joint, and spend five hours buying a dress, and underwear, and shoes, the whole shaggin' lot! Despite herself, she gulped back the last of her drink, and left.

Back on Grafton Street, she paused at Brown Thomas's window, and gorged herself again. Ah! she was only annoying her head, and she swept down the street. Her momentum carried her into Wicklow Street and, against all her intentions, she stopped off at the International Bar for another drink. After this one she would go home and have sense, and maybe write to Marian, and tell her her woes, and ask her had she room in her flat in Berlin, for a week, or maybe forever. This time she had less inhibitions about drinking quickly. She couldn't care less if she never talked to another human being ever again, much less chat up a man, and her dreary flat seemed like the only haven she had ever dreamed of. She finished her drink and stood outside the bar, looking up South William Street.

'Come on,' she said to herself, 'go home,' but instead she went to Grogan's.

Although it was past nine o'clock there were still empty seats by the tables in the lounge. Tommy greeted her and brought her a gin and tonic, and she took several quick sips before taking in her surroundings. There were a lot of paintings on the wall since she had last been, and a few sculptures, by the art students, she supposed, without studying any of them beyond a glance. Across from her was a big old black and white photo of Killiney Bay and Wicklow Head. So, the changes in the pub were superficial, and she took comfort from the familiarity of the photograph.

Under it, two couples of late middle age were talking and laughing, but to her surprise, they were drinking pots of tea. She looked at them openly, admiring their lively, intelligent faces. She knew them to see; perhaps she had seen them here before, and she guessed they had not always drunk tea in public houses.

There were no art students in as yet; most likely they were in the bar, but there was a vociferous group in the seating next to her, all much younger than her. The fantasy her hopes had burgeoned on were fading. She had money for two more drinks, but already her isolation was bearing in on her. The couples under the photograph were leaving, and they were the only group she had warmed to.

To take her mind off herself, she looked hard at the photo, traced the line of the railway overlooking the beach. She remembered then that it was the Wexford line, the one Mungo would have travelled on, in what seemed an eternity ago. She wished he was here. Those brief hours on a few afternoons had kept her going. Now she did not even have the stories, those comforting lies they told each other, to keep her brain alive.

He wouldn't be back. It had been an interlude, and he had returned to his wife, choosing comfort before passion and imagination. And as she looked at the photo, she realized why there were no art students. It was summer.

Someone in the group next to her got up to get a round of drinks, and a young man pushed back his stool to make way for him, hitting against Tess's table and upsetting her drink. Embarrassed, he turned to her.

'Please excuse me!'

'Oh, it's fine,' she insisted. 'No harm done.'

'Allow me to buy you another drink.' He stood up. 'What is it you are drinking?' He smiled. 'Please.'

'You've twisted my arm,' she said, grinning. 'A gin and tonic.'

He wasn't a day over nineteen, she thought as she watched him at the bar. Tall and thin, with narrow hips and a tight cut on his hair, as if he had just finished military service. It was only then she realized he was German, and she swallowed hard. He was no Sascha, there was no experience in his clean cut, open face, no sensual charm; she couldn't imagine him having the daring to sweep her into his arms. He returned with the drink.

'Are you German?'

'Yes,' he said, bringing his drink and sitting before her. Jesus. It was as easy as that. She had forgotten. 'From Köln,' he said, 'do you know it?'

'No, I can't say I do.' Why couldn't he have been from Berlin?

'Perhaps you know it as Cologne,' he said. His grin was getting wider and she could see he thought she was easy. She grinned back.

'Ah yes, I have you now.' He was drunk, which was fine, but she didn't want him too drunk. His name was Max. The pub had filled suddenly and it made her feel more secure. She finished her first drink. Remarking how hot it was, she took off her jacket and saw his eyes widen a little in appreciation.

'I have a friend in Berlin,' she said, but he had never been there and wasn't interested in talking about Germany. His head was full of Ireland and Irish music and the wonderful pubs where you could meet people so easily and people liked to talk. So she went along with it as if that was her world too, as if she was immersed in it. She bought him a pint. They toasted each other. She told him what she could remember of a Fleádh Cheoil she had been to years before. The families of musicians, the drinking, the wildness, the *craic*. He loved it, knew more about it than she did.

'Where are you staying?' she asked as the barmen began to call time.

'In a hostel near Christchurch,' he said. His eyes were watery from drink, but they had sex in them. Perhaps her own were the same.

'Oh. I live near there.' She hesitated, waiting for him to pick up his cue, but he just continued to look into her eyes. 'Maybe you'd walk me home?'

Like the schoolboy he was, he grinned at his friends as he left with her, and they grinned back, men and women of the world – but Tess laughed, knowing who was picking up who. He had bored her, though she tried to deny that to herself, concentrating all evening on his body. One night was all she wanted, and then he would be gone. She set a quick pace, bringing him down through Temple Bar and across Grattan Bridge, opening her door and letting him pass in without a word.

'The toilet's up there,' she pointed. She had just remembered the question of condoms. She wasn't going to fuck him without condoms, and for a few desperate moments she wondered if Mungo had left any behind him; but no, she would have come across them by now. The toilet flushed. There was no other way. She was going to have to ask him straight out and if he hadn't she would jerk him off where he stood and send him back to the hostel. Maybe it was enough just to know she could seduce him. Then he stood before her, looking down on her, and she knew it wasn't enough, knew she wanted him, all of him.

'Have you condoms?'

'Yes.'

She smiled, relaxing, and stood up on her toes to kiss him,

her tongue sliding into his mouth.

'I won't be a minute,' she said then. 'The bedroom's over there.'

When she went into her bedroom she caught her breath. In the bathroom she had been nervous, wondering if all this was real, but now the sight of him, standing naked, made her forget herself and she smiled, looking him up and down.

'You're very nice,' she said.

He smiled. She could see he was nervous, and his large, flaccid cock hung like a perished white tube. She went to him and kissed his chest, running her fingertips over his nipples. So the dream was coming true; but then he reached down and clutched her buttocks and she was brought back to earth as he tried to pull her frock over her head. Whatever else happened he was not going to see her completely naked, so she stopped him, putting a finger to her lips.

'Get into bed,' she whispered. He grinned, and slowly obeyed, watching her all the time. Before turning out the lamp, she saw that a condom was opened from a packet of three on the bedside table.

'Why do you turn out the light?' he asked from the darkness.

She didn't reply, but trembling, she undressed and lay on top of him, kissing him deeply. She thought she would pass out as he turned her on her back and roughly kissed her neck and breasts, passing his fingers between her drenched lips. This was basic stuff, but her imagination had made her ready long before, ready for anything.

Then, to her consternation, he stopped and took his fingers and body away from her, so that she was stranded in the dark. Her rasping breath slowed, and she heard a low curse in German. She could hardly believe it in one so young and big, but it was obvious what was wrong. He was kneeling back on his heels, and she knelt in front of him, taking the head between her fingers and thumb, flicking her tongue into his mouth, squeezing her eyes shut to hold onto her own pleasure and anticipate the pleasure to come, and very slowly he responded and grew hard.

She groaned as he entered her deeply, but though he took a long time to come, she did not peak herself, and long after he was asleep, she lay awake wondering if she had won or lost. At least – at the very least – she had played.

When she woke, it was bright and Max was at the toilet. Her first thought was to don a tee-shirt, and when he returned, unabashedly naked, she kissed him quickly and went herself. She took off what remained of her make-up and after she had washed, she pondered whether to put some fresh stuff on and decided that no, he could see her as she was, her face at least. She had bedded him, he would be gone in an hour or so, and that was it.

She expected him to be dressed when she returned, but he was propped up on an elbow in bed, smiling that knowing smile, and she noticed that another condom was opened on the side table. Here we go again, she thought – but why not? She laughed and got in beside him and immediately his hand was on her naked crotch.

'Take off your clothe,' he said firmly. 'I want to see you naked.'

'Who's full of beans this morning, then?' she countered. She had to think quickly. *Clothe.* He made to take it off himself but she stopped him. 'Isn't it enough to feel me?'

'No. I must see you also.'

'Only in a special way, then ...' Perhaps there was a way out of this, a way which would fascinate him and perhaps her too.

'You are making rules?'

'Maybe, but I think you're going to like it.'

'*Ja?*'

'Kneel up in the bed, away from me, and close your eyes. If you do that, I promise I'll take off my tee-shirt.'

He hesitated, but she knew by his half smile that he was intrigued.

'But I still won't see you,' he half protested.

'You will, in a very special way.'

Warily, but nevertheless smiling, he did what she asked.

'Alright,' she said, 'I'm taking it off now, but if you turn, I'll throw you out.'

'Understood.'

She waited a few moments to be sure, not trusting him for an instant. Then she rolled up her silk scarf and put it around his eyes.

'*Was* ... ?'

Then, and only then, did she take off her tee-shirt.

'I'm completely naked,' she whispered. 'Now ... I'm going to get out on the floor and do a sexy dance for you, and I'll show you every part of me.'

'*Aber* ... how can I see you when you have made me blind?'

She tapped his forehead. 'Here. You will see everything here.' He put his head to one side, doubtful, and now that he could not see her she felt confident and in control, and she trembled with pleasure. He would do anything she wanted. She had dreamed of this, or something like it, for a long time without ever believing it would come to pass, and now, with a simple device, she had made it happen. As an afterthought, a final delicious touch, she guided his fingers to his stiffening cock, and he took the cue. Now! Now it was up to her. She stood on the floor, not knowing quite where or how to begin.

'Can you see me? In your mind, I mean?'

'*Ja*. Yes. I can see you very well.'

'Good.'

She cupped her breasts in her hands, watching closely as he became hard beneath his fingers.

'I'm caressing my breasts,' she said, a tremor in her voice, her breath becoming short. 'Can you see me?'

'Yes.' His mouth was lax, his chest was rising and falling.

'Can you see what my breasts are like?'

He hesitated a moment, as if bringing them into focus, and affirmed that he could. She admired them herself, kneading them softly, becoming more preoccupied with the erectile changes in her own body than in his.

Her hands moved down to her belly. It was a part of her which had stretched beyond her to contain a miracle, and for the first time she enjoyed it, was grateful to it, felt she loved it as her own.

'My belly,' she whispered hoarsely. 'Can you see it? Do you like it?'

'Yes. Yes, it is soft and white. I am kissing it, I am licking it.'

She sighed, adoring him kissing and licking her smooth, soft white belly and she began to groan, her eyes closed, her hips moving so that the floorboards creaked beneath her. Very slowly, because she wanted it to last, her fingers moved into her crotch.

'My hips, my bush, can you see them?'

'Your bush … ? Yes, I love them.' He was now engorged, his mouth open, his head held back, his chest heaving.

Her fingers lingered along the V towards her mount, then moved between her legs to either side of her lips and lingered there. Her moans and sighs mingled with Max's grunting, and her juice leaked and trickled down her thighs.

She thrust her pelvis forward and gasped as her fingers slid between her lips.

'My cunt … my cunt … can you see it?'

'*Ja* … Yes!' He was frantic. She could see it through her own clouded eyes. He was frantic. She staggered, possessed by a greed for his cock. She took the condom and wrenched away his hand and put it on. She knelt in front of him on the bed and lowered that urgent hardness until it probed her lips. Impatiently she manoeuvred herself, it was awkward at first and he was no help, but then it happened and she was impaled. She rode him hard and loud, abusing her breasts and clitoris, out of her mind. His hands were around her waist and shoulders, she hardly knew and didn't care as long as he kept up that pounding rhythm with her and she arrived at where she craved to be, and as his groans became louder and she sensed he was not too far off, she pummelled her pubis, her head rolling from side to side, and rode him deeper and deeper, until after he had come she screamed, the waves of pleasure overcoming her, and she fell away from him onto the bed and curled into herself.

For some time she lay there, dazed and trembling, spasms jerking in no particular sequence through her body. Vaguely, she wondered about his silence, if, perhaps, he had already gone. He had not reached out to touch her. Maybe, just maybe, he was as dazed as she was. When eventually her body quieted and left her instead with a peace which seemed to stretch into the distance, she took a deep breath and looked around at him through half-closed eyes. The blindfold was off and he was sitting in a semi-lotus position and watching her as if she was a strange animal he was cataloguing.

'Did the earth move for you too, darling?' She laughed and stretched, pleased with herself and pleased with the world. He did not laugh, and continued to look at her in silence, and she went cold as she realized he was looking at her belly.

'Would you like some breakfast?' she asked as she took her dress and turning away from him, put it on.

'I have no time. It is now ten and I'm going to Galway on the eleven o'clock train.'

'Oh.'

They both dressed in silence, and she went out to the living-room to wait for him as he finished. They were awkward as he hesitated at the door.

'Well, good-bye then,' she said. He nodded.

'Good-bye.' And he was gone. For a moment she thought he was going to shake her hand. No kiss, no embrace, not even a smile. Just a hesitant glance. She went to the window and watched as he crossed the road and walked by the river to cross at Grattan Bridge. He was so tall, she thought, and so young, and how would he remember this morning, and would he remember it when his own body wasn't perfect any more?

She would always remember him, for all his boyish confusion. She had lived this long before realizing she was free after all – or at least far more so that she had ever imagined. Long after he had disappeared into Parliament Street, she was smiling, a vacant, lost world in her eyes.

She went to see Arthur that afternoon. He was playing with some children on the street so she let him be and talked instead to her mother; and for once, with all her tensions drained away, it was easy, and the ordinary gossip which usually got on her nerves was entertaining. Her mother looked at her knowingly, and although she would never verbally approve, Tess noticed her faint, quizzical smile. Arthur's face lit up when he came in for his dinner, but at the table he was shy and looked at her curiously several times and she became uneasy. When she left he kissed her in the usual way, but he held something back.

It troubled her on her walk home. Maybe she had imagined it, or maybe she was projecting guilt and the child picked it up. This angered her, although whether she was angry with herself or Arthur was hard to tell. Whichever it was, she refused to believe she could be guilty about the best thing that had happened to her since Arthur was born. She had waited long enough and the odds were that its like would never happen to her again. Happen to her? She had made it happen, and she broke into a smile.

She dreamt of Arthur that night, but in the morning she could only recall the faint ghost of his face. She forgot about it and, as she queued in the dole office, fancied she still tingled from her hour of glory, and the smile stayed put. With her money in her bag she went to Stephen's Green and lay in the sun, her skirt hitched well above her knees, and daydreamed about her seduction, going over it in detail and marvelling that she had done it, as if for a while she had become a different person to the one she had always known, and she vowed not to rest on her laurels. She sighed at the luxury of it, and smiled again.

She rang her mother to tell her she would not be over that afternoon, as in her light mood she had said she would. There was no denying it, she thought as she walked down Grafton Street, although she would never admit it to anyone: with that young German she had been a *femme fatale* and she had loved every minute of it, and because, as she reasoned, she could not be a mother as well as a *femme fatale*, she was afraid of her son and his unknowing judgment.

There was a card waiting for her when she got home.

'Dear Tess. I will be in Dublin on Friday. I'll call about twelve, hoping to see you. Love Mungo.'

Short and without ornament, as usual. Reading it over several times, she was at a loss as to what she was supposed to feel, finally deciding as she slowly ascended the stairs that what she should feel was resentment. In all the time she had needed him, he wasn't around. Now that she was feeling good and strong, he was turning up on her doorstep, full, no doubt, of woe.

She wondered if she should tell him about the bold Max. Not in every detail, of course; she couldn't do that even in the guise of a story. This reminded her of their stories, and how she missed them. In truth, she also missed him, and that night she lay awake in bed for a long time, listening to Schubert, unable to think out how much Mungo meant to her, but the question stubbornly remained.

The next morning she rose early and went shopping for lunch, presuming he would like ham and cheese with his salad, and she stretched her budget to a couple of bottles of beer. As she checked her face in the mirror she reflected with a smile that with Mungo there was no need for make-up, but the smile faded as she wondered if they would end up in bed, and if she would be disappointed if they did not. She still felt sated, and maybe if she wanted anything now, it was tenderness, and maybe their stories. Her story? She hadn't a clue, but he was sure to have one, and that would carry their time together.

The bell rang at twenty to twelve. He was quiet, diffident and somehow he had aged in the interval, despite his deep tan, and for the first time she noticed the flecks of grey through his brown hair. His face lightened when he saw the table set, and she immediately brought out the plates of salad and two bottles of cold beer.

'I thought you could do with one of these after the journey,' she said.

'That's very nice of you.' He smiled, and sat in to the table.

Nice? It hurt. He had said it as if he was being polite, as if they were strangers, being nice to each other.

'I'm sorry about your mother,' she said, remembering.

'Thanks. It's … ah … it's been a difficult time for me. One way or another. A lot of problems I'm not used to. Responsibilities, debts. I'm up to sell the house here in Dublin. To put it on sale, that is.'

'Oh. So you're settling down there.' She hadn't bargained on this and was surprised at how much it upset her.

'So it seems. I've missed you.'

'Have you?' She composed herself and looked up, meeting his eyes. 'Have you?'

'Yes. Very much. You. The way you are. Your body. The stories … Somehow you gave a … a texture … I don't know what I'm saying. I missed you. Your stories. What happened then?' he asked, almost plaintively.

'When?'

'Your dinner-party lover.'

'Oh.'

They looked at each other, and she knew that he knew this wasn't the right moment. It didn't do any longer to just launch into their tall tales, avoiding everything else they needed to say. But however faintly, the lines were open again, and he put his hand on hers, and she grasped his in turn.

'I can't remember what happened next. It's been so long, Mungo. I'll have to think about it.'

They ate, and she got him to tell her about the farm, his mother's death, about living in the country.

'It's pleasant in the summer, and of course the children love it – the freedom, the things to do. But I'd prefer to be here.'

They were quiet again and she knew he wanted to make love to her, but they ate and drank and talked again and time passed.

'I've to meet an agent at two,' he said. 'If I could see you this evening I wouldn't go back to Wexford, and we could relax together. What do you say?'

She would love to. She had to meet her son, anyway. They could meet on Sandymount Strand, at the Irishtown side, between four and five, and decide what to do.

When she went to Ringsend, she discovered that Brian had been to see Arthur the previous day, and Arthur, his face alight, told her how his father had brought him to the park and had played football with him until they could no longer see the ball, and implied that Brian was a far better ball player than herself. She was pleased that Brian had done it, but it was so unlike him that she felt uneasy.

Arthur was doubtful when she suggested an outing to Sandymount Strand, but once it was arranged that his friends could also come, he warmed to the idea. The tide was out, and they played ball along the sand, breaking off to chase gulls, or parody the gentle trot of a pony ridden by a girl who knew she was rich.

Barefooted, Arthur was having a wonderful time, and for a while Tess forgot about Brian; but he crept back into her thoughts, and she wondered if, with the freedom he had with Arthur on holiday, he had found a woman, and if perhaps his happiness had made him generous towards his son. She recalled her battles with him over the videos. A man like that would think nothing of going to a massage parlour if he had the cash, and she drifted on from there to a throwaway sentence in one of Marian's letters that had stuck at the back of her mind – something about red lights on ordinary streets, where men casually stepped into such houses in front of women and children, but no one took any notice. The sun had made her lazy and she had given up mulling over Brian's sex life when Mungo spotted her and called out her name. She sat up, blinking, to greet him.

'Hello. Did you get your business done?'

'He's coming out to see the place tomorrow,' Mungo grinned. 'So I would have had to stay over anyway.'

'Have you rung your wife?'

'Yes.' His smile disappeared, but he soon rallied. He had aired the house, and he wanted her to stay the night with him there. She didn't answer. She had noticed how Arthur had stopped playing and was glowering at an oblivious Mungo.

'Don't act too intimate with me.'

'What?'

'I think my son is jealous of you. Tell me how to get there and I'll meet you at eight.'

'I see what you mean,' he said, discreetly watching Arthur who had just kicked the ball very hard. He wrote down his address and drew a rough map and when Arthur looked around again he was gone.

On the way home, Arthur walked ahead of her with his friends. When they were gone, he waited a while but she could see he was bursting with righteous indignation.

'Who was that man on the strand?'

'Hmm?' She was ready for him, angry in turn but determined not to betray herself. 'Oh you remember! He's the father of that little girl you liked so much.'

'I did not!' he retorted. But he was blushing, and he never mentioned it again.

It was strange, being in another woman's house, alone with her husband. In many ways it was like her own abandoned home. Mungo showed her around as if she was a prospective buyer. He had a meal ready: fish, complete with sauce, potatoes and broccoli, with a cool, Italian white wine, a second one in the fridge. He even had paper napkins. She felt she was being courted and it was a nice, almost forgotten feeling.

When they had finished the meal they went to bed. It was as simple as that. He had been patient, but she knew from early on that he wanted her badly, and although she felt strange in another woman's bed, she enjoyed him without losing herself to his thrusting body. It didn't matter. She stroked his head as he lay still on top of her, glad they had made love, glad they were together. He was so still, for so long, his hands on her shoulders, his face buried at her neck, that he seemed unwilling to leave where he was, entwined in her thighs. There was satisfaction in that. Her thoughts drifted pleasantly to Sascha, and little by little, her story pieced itself together. Afraid that Mungo might fall asleep, she nudged him after a while and he climbed off her, his eyes heavy. Now was the time.

'After that first night with Sascha,' she began, and laughed as he perked up. 'After that first night with Sascha, I began to see him constantly. He was a strange one. Sometimes he refused to come, said he wanted to conserve his essence.'

Mungo laughed, settling into her story like a child. She was amused too, not knowing where that last bit had come from. Encouraged, she took a deep breath.

'Another afternoon, he blindfolded me and made me touch myself while he talked dirty about his body. Could you believe it,' she laughed, rubbing his nose with her finger, 'the things men dream up.'

He grinned.

'It was all squeezed into an hour in the afternoons, though, that was the trouble, so it was all frenzy and madness. I could hardly ever see him in the evenings because I couldn't afford a baby-sitter so often. He wanted to pay, but it's best to stay independent in these matters. And then somehow, Arthur seemed to sense what was happening and became very difficult and wanted his father back. He's usually quiet and easy-going, but Arthur is a jealous young man as you discovered this afternoon.'

'So I did.'

'Once, after a particularly heavy session with Sascha, I arrived home late and I suppose a bit all over the place, and he was waiting for me at the door. I had been late before, but I usually had some shopping in my arms so that was fine – that's what mothers are supposed to be doing in the afternoon. But this time, this time he no sooner had me inside the door than he charged at me, kicking the shins off me. Well! Well I lost the rag myself and I beat him around the room – but the little devil fought back and the two of us were black and blue before we fell into a heap, worn out. Needless to say, I didn't see Sascha for a few days after that, and when I was on the street I wore dark glasses and black tights.'

'You better watch your step, so.'

She hesitated.

'I still had my dark glasses on about two days later and I had just finished shopping in a market, and when I came out into the strong light I was blinded for a moment, even with the glasses – they were a cheap pair. There were a couple of bookshops across the road, and when I could focus again I saw a man browsing at one of the outside stalls. I noticed him because he was so restless and he looked familiar. Then I realized it was Brian – my husband. Now it was mid-afternoon so he was probably on his lunch break, so that was fair enough, but I knew he wasn't in the area to see me, as he didn't know where I lived any more – or so I hoped. And I knew he wasn't interested in books, so I decided there was something fishy and that instead of dodging him I sat down on a bench and watched him. He was like a cat on a griddle, and when I noticed a red light on a building half-way up a side street, I realized why. All of a sudden he moved off like a shot, went down a few steps and disappeared. Well now, it was really none of my business, I mean, we weren't divorced but we were separated and so it was his own affair what he did, but for some reason I just sat there getting angrier and angrier, and eventually something snapped. I took my groceries in my arms and ran up that street. I expected to find some kind of door with a buzzer, or something, or a bouncer, maybe, but all there was was a red bead curtain and you could see men sitting inside in a kind of red glow. Well, that took the wind out of my sails for a second.'

'Jesus.' Mungo grinned.

'Only for a second, mind. The fact that it was all so open made it worse, somehow. I was furious, and I jumped down those steps and through the bead curtain, and the men jumped up with a wild look on their faces, as if I had a machine-gun or something, but Brian wasn't one of them. Then some of them started shouting at me. They looked unreal in the red light. Everything was red – red velvet, red lamps and even the horny photos looked red. It took my eyes a few seconds to adjust, but then I saw that the moans and groans were coming from a video in the corner. Then this enormous woman, fully dressed, appears and shouts at me in German, but I didn't give a blind tit for her and I gave as good as I got. "Where's my husband?" I shouted in English, and you should have seen the boys, looking nervously at the street in case their wives were about to jump into the room too. Then the big lady started shouting something about the police and I laughed, I just laughed at the idea of the police coming to throw a woman out of a brothel for disrupting business.'

Mungo laughed. It was a good one alright.

"I'm not leaving here without my husband," I screamed. I suppose I was a bit off my head, little ol' me in a place like that, but I nearly freaked out altogether when I saw Brian coming out from behind a curtain with his whore in tow. The two of them were standing there with their mouths open, as if the Last Day had come without warning. He had all his clothes on at least, but she had nothing on but a G-string. I went to clobber Brian, but as he stepped back I got a good look at her face ... and her hair ... and her body ... and I nearly flipped my lid. She was my double. I lost the head altogether then and knocked her to the ground and somehow or other I knocked her out cold. There I was in a Berlin brothel, my groceries scattered over the floor, lying on top of a naked woman who was the image of me. I ran out of that place like a scalded cat, and gave Arthur beans on toast for his dinner for the next three days.'

- *Twelve* -

Mungo woke in grey light as Tess eased out of bed, stretching along the inside, and for an instant the line of her body made an image, as graceful as a wild animal, which he would never forget. He heard her piss into the bowl downstairs, then silence, until the toilet flushed. She came back, oblivious to him, and he marvelled at her female composition as if he was looking at a woman's body for the first time, with the miraculous suspension of her breasts, and the perfectly balanced triangle between her hips. Her breasts hung as she leaned forward, peering at the floor to find her scattered clothes.

'Good morning,' he said softly.

'Oh. Did I wake you?'

'No.'

'What time is it?'

He reached over to the bedside table and peered at his watch. 'Ten past eight. It seems a lot earlier.' He yawned, but watched her through squinted eyes as she went around the bed to pull back the curtains. She examined the sky and groaned, as if the heavy grey clouds had no right to be there. She glanced at him and grinned.

'What are you looking at?'

'The loveliest sight I have ever feasted my eyes on.'

'Am I now?' The smile had vanished, and she sat back on

the bed. 'I know you're a smooth liar, but thanks all the same,' she said, and kissed him.

'You've got breath like a stale floor cloth in the mornings,' she said, screwing up her nose.

'You're no spring breeze yourself,' he countered, and they laughed. He knew he had made her happy, if only for a while, and he felt as if his senses had rounded out.

'What's your hurry?'

'I've to get Arthur his school stuff.'

'School? But that's not for another few weeks, is it?'

'Come on,' she said as she dressed, 'get up and have breakfast with me.'

He wished she hadn't mentioned it, reminding him that Connie, being a planner, would probably be in Gorey doing the same thing, his children apprehensive about their new school. Even more than his mother's death and her will, it brought home to him how events were conspiring against him.

'Well, come on, glum face,' she demanded, pausing at the door.

When he went down she had found everything and had made toast under the grill. It was as if it were her kitchen, had been for years, and he felt an odd displacement as he put his arms around her and kissed her neck.

'Did you say the agent was coming today?' she asked over breakfast.

'Two o'clock,' he said, his mouth full of toast. 'What am I to do till two o'clock if you're not going to be here?'

'You'll find something.'

'I could stay in town another night if you could come back this evening ... ?'

'Randy, aren't we?'

'Thank you, ma'am.'

'I'll leave Arthur with his father's parents. They wanted him back, anyway. Well then,' she said rising, 'if I was back here about five?'

'Grand,' he concurred, rising with her.

'I'll get something to eat. You get wine or beer or whatever, if you like ...'

Her voice trailed off into a whisper as he embraced and kissed her, his lips brushing lightly along hers.

When she was gone he sat against the table, his mind blank. Then he saw the washing up from the night before piled in the sink. He pulled himself together, intending to obliterate all traces of recent occupation before the agent arrived. He stopped as he stripped the beds which like much else had been left as they were before the family had moved to Wexford, as they thought, for a few weeks. Why should he facilitate the sale? If they couldn't sell the house, then in all likelihood the farm would be unviable, given the debts, and it would have to be sold instead. He lay down, staring up at the ceiling. It was too late. He was trapped and he knew it. What a sleepwalker he was!

He rolled off the bed and went for a walk, recalling the time, which seemed so long ago, when he used to jog. Inevitably his perambulation brought him to the Phoenix Park where, crossing through the People's Garden, he took off his shoes and ran over the grass to the Wellington Monument, circling it once. Sweating and out of breath, he stumbled onto the lowest step of the plinth. He wasn't fit any more, that much was certain. The humidity was awful. His life was awful. No matter which way he turned, there would be sacrifice and hurt.

The agent came as agreed and assessed the house, and they settled on a sale price. When he had gone, Mungo walked through the house as if bereaved, imagining his children running through it, pausing at the foot of the stairs as he watched Connie's ghost and his own stumble up the stairs to make drunken love.

He shook his head. He was being sentimental. Nevertheless he went upstairs and looked into his bedroom, which seemed unnaturally quiet. They had made their children here, they had quarrelled and lain back to back in anger and bewilderment. How many dreams had passed through this room. And nightmares, and tears, and groans of passion? And Tess's ghost had come between him and all of that, and he didn't know if he had betrayed or escaped it.

He went into the children's room, imagined Ethna sleeping there, her thumb in her mouth; imagined himself pulling the cover back over her shoulders on a winter night. Then he turned to Aidan's bed, saw before him what had happened there, what had changed his life – the flames, the screams, the nightmares – and yet, also, the closeness and tenderness as he comforted his children.

The mugginess of the afternoon finally got to him, and he lay back on Aidan's bed and fell asleep. He woke an hour later covered in clammy sweat, not knowing whether he had dreamt of a thunderstorm or not, or of a low-flying jet, circling to land or curving away to its journey over the Irish Sea. A light rain streamed down the window.

He rang Connie from a phonebox in Stoneybatter. It took her a while to answer and she was breathless when she did.

'We're just in,' she said. 'How did you get on?'

'He didn't turn up, so I rang him a minute ago and he said he'd come round at six.'

'Oh. So you won't be home this evening.'

'No. And I don't know if I'll make the morning train tomorrow, so don't expect me home till the evening.'

'What are you going to do up there all day on your own?'

'Oh, read the papers, I suppose. Go to a film in the afternoon, maybe. Or maybe I'll just go for a walk in the park.'

'You really like it up there, don't you.' She wasn't being sarcastic, but warm and understanding.

'Yes … I do. I love it, in fact. I'm running out of money,' he said quickly as the warning bips sounded, 'I'll see you tomorrow evening,' and, as she hesitated, the phone went dead before she could reply. He took a deep breath, held it and let go again before replacing the receiver.

On his way home he bought three bottles of wine and a bunch of carnations, making a mental note to get rid of the empty bottles and redundant flowers before returning to Wexford. The flowers brought the room to life again. He put on the immersion, and, realizing he hadn't listened to music for a long time, chose his favourite cassette, Rodrigo's *Concierto de Aranjuez*. Lying back into the sofa he imagined himself in Spain, with the rolling guitars and cutting violins. This was the very life. The water was lukewarm, and he left the bathroom door open as he showered, listening to the music, and he smiled, thinking his taste must make him a romantic. Whatever about that, he felt good and let the water run cold. He hadn't many Spanish tapes, but he played them all until Tess came, almost an hour late.

'God, I've had a terrible day,' she said, her face drawn. 'Can I have a shower?'

'Sure,' he said, and he turned on the immersion. 'It'll take a while.'

'Hold me,' she pleaded. 'If you can stand the smell of sweat off me.'

He held her tight, his face in her damp, straggled hair.

'The bastards are finally going to throw me out.' She leaned back from him a little to face him and laughed bitterly. 'In a week's time I'll be homeless.'

'What?'

She moved away from him and sat at the table, and then, in agitation, turned. Then she saw the carnations. Leaning across the table she smelled them and closed her eyes.

'They're lovely. Are they for me?'

'Of course. What do you mean, you'll be homeless?'

'Homeless. No home. No door to close after me at night. I can't afford anywhere else with the price of flats. Not even those boxes they call bedsitters. It was too good to last but now the number's up. There was a solicitor's letter waiting for me in the hall when I went back this morning. God!'

'You can stay here.'

'What? But you're selling the place.'

'I know. But it mightn't be sold for months, and then you could still be here for a while after that – it'd give you a breathing space, if nothing else.'

'That's good of you Mungo, but it's not on, really. I like the house but it's not my place, do you know what I mean? And what if your wife decided to come up and check on the place – what'd happen then? I'd be out in the rain in five minutes, and you'd probably be out with me.'

'She won't come near this house if she can help it. She hates it and she's as happy as a fly on a dungheap down there.'

'Oh I don't know. We'll see. I might have to yet. Thanks anyway. The alternatives are going to live with my parents which is not really an option, or going back under my husband's roof, which is not an option at all. Is there by any chance a hair-dryer, or even a blow-heater in the house?'

'A blow-heater? Sure, just there.'

'Oh, *wunderbar!* And have you a spare shirt?

'Yes.'

'Great,' she said, getting to her feet. 'Let's get this meal on the road, and I can have my shower then. I want it *hot*!'

She launched herself into the preparation of the meal, and again he noticed how easily she took Connie' place.

'Put on some music,' she said, washing the rice at the sink. He rewound the cassette and switched on the Rodrigo. When she had the vegetables ready she sat with him on the sofa and listened. The adagio began.

'I know this,' she said quietly. 'It's beautiful.' She leaned into him until the movement ended, then went back to her cooking without a word.

'What are you making? Or does it have a name?'

'Lamb Shashlik, I'll have you know.'

'*There's* posh.'

When she was satisfied that it was in progress, she dried her hands and turned to him, leaning against the sink, but said nothing until the cassette clicked off.

'Where's that shirt you promised me? The water should be hot now, shouldn't it?'

She took the shirt and locked the bathroom door behind her. He turned over the tape and listened to the Castelnuovo-Tedesco.

'Can you set up that blow-heater for me?' she called from the back. He went out to see her hanging her dress and knickers on the line in the backyard. She was wearing his shirt, her hair stringy after the shower, and once again he was pierced by how natural it seemed that she should be with him like this.

On her instructions, he checked the food as she dried her hair, smiling at how she was organizing him, and wondered how long he would put up with that if they were together. For now, of course, it was part of the magic. He opened the wine. The evening had turned cloudless and pleasant.

Over the meal they talked about music while another Spanish cassette played at low volume. He had been shaken by desire for her as she walked about in nothing but a shirt, his shirt, but he had constrained himself, and now, with the food, the wine, the music, the flowers – her easy sensuality had blended into an erotic atmosphere. She talked on as if oblivious to it, how she had hated her mother's classical records and her mother's attempts to teach her simple classical pieces on the piano, but in her late teens had read biographies of Schubert and Schumann, and how their lives had appealed to her romantic phase.

When they went to bed they were both drunk, and she was maudlin, and turned away from him, crying silently. 'Why are you crying?' He knew it was foolish to ask, but to say nothing was unbearable. And he was bewildered. The evening had been perfect and he could not understand how it had come to this. A crystal stream flowing into a quagmire, that's how he thought of it. Shag it. He stroked back her hair, but she was quietly inconsolable. When she spoke, after an interval which seemed much longer to Mungo, her voice was plaintive.

'What happened when you got to Barcelona?'

'Barcelona?' He paused, gathering his befuddled wits. The train. Yes. If he could gain time by finishing the train journey, the rest would fall into place. He took a deep breath, wondering if he had the strength.

'I had fallen asleep on the train, and when I woke it was full light and we were travelling along the coast, somewhere

- 175 -

between Tarragona and Barcelona, in view of the Mediterranean. A fleet of American warships seemed to be at anchor
off-shore, squat and black in the glistening morning water. We
were travelling at speed now, and there was an air of
expectancy in the train, though we still had some time to go.
Ahmed was asleep, nestled among his family, and I felt sorry
that I would probably never see him again.

'Connie was waiting for me at the station. She was two
months pregnant at the time, and mad at me for staying
longer than I said I would in Vigo, but I'd had such a good
time I was easily persuaded. I suppose it was hard to blame
her, in her condition.'

'Very hard.'

'After Franco's death, the place had got very exciting. The
King was crowned and he wasn't the fascist puppet most
people thought he would be. Then there were huge marches
in Barcelona. Kirsten, our flatmate, Connie and I were plan-
ning to join one when Connie had a miscarriage.

'She was three months gone and she was devastated. We
both were, but I don't think she ever recovered. When I went
to see her in hospital the following day, she wouldn't speak to
me, and the nurses looked at me as if I was some kind of dirt.
Maybe that's why I said I would marry her when we came
back to Ireland for the summer. As soon as I left the hospital I
went on the piss.'

'How very male.'

'Well, I was hurt and confused. A part of me was gone too,
even if it was a nuisance, and we had talked on about marriage, leaving it on the long finger. We were very young. We
didn't have work permits, so we weren't sure if we could
marry in Spain.'

'Did you go on the demonstration?'

'Yes. I was dying, of course, after drinking all night, but I
went.'

'Well, don't just lie there! Tell me about it?'

'Now?'

'Yes, now!'

'I was very hungover, and exhausted. I don't remember much about it. Except that there were thousands. Hundreds of thousands.'

'What else? Surely you must remember more.'

'More? There were lots of banners, mostly in Catalan, and Catalan flags, which I hadn't seen much of before. I wasn't very aware of things Catalan, most of which had been banned under Franco. Except they spoke Catalan in one of the offices where I taught. I went with Kirsten,' he added as an afterthought.

'Aha. Now we're getting somewhere.' Tess didn't seem to be maudlin or very drunk any more. His own head was very clear, and aware.

'Well, we had gone to see Connie in hospital. Connie was so depressed that we didn't stay long and Kirsten and I went for a drink, and when I asked her did she want another, she said no, she was going on the demonstration. It was only then I remembered it, to tell you the truth. A curious thing about Kirsten. I never saw her without gloves. Connie said it was because she had lost the fingers on her left hand in an accident, and it must have been true because she had only one glove on this particular evening. Buff-coloured, and kidskin, I think. I don't know why, but it intrigued me. We were attracted to each other, there's no doubt about that, but I wasn't going to betray Connie while she lay on a hospital bed, her heart broken. We spent a pleasant half an hour, that's all, and then we set off for the demonstration. It began in Plaza San Jaime, where even though the march had long since begun, the crowd never seemed to get any smaller. Eventually we found ourselves out of the square, heading towards the port. We turned right, down past the Columbus Column, and right, into the Ramblas. I had one of those hangovers that worsen as the day goes on. My head was splitting, and at the first café I saw I persuaded Kirsten to leave the march to get a brandy.'

'Tut, tut.'

'I didn't intend abandoning it. Not at all. I just needed a cure. Kirsten wouldn't have anything, so I knocked it back and she dragged me by the hand back into the thick of it. On the reservation, the flower sellers and flag sellers were doing fast business as the marchers broke ranks to equip themselves suitably for the evening. The brandy had hardly any effect and it wasn't long before I dragged Kirsten away for another. The cafés were doing a roaring trade, so I wasn't the only one. I knocked it back again and Kirsten looked at me anxiously but I wasn't drunk. I was like a flower pot that hadn't been watered; it seemed to evaporate inside me.

As the march got nearer Plaza Cataluña, it slowed. There seemed to be more huge banners and the chants were getting louder. We were at a standstill for minutes at a time. I needed another drink. Kirsten pleaded with me.'

"Mungo, sip it, sip it, or you'll have a heart attack."

"Sip it. Okay. Maybe you're right." I took a sip and then put it under my jacket and walked out, back into the heart of the march. I suppose I was drunker than I had thought because I drank the brandy, sipping as Kirsten had suggested, by the ring of the glass, and as she so rightly warned, I could easily drop it that way. Then I heard sirens and there was shouting and people backed into us and I spilt most of my drink. The grey jeep, full of heavily armed *Grises*, had mounted the centre of the Rambla at high speed, scattering everyone. You could feel the fear and see the reason. With all of us jammed there so tightly, they could have pointed their submachine guns and killed hundreds, though they were now a good way down. I started shouting angrily with hundreds of others. I suppose part of it was delayed fright. Anyway, when I looked down, my hand was bleeding profusely and the glass was smashed on the ground.

"Oh God," Kirsten said, "they'll think you're shot. Let's get out of here before there's a riot." I hadn't thought of that and I didn't argue. I hid my hand under my jacket and we hightailed it down a side street, where Kirsten examined my hand. "It's worse than I thought," she decided. "Hold it up." We walked on, my bloody hand in the air, for what seemed an age. I think we were lost. Then Kirsten spotted a pharmacy, bought a bandage, and bandaged it on in the street. "Hold it up! I think you need stitches. We'll have to get you to a hospital."

We got a taxi. The driver was doubtful but he took us. We said we'd been on the march when he asked what happened and that seemed to satisfy him. Kirsten had to keep reminding me to keep my hand, which was now very sore, in the air. Then, without warning, she kissed me, forcing her tongue in as far as it would go. I was startled of course, and then I responded, trying to remember to keep my hand upright. She withdrew, kissing me rapidly on the face and neck, then resting her head on my breast. I glanced in the mirror and saw the driver was keeping an eye on us.

We arrived at the hospital, an old building from the last century, and I had to wait quite a while in casualty. I obviously wasn't the only one to have a minor accident on the march. Kirsten said she'd take some air and wait for me in a café across the road. Then a friendly young doctor with an open-necked shirt stitched up my hand, chatting pleasantly as he worked. He seemed pleased that I had been on the march and was convinced that Spain would soon be socialist and was very happy at the prospect. There were two children waiting with their mother in the queue, and I realized they were staring at me and for some reason they made me nervous. I could see the mother had been beaten up and was pretty dazed. The nurse sent me on my way, no charge, and I thanked her, but once she had turned away I couldn't take my eyes off the children and they were looking at me in a very hostile way. They were about the age of Arthur, say, and Ethna. Come to think of it, they looked vaguely like them too, apart from their brown eyes. They made me so nervous as I passed them that I backed into the wrong door, and found myself going up a stairs. This was so obviously ridiculous that I turned back, only to see the children had followed me. I can't explain why, but they terrified me, so up I went the stairs again. I looked around and the little devils were following me, and not to put a tooth in it, I fled.

'I didn't know where I was going, but no matter how quickly I walked, when I turned, they were there, side by side, staring at me. I reached the end of the hospital, but the doors there were locked, so I had the choice of confronting them or going up another flight of stairs. When I reached the top of those they were still there, no more than twenty paces behind, whether I walked fast or slow. It occurred to me that they were wary of coming closer, but that didn't lessen my fear of them. By now I was walking rapidly and sweating heavily. When I got to the end of the corridor, back where I started except one floor up, a crowd of off-duty nurses were waiting for the lift. There was nothing for it, but up the stairs to the third floor, my tormentors in pursuit. By now I was tiring fast, and the more tired, the angrier I became, and I pushed through two heavy wooden doors and stood rigidly still. The doors swung back and forth for a while, and when they had stopped I glared through the oval glass panel at the two. They stared back, but for some reason they retreated. Then a low moaning made me turn. I could see nothing, as the doors were at a T-junction, but then an appalling sight passed before my eyes. A child of about eight was being wheeled on a trolley, obviously to an operating or dressing theatre, by two indifferent orderlies. The child, whose body was covered in loose dressings over what I guessed were burns, was otherwise naked.'

Mungo faltered, in obvious distress, and Tess took one hand and squeezed it, and with her free hand she caressed his face. He gathered himself again, as if for one last effort.

'I knew ... I knew that even though he was heavily drugged, he was in too much pain to lie down. They passed on, out of sight. I turned left, away from him, and then right through another pair of heavy doors until I came to a second very long corridor, bare of humanity until an orderly in gleaming white came through the doors at the far end. Then he started running at me with tremendous speed, and as he passed me his face was grotesque with fear. I burst through the doors, gasping. When I turned, I noticed that the orderly had in fact only walked a few metres, and was looking back at me as if I had done something odd, but was otherwise calm. There was no sign of the children, which was what I was really interested in, and I took off my jacket and used it to wipe the sweat from my face. Looking up, I saw that I was standing under a glass dome, and that the evening sky had turned vermilion. At the far end of this area there were stairs, and I went down the three flights into the hospital garden where there was a seat under a tree, and I rested there for a while. I can't tell you how soothing it was to sit under that tree, the leaves rustling. It was a feeling of great and sudden freedom, and looking up at the old sandstone building I felt that I had been a prisoner there for a long time, but now I had finally and permanently escaped.

'Across from where I sat, there was a large wrought-iron gate. It was locked, but I saw there was a turnstile beside it and when I tried it I found myself on an unfamiliar street. I reckoned I could find my way around the block to the café where Kirsten was waiting. Half-way along the street, I stopped to let a truck enter a yard. Curious, I saw that it was trailing drops of dark blood, and I watched as the truck stopped beside a small crane. The driver and his helper jumped out, laughing, and opened the back. Their cargo was a dead black bull, the sword of the *torero* still in its back behind its neck. The men called several of their work-mates over, and they laughed and joked about it. One of them jumped onto the lorry then, and tried to remove the sword, but couldn't. Then each of them tried, with equal lack of sucess. The two of them tried together, but they failed too.

'Finally they gave up, manoeuvred dirty canvas strapping under the bull and hooked it onto the crane. For a moment I thought the bull was too heavy for the crane, or that the canvas would snap, but suddenly it was suspended high above the yard before being lowered onto a trolley and pushed into a low, white building, and the workmen pulled the doors behind them.'

- Thirteen -

Tess stayed overnight in Fairview to ease Arthur into his first day back at school. It distracted her from Mungo and her worries about where she was to live. He had insisted on giving her a key and in the end, she reasoned, she didn't have to use it. Meanwhile it nestled in her bag, an embarrassing secret. Arthur didn't seem to appreciate that his freedom was over, and she let him play on the street till nine, when she had finished ironing clothes for the coming week. Then she went through his books and copies with him, and he looked at them as if they contained a judgment.

But he had a bath and went to bed without fuss. She assumed that playing all day had worn him out, but when she looked in on him, expecting him to be asleep, he was reading. She was put out. Not long before he would have demanded that she read him a story, if only as a proof of her attention. Now he was growing away from her. She should have been pleased but she wasn't, and when she sat back in the armchair to watch a film she had looked forward to, it was with a long face. Brian said nothing. He put a bottle of beer to his lips.

At the commercial break she asked him if he would like a cup of tea. This for some reason surprised him.

'That'd go down well,' he said then.

Her heart sank as she spotted his smile. She had only suggested it as something neutral to say, expecting him to refuse because of the beer. But he had taken it as a conciliatory gesture. As she foresaw, the serving of the tea and scones created an intimacy. It was the closest they had been for a long time.

'These are delicious,' he said, regarding his half-eaten scone. She had baked them for Arthur, primarily, and she thanked him for the compliment. He waited till he was almost finished, and cleaned his teeth with his tongue. Then he looked into the dregs of his tea, and swirled them around. Such a cliché! she thought, as she waited for him to speak.

'Tess ... I've been a bollocks, I know.' She looked at the floor. 'I was under a lot of strain ...' She knew he was put out that she wasn't responding. The cosy little scene hadn't worked, and now he would blow his lid and prove that he was still a bollocks. But to her surprise he composed himself and spoke softly, reasonably.

'Look, things haven't been perfect – but what marriage is, for Christ's sake? I ask you. And I've been pulling myself together. I've given up the gory videos, and the porno – did you know that?'

'Yes, you told me.'

'*The Sound of Music*,' he guffawed. 'That's what I'm reduced to now!'

'I thought you had that out months ago.'

'Yeah, well, that kind of stuff, you know? I get them out for Arthur. We watch them together.'

'I know. He told me. *The Everlasting Story* is his favourite.'

'That's right! Christ, I've watched it twenty times if I've watched it once. Good film, mind. Great imagery.'

It was the end of that lead and Tess was trying to keep track of the film which had long since resumed. He slumped into the armchair and stared at the television, but at the next commercial break he rallied again.

'Tess, we've had our bad times, but we've had good times too, remember?' She didn't reply. 'Jesus ...' he whispered. 'What am I supposed to say? I fucked it up, I know. I'm sorry. But there's two sides to every story. You're no angel yourself.'

'I never pretended that I was.' It was a mistake to answer him and she knew it, but silence had become impossible. He relaxed and rearranged himself to face her.

'Look, Arthur needs the two of us. Why don't you move back in? We can take it easy for a while, see how it goes.'

'I'm here every day, Brian.' He was clever, she had to give him that. The film resumed and she pointedly turned to watch it. He seemed at a loss for a while.

'Well, I've laid my cards on the table. It's your hand now. I'm off to bed.'

Tess stubbornly watched the film to its insipid end, before pulling out the bed-settee and retiring in a trough of gloom. She lay awake in the dark, tears drenching her pillow. She gave him credit for making an effort in recent months. If he had done so two years before, she could have responded, willingly. But now it was too late. He was trying to persuade the woman who didn't exist any more. She reflected on how true that was. It was tragic, in a way.

Brian left early, banging the door behind him to make sure she woke. She dragged herself out from the clammy duvet and coaxed a dazed Arthur out of bed. He was difficult. He dragged on her nerves at every move. He baulked at his uniform, the way an animal refuses clothing, and she almost hit him in despair; but she drew back, knowing that if she did she was lost.

Inevitably they were late, and she had to push him through the class door, but it was the first morning back. It was almost expected, and they wouldn't be doing much today, the teacher said. Arthur looked around him as he sat in the desk. The reality, it seemed, wasn't so bad.

On her way back to the quays she made up her mind: she would move into Stoneybatter for a few weeks, use it as a base to get a job and get some money together for her own place. If she was going to sort herself out, she needed that at the very least. It would have to be cleaning or waitressing, and on the black, but so be it.

She stopped off at the supermarket in Henry Street to buy

refuse bags and, back at the flat, immediately began to fill them. Her books were neglected and she thumbed them open, raising little clouds of dust. She sat on the floor and began to read through blurbs.

Her packing took all morning, and when she had finished she wasn't so sure about Stoneybatter any more. She washed herself, went to The Winding Stair for soup and a roll, and braced herself to traipse around every restaurant she could think of to ask for a job. Because of Arthur, it had to be in the evenings, so that narrowed it down further. She lied about her experience, but it was no use, there was nothing. Maybe another time. Maybe. She saw that most waitresses were far younger than her, light on their feet, capable of pleasing customers, who would in turn part with a tip, perhaps. She was useless, good-for-nothing.

Back in the flat she lay on the living-room floor, exhausted and sorry for herself. God, she hated poverty, how it cramped her life, how it stopped her from being who she could be. Somehow, it hadn't been so bad when Mungo had been poor too; it had been normal, and funny in a way. The tears streamed back over her ears. Now he had a fucking farm, living in ease with his fucking wife. A current of energy seized her and, jumping to her feet, she grabbed a bagful of books and, despite the weight, swung it against the door. Several books spilled from a gash in the plastic and twisted as the weight crushed them this way and that.

She stared at what she had done. As usual she had injured something she loved for the sake of a moment's release. To cap everything, she couldn't afford a taxi until doleday. She left the carnage where it was, unpacked her tape-recorder and some cassettes, lay on her bed and played 'The Wanderer'. She fell asleep before it ended and woke about two, her head clear, racing through her preoccupations: Berlin, Fairview, Stoneybatter, her mother, Arthur, Mungo, schemes for earning money. It never solved anything but she could not stop, and the hours passed that way. She got up and watched the bleak light of dawn on the Liffey, the gulls gliding low over the water, smooth and shiny as glass, an occasional car disturbing the silence. For the first time, sorrow at leaving here replaced anxiety at finding somewhere new.

She went back to bed and awoke at noon. There was nothing to eat but she made black tea, went to the park at Jervis Street and sat there with a book on the tarot until it was time to collect Arthur. She wondered if he was old enough to be embarrassed at being met by his mother, but she put it out of her mind and hurried him home. She was starving, and it would have to be filed away with all the other things she had to think about. Later, she justified her humiliation in asking her son for the loan of a pound by persuading herself that it would make him feel grown-up, and in fact, he seemed pleased about giving her the money.

'Ten per cent interest,' she promised.

'Oh that's alright,' he said, waving away her offer. 'What's ten pence these days, anyway.'

Taking some butter and hoping it wouldn't melt, she bought milk and bread on the way home, so tea and toast was assured for breakfast.

The questions piled up as she sipped tea at her front window. Did she love Mungo? Was she harming herself by loving him if she did, as she would have to endure the long weeks of loneliness between seeing him, to be rewarded by a few snatched hours? Should she fall deeper into the trap by living in Stoneybatter for a while? Was he using her? Did he have a real case in staying with his family or should she confront him with a choice? What, in the end, was at the root of her predicament?

The tide was out and the river was low enough to see the Poddle river flowing out in front of the Clarence Hotel. It came for miles, and mostly underground. She only knew its route took it under Dublin Castle with its history of power and imprisonment; under the Olympia Theatre, with its ghosts of laughter and dancing; under the Clarence – and who knows what dreams had been played out in its rooms? Did she love him? Yes. No. She missed him badly, and yet there wasn't that x factor she thought should be associated with love. Maybe it came down to a decision. She needed a dandelion or daisy. I love him, I love him not. Was she harming herself if she did? Yes, but she was harming herself either way, as she could think of no other way to redeem herself other than through her few hours with him. Perhaps her willingness to be hurt spoke of a kind of love. She should go to Stoneybatter if for no other reason than that she wanted to; she wanted to occupy a place that wasn't hers, as if somehow, if she couldn't have a happiness rooted in herself, she could at least strike a vicarious blow at Connie, or whatever her name was.

Was he using her? Yes, in the same way she was using him, so that cancelled out. And what was the other? Oh yes: the choice. That would be a wielding of power, but she realized that what she would lose or gain in the end by wielding it would reveal something about herself, something fundamental perhaps. At her age, it seemed vital to be able to flush out something she could recognize as being truly belonging to her, something basic about which she could say, well, maybe I don't like it but it's me. I can build on this and go with it in the direction it takes me, because I know it's true. Even if it meant self-destruction. There was another question she had posed, but she couldn't remember what it was, and her tea was cold.

The next morning she hauled her belongings downstairs, got her welfare money and took a taxi to Stoneybatter. She sat at the table and looked at her black bags lying on the floor. This was only temporary. Mungo would be back in two days. She would tell him then. The house wasn't the same without him and was far too quiet. She put on one of his Spanish tapes and began to nod, then sway to the guitar, and then a wild thought occurred to her. What if she could pick up someone and bring him back, and fuck him in Connie and Mungo's bed? What about that! And have Mungo catch them on Friday morning ... Would he be violent? Would he care?

She didn't carry it through, not knowing if she hadn't the nerve or if it was just the anarchic thought of a woman on edge. For all that, it preoccupied her over the next few days, and she concluded that she liked being in the house like that, on edge, as if she was about to be caught doing something shameful, or at least unapproved.

Mungo surprised her by arriving early on Thursday and, although he said nothing about it, she could see he was pleased she had moved in. Her bags were still on the floor, unpacked, and she apologized, offering to move them under the stairs, but he stopped her. There was someone coming to see the house; it would give the impression they were in the process of moving out. Before she grasped what he was saying, he kissed her and held her close. It was what she had wanted for days, hardly knowing she did, and she gave herself up to it.

'They'll be here in a while,' he whispered.

'Oh.' They touched each other lightly, hardly breathing, stealing glances at each other. 'We have to talk,' she said, brushing a stray hair from his brow.

'Right,' he said, lowering his gaze. Maybe he had looked forward to a morning of uncomplicated pleasure; maybe he had hummed and smiled to himself all the way up on the train, feeling light and free, and now here was a woman full of complications. Life was never simple. Certainly his face had become older in an instant.

'I'll make some tea,' she said, breaking away from him. In the kitchen she reflected that it might be easier to tell a story, and in truth, though she felt the need to talk, now that the moment had come she had no idea what she wanted to say. She would just have to blunder into it.

They drank their tea in silence. It was excruciating.

'Are we going to just go on like this?' she asked him.

'Do you have a suggestion?'

'No.' She hated her questions answered by a question. It was a sure way of going round in circles. 'I thought you might have.'

'Sorry. I'm at a loss.'

'I'm only going to stay for a few days, till I get a flat of my own.'

'Right. I want to tell Connie about you,' he blurted.

'What?' She felt a wave of panic tinged with pleasure. She wasn't ready for such a thing, if she ever would be. 'Don't be foolish, Mungo!'

'Well, I want ...' The doorbell rang and he went to answer it. It was the estate agent with a young couple, and Mungo invited them in.

'Good morning, Mrs Kavanagh,' the agent nodded to her. Mungo found that amusing, but her mouth dropped open and she stared at the agent. Shit. She had to get out of this house as soon as she could. The young couple came forward, smiling, to shake her hand, and she rose and found the grace to respond, though a voice was screaming in her head that she should run.

'Excuse us a moment,' she said, and took Mungo to one side. 'I'm going. Are you staying this evening?' He nodded. 'I'll see you about seven then. Maybe you could make dinner.' She tried to smile, and left him with a swift kiss on the cheek.

That evening, as she left Fairview, she was reluctant to go to Mungo, but for the moment she had little choice. As she walked through Phibsboro and into Rathdown Road, she dragged her feet, perversely hoping the dinner would be ruined by her late arrival. It was nearer eight than seven, and would do no harm to keep him on tenterhooks. When he opened the door she was pleased to note his anxious face, but he said nothing. He had waited, cannily enough, before cooking the food, and over a glass of wine they recounted their day, he doubting whether the couple would buy, and carefully avoiding the questions of the morning until midway through the meal.

'I want to see you on a regular basis,' he said, 'once a week, say.'

She didn't reply, still unsure whether she wanted this or not, while enjoying his need for her.

'Don't tell your wife. Tell her you need to get up once a week or whatever. Tell her anything, but don't tell her the truth. Life is difficult enough.' Then she turned away. 'All we need now is a fire.'

He lit a small fire, while she put on the theme from *Elvira Madigan* and they finished a bottle of wine, together on the sofa.

'Is that a pack of cards I see on the mantelpiece?'

'Yup.'

'Let's play poker! I haven't played for years!' So they played for pennies.

'You haven't told me a story for a while.'

'Heh?' She had a full house. 'A story? Wait till I clean you out, then I'll tell you a story.'

They played for an hour, and she won most of the time, which put her in excellent humour.

'Alright then, I'll tell you about Berlin. Any wine left?' He opened another bottle.

'Where did I leave off the last time?'

'The brothel.'

'Oh yes.' She giggled. 'The brothel.' She snuggled in to him and settled. 'Well, that cut the corners off him. He found out where I was living, and begged me to go back to him, would you believe, but I wasn't going to live with a man who went to brothels!' She had meant this to be humorous, but somehow it wasn't. 'He said he had just gone on the spur of the moment, that he wouldn't do it again – he nearly went on his knees. So I gave in, said he could have Arthur at the weekends. That's the one thing I admire in him, the way he looks after his son ...

'So I got a job in a hotel as a cleaner during the week, and I worked in a restaurant kitchen at the weekends, and that's how I got by. It was okay, even if I didn't get out much. Of course I saw my lover some afternoons, but he was away a lot.'

'Sounds familiar,' Mungo interjected.

'It does, doesn't it.' She touched him lightly on his neck, absent-mindedly tugging the hairs which sprouted there. 'And then of course,' she said, moving on quickly, 'I had the odd beer with the girls at work, only one of whom was German, mind, and good old Marian kept me afloat. Apparently Frau Pohl had been asking about me, so we arranged another evening. Her beautiful granddaughter let us in with a big smile. "This way, girls," she laughed, as if we were in for the time of our lives, and she led us to Frau Pohl's room with such a bounce in her step I thought she was going to break into a dance. "Granny, your visitors!" she announced in English, and Frau Pohl nodded, with an indulgent smile, to her granddaughter.

"Good evening, ladies. You are welcome. Dorothea, ask Yeliz to bring us tea and biscuits. Or," she asked us, "would you prefer chocolate?"

'She was seated in her bed, supported by pillows and satin-covered cushions, as before. Tarot cards were spread out on her bedside table.

"I thought that perhaps this evening we might listen to some music."

"That would be lovely," Marian said. Turning to me she said: "Frau Pohl has exquisite taste in music."

"Dorothea – won't you join us?"

"Yes Grandmother. You want me to pour the tea?"

"I thought the ladies said they wanted chocolate?"

'We had said no such thing, of course.

"Yeliz?" Frau Pohl called. "Yeliz has a wonderful ear for music, you know. Dorothea, will you put on Mahler's Eighth?"

"Ah," said Dorothea. "You want me to be disc jockey."

"It would seem that Dorothea's in love," Frau Pohl said. "She reveals all the signs. But she will not gratify her grandmother by confiding in her."

"I am simply full of the joys of life, as always."

"Not always."

"But who is?"

'Yeliz came, going directly to Frau Pohl, who spoke quietly to her in German. Yeliz smiled at us and took a seat as Dorothea found the record and put it on.

'It had been a long time since I'd heard the Eighth. My mother used to play it when I was a child, on a record player not unlike Frau Pohl's. She played it when she was in one of her dark moods, and, I remember, she used to close her eyes, her head back, as the opening chorus began, and now I knew I was doing as my mother had done all those years ago, my head back, all my frustrations cast away on the great tide of the chorus.

'I wished I could be there forever, in that room, at peace, with Ireland far away. It seemed that life should always be like this: beautiful, grand, plumbed and made meaningful by great music, great art.

'The first choral section ended and I opened my eyes. The others had their eyes closed too, except Dorothea, who stared peacefully into the distance. For a few seconds the room was perfectly quiet, and then that slow orchestral movement began. It haunts me, I don't know why. I felt like crying. Why had life to be so difficult? Always, always, it was relentless, from bed in the morning to bed at night. And listening to the slow, quiet music, I felt I could hold that recognition in my hands, and examine it from all sides, and see that it was true. Then the chorus slowly entered the orchestra again. And then the powerful tenor. As long as we have strength, I thought, as long as we are strong enough for the burden, and come out the other side – at least to some kind of understanding.

'The first side ended, and Yeliz was there, pouring our delicate cups of chocolate. It seemed like an ideal time to gossip, or something. Having been in the clouds as well as the depths I felt stranded, and I felt like a young girl and wanted to say something girlish. I wanted to talk to Yeliz, but I didn't know how to. She looked so dignified and at peace with herself. And so young.

'Frau Pohl looked tired, and for the first time I thought of her as old. We had finished our chocolate, and she nodded to Dorothea, who lay the needle on the second side. In a few moments I had forgotten everything but the pleasure of the music and those soaring voices, or the depths of the bass, unaware of the lyrics, except for their whispering or exultant sounds. It is beautiful to be softly tugged in different directions, not caring where it leads, knowing only that the journey is full of wonder. I'm not sure where – I think it's where the soprano and two altos sing so gloriously together – I realized something was amiss and I opened my eyes.'

Tess went pale and stared.

'Are you alright?' Mungo asked.

'Ahm, I think so,' she smiled, her colour returning. 'But ...'

'But?'

'But you're not going to believe this. What matter. It happens to be as true as you could wish.'

'Of course.'

'I was suspended,' she laughed. 'Ah what the hell! I was suspended almost two metres above the floor, as if I was in a trance.'

'Janey Mac!'

'At first I didn't realize what had happened, as I looked straight at Frau Pohl, who was perfectly at peace. Perhaps I would have closed my eyes again, but I noticed that her quilt hung like an ice-cream cone beneath her. I looked around me. We were all weightless, and if the ceiling was not there we might well have floated out into the night. But that wasn't all.

'Dorothea was gazing at a small, exquisite pastel of a maid on her way to serve chocolate. She was an eighteenth-century girl – of that I'm quite sure – carrying a wooden tray with a glass of water and a delicate, tall china cup on a saucer. The flesh tones of that chaste maidservant were perfect, and so were the tuck and flow of her clothes. But the glory of the pastel was the girl's apron. Each crease was so finely done you could almost hear the starch rustle. No wonder Dorothea considered it in rapture.

'I had for a moment confused Yeliz with the chocolate maid, but not at all. She was wearing the dark, modest clothes of her Turkish mother, and carried a basket of fresh vegetables on the crook of her arm. She looked proud, like a woman sure of her station.

'I wasn't sure what had happened, whether I was hallucinating, projecting my own idea of what made these women happy; or whether the music had revealed them to me. And so I was afraid to look at Marian. Or, to be more precise, I was afraid of the jealousy I had felt for her since our schooldays. She had always got her heart's desire without any effort that I could see. But I also know that she had the courage to do things that I had not, and so she deserved her success, waltzing around from one city to the next, lapping up the good life. Imagine, I hated the guts of my best friend. So my mouth fell open when I saw that she was suckling a naked baby girl, her breasts full of milk, her face flushed with pleasure. To think that that was what was beneath it all. A Mother Earth. The sly bitch.

'And that left me. And no, I'm not trying to hide the truth, but the fact is, I couldn't see myself. By now I was drowsy, and my eyes closed again. The choir was singing the Mater Gloriosa and I was swept away. I wanted to cry. I wanted to scream *No no no*! It mustn't be like this! I was thinking of happiness. I feared it like hell. I feared being obliterated by it. And sure enough I went cold, as if, as I feared, I had died. Died of happiness, a no more deadly murderer.

'But when I opened my eyes I realized it was the coldness of the night air. I was floating above Berlin, being carried along by a light wind. I had travelled away and was now above the city centre, above the Gedächtniskirche and the sex joints. The smell of burgers and sausages wafted up to me and I beheld the Mercedes-Benz star; and on a rooftop garden I could see the clients of a women's sauna cooling off.

'I crossed over the Zoological Garden and didn't hear a sound. It was too much, and I closed my eyes tightly, hoping this was a dream from which I would awaken soon. But I flew on at speed, I could feel it, and tears drenched my face and my body was stiff, the air was so cold. In the distance I could hear a police siren and the groaning of the S-Bahn. And yet I could still hear the music surrounding a tenor voice which I knew was somehow keeping me afloat. It went on and on, and as it died away I felt my feet touch the ground.

'The final chorus, the Chorus Mysticus, began then. When, very frightened, I opened both my eyes I was in darkness. Wouldn't you be scared? But it wasn't pitch darkness, and I realized I was in a large arena. A sports arena. In fact I was in the Olympic Stadium. I was on the track where Jesse Owen had mortified Hitler in 1936.

I took off my shoes and ran. I only intended to warm myself up at first but then I began to enjoy it, and I laughed at Marian back in that apartment, suckling a baby. I had done all that. The choir sang on, filling the stadium with a powerful sound. I ran faster, wheezing like mad, and I knew I would have to stop. But I didn't want to stop, and instead I ran faster, and faster, and faster, and faster.'

- *Fourteen* -

They caressed each other, tentatively. They were falling apart instead of coming together, and there was nothing he could do about it. After a while they gave up their attempt to make love and simply lay in each other's arms.

She switched off the light and he brushed back her hair with his hand, again and again. They had hardly spoken since she had finished her story, and he could think of nothing to say. She turned away from him. He lay awake, knowing she was awake too, but he must have blacked out, because suddenly he found himself in the middle of the night needing to piss.

Instead of going back to bed, he hesitated at the door of the children's room before going in. Their two bunks were bare, and without their chaotic presence the room looked desolate. He remembered Ethna, huddled in sleep, thumb in her mouth, and he wished she was here, where he felt she belonged. And Aidan ... He lay back on Aidan's bed, new since the fire, the fire which had repeated itself so often in his son's head. For all its terrors and responsibilities, its fights, silences and boredom, this house was where life had happened for him, and now he was throwing it away. There would be one last story between Tess and himself. He did not know what it was, but he knew it was important that he make it count.

He woke at dawn, chilled, vaguely aware of Aidan's dreams, and slipped in beside Tess.

When he woke again she had showered and was at the end of the bed, beginning to dress.

'Hi,' she said.

'Hello.'

'Where were you last night?'

'Screwing another woman.' He yawned.

'Huh. Nothing would surprise me.'

'I'm going to miss this house, Tess,' he said, pulling on his trousers. He turned to her. 'Now I'm going to miss it even more.'

'Your children mean everything to you, don't they?' she asked him over breakfast.

'Not everything,' he said through his mushed corn flakes, 'but an awful lot. I suppose Arthur comes first with you?'

They talked about their children then, the anecdotes, sad and hilarious to the universal parent. Mungo still omitted the story of the fire, though it loomed large, and partly because of this preoccupation, they faltered after a while. He put on some music to fill the gap, and they washed up. A waltz began, and he pulled back the table and chairs to make a space and hauled her into the dance.

'What are you doing?' she laughed, half resisting. 'You're crazy, at this hour!'

'What does it matter what hour it is?' Their time was short, and he knew she knew it was a way of being close, and they danced in silence, and he read in her eyes and parted lips what she could no more put in words than he could.

The music changed to a reel, and he plunged them into a wild, formless dance.

'I forget how to do this!' she shrieked.

'I never knew in the first place!'

Whooping, she threw herself into it with him until one lost balance and brought the other into a heap on the floor. In a moment, breathless, they were undoing each others buttons and zips.

Afterwards, they showered together, soaping each other, sharing the same towel. Later, she saw him off at Connolly Station. He had to ring Connie, and his heart pounded in case his voice betrayed him as he felt sure it must do. But Connie, good old Connie, was brisk and to the point. She would meet him, but she might be late because of the children. He left down the receiver, relieved. Tess was looking away. He led her to the bench beside the toilets and they sat.

'I shouldn't have come,' she said quietly. And then she said: 'You lie so well.'

'I didn't tell a word of a lie.'

'Mungo … Can you loan me the money for a deposit?

'How much?'

'I'd say one hundred and twenty, if I'm lucky.'

'I'll see what I can do.'

She looked away from him, embarrassed. He took her hand, but she kissed him suddenly and walked away. He was dazed as he went to the train, but he knew that Tess was right. By the time he reached Gorey he would have recovered enough to pretend nothing had happened, with total conviction, talking only of business, keenly interested to know what had gone on while he was away. Yet, he turned the same question over again and again.

All along they had spoken to each other by means of a story, which had not only satisfied them but seemed necessary. Now her last story seemed to be just that: her last. As he walked the fields over the following week he could not reconcile the passion of their last hours together with the end of passion and, worse, the end of friendship; but it seemed that forces outside their control were working towards that end. Connie noticed his depression.

'I don't want to sell our home in Dublin.'

'But we have to.'

'Yes, I know. We have to. Don't you find that depressing?'

But Connie was glad to be out of Dublin. She had blossomed and had quickly got used to the extra money which was, for the moment, available. And she only had to point to the children to prove how right she was. For the time being, the subject was a useful veil for the real source of his depression. His only problem was to get the money for Tess, which he solved by getting a small loan from a different bank. He would use the surplus for the initial repayments and worry about the rest later.

A letter arrived from the estate agent. Three clients had seen the house in the past week, and one was interested and would view again in a few days time. He had to get Tess out of there fast and used the excuse of airing the place to go to Dublin early.

'There've been tribes here since you went,' she greeted him.

'I know.'

'It's murder.'

'I know. We'll get you a place, don't worry. I have the money.

'Oh.' She seemed to have forgotten about that, or not believed he would remember, or that he'd forget on purpose. He brought her into town and read the evening papers over tea and cake in The Winding Stair. She rang three numbers, two in Rathmines, one in Heytesbury Street. They were all tiny, but despite their dilapidation both Rathmines bedsitters were already taken by someone ahead of them in a long queue, so that when she found herself at the head of a queue in Heytesbury Street, and despite the claustrophobic, cramped space, she took it. The landlord, still dressed in his Garda uniform, asked if she was working.

'Waitress,' she said quickly, praying he wouldn't ask where, and check if she lied, but when she produced the one hundred pounds deposit he showed no further interest.

'I took it,' she said brusquely as she walked past Mungo who was waiting outside the door. She checked the phone number in the hall before leaving.

'You don't look too happy about it,' he said, catching up with her on the street. She turned on him.

'It's a hole, and a hole in the wall, to boot. I'm thirty-four, I've to share a bathroom with six others. I've to cook where I sleep and I've to pay most of my dole for the privilege. Do you expect me to be giddy with happiness? Come on, I might as well move in.'

They hailed a taxi outside the hospital, went to Stoneybatter and loaded her belongings into the car. Then she asked the driver to wait a minute and led Mungo inside. She gave him his key and her number.

'I'm going back on my own, Mungo. Don't contact me for about a month. I need to lick my wounds.' She turned to go, then stopped without facing him. 'Thanks for the money. I don't know when you'll get it back, but you will.' She hesitated again. 'Ring me. Or write me a card. Something.'

And then she was gone. He stared at the door, then sat in the armchair, staring into space. Eventually he roused himself and walked to the Phoenix Park. He walked through lush pastures and scrubland, past a herd of deer peacefully grazing, out past the Papal Cross, until hunger drew him home again. There were the remnants of a loaf, the dregs of a carton of milk, some butter, and he made tea and finished it all. He was tempted to get drunk and had enough money to do it properly but he went to a mindless, violent film instead. He hated such films, but they were noisy and he needed distraction. On the way home he stopped in Hughes's pub, and listened to the musicians over a few pints which he hoped would make him sleep.

When he pulled back the covers he saw that she had left a few hairs and a stain. He switched out the light and fell into bed, wondering how it could be that the woman he already missed so much could have been here twelve hours before. He shook his head in bafflement, and then, finally, a few tears came. There was nothing for it but to endure.

In the morning he took the sheet and put it in the refuse bin. The stain was light and had not seeped through to the mattress. He tidied the house and washed himself, and the agent and his couple arrived. They were young, already had a house in the suburbs but wanted to move close to town.

'You won't get much closer,' the agent beamed.

'Any children?' Mungo asked to be pleasant, although he felt awful.

'One,' the woman said. 'He's in the crèche this morning.'

'Oh.'

They looked over the house again, discussing how they could make it as open-plan as possible. Mungo leaned against the kitchen sink, wishing he was far away. The deal was done. Now it was a matter for the solicitors.

In the station, he sorely wanted to ring Tess, ask how she had settled in, anything to hear her voice, but he didn't. Instead, he rang Connie, who was delighted with the news, and he told her he was on his way.

The weeks passed, and he dealt with his pain by working himself to exhaustion until light faded. His one pleasure was to watch the leaves of the oak in the big field change to yellow and then brown as they accumulated around the tree. With the children at school he stayed out of Connie's way until they came home. He was asleep by the time she got to bed, up before she woke, so that hardly an unnecessary word passed between them from one day to the next. The farm was getting back into shape through their labour, and this seemed to be enough.

There was a brief Indian summer. One afternoon was particularly warm and he sat under the oak to rest. He leaned back into the trunk, as if it exuded comfort, and realized he had hardly stopped to take breath for weeks. Tess had asked him to ring in a month. It was now long passed a month, but he was reluctant to revive the pain and to what he perceived as little purpose. Then he remembered his last story. An inkling had come to him the night he had slept on Aidan's bed, but he had pushed it from his mind. In the weeks since, it had come back to him in fleeting moments, but each time he had rejected it, just as he had rejected any deep feeling about what had happened his child. Aidan had broken into the last story he had told her. He had come from nowhere, from an unseen corridor in a labyrinthine hospital, in great pain, being pushed by two strangers whose thoughts were elsewhere. His train journey was leading him back to the beginning, when his life was changed, and Aidan was marked for life. There was one last train journey then, on – what were they called? *Tranvías*, the local trains. One last journey on a *tranvía* along the coast. Both Aidan and Mungo loved a train journey by the sea. That was it – a trip to the Costa Brava. And an outing to an abandoned church overlooking the sea. He jumped up and went to the house.

'Connie! Do you want anything from the village? I'm going to get a few beers.'

'Get something for the rest of us. This is worse than summer.'

What did she mean, 'worse than summer'? Weren't the goddamn winters long enough for her? She'd soon find that one out, up here in the hills. He drove through Monaseed and on to Hollyfort, bought the drinks and made sure he had enough change. It occurred to him that she might not be in on such a fine day, but she picked up the phone just as it rang.

'Tess?'

'Yes. Mungo?'

'I was afraid you might be out on such a glorious day.'

'Is it fine down there? It's pissing rain here. Ah ... Mungo, I was just on my way out to work, and I'm late.'

'You're working? Since when? What at?'

'Waitressing. It's handy hours, early afternoon and evening and I need the money. I've got to –'

'What about Arthur?'

'He goes home himself now. Listen, Mungo, have you any plans to come up? It'd be nice to see you.'

His spirits rose.

'Do you fancy a fancy-dress party for Hallowe'en? The girls in the house here are all talk about it. You could come up on the evening train and meet me after work. Do you know The Ranch?'

'I know where it is. A fancy-dress party? I wouldn't have a clue what to go as—'

'Wear your father's uniform you were going on about. I've

- 202 -

got to run, Mungo, I'm late already. Eleven o'clock, Hallowe'en, The Ranch. Right?'

'Right.'

'Byeee!'

His father's uniform. Jesus. There was something scandalous about wearing it to a party. He shuddered and replaced the phone. There wasn't much room in her life now, he thought, as he drove the long way home, north, then across the side of Annagh Hill – but at least she's squeezing me in. His thoughts now with the autumn landscape of the valley, now with Tess's offhand inclusion of him in her plans, he wondered if there would be time to tell his story. He realized he was at peace, as if something wild and mournful had settled in him. Perhaps it had something to do with the valley, its colours dying to make way for winter on this beautiful day.

'I rang the solicitor to see how things were going,' he said over supper, 'but he was out. So the secretary offered me an appointment for Thursday morning, ten o'clock.'

'Sure these things take months, Mungo.' Connie buttered a slice of bread for Ethna. 'Anyway, I thought you didn't want to sell the place. What has you so anxious to get rid of it now?'

'For one thing, let me remind you that it's sold. And if it's sold we might as well get the money as soon as we can, seeing as we're not millionaires. And you have to push these people!'

'Alright, alright, you've made your point – Ethna, don't spit out good bread!'

'There are children starving in Africa, you know,' Aidan lectured, repeating what his mother had said so often. Ethna replied by hitting him on the shoulder with her knife, the flat end, with enough force to hurt.

'She stabbed me, she stabbed me!'

'Stop it, stop it both of you!' Connie yelled.

'Cop on, Aidan,' Mungo said. 'And don't you hit your brother with a knife again, Ethna.'

Ethna and Aidan scowled at each other, but peace returned.

'I'll go up on the evening train on Wednesday,' he said to Connie.

'Wednesday? But you can't go away on Wednesday – it's Hallowe'en!' Aidan protested.

'Hallowe'en?'

'We have to have a party for Hallowe'en!'

'A party, a party,' Ethna joined in, clapping her hands.

Mungo's heart sank, but then he had an idea, and opened his arms wide and smiled a generous, paterfamilias smile.

'Well then, we'll just have to have the party before I go, won't we?'

The children cheered.

'What do we need?'

'Apples, and monkey nuts,' Aidan said, none too sure.

'And crisps,' Ethna nodded.

When Connie had settled in front of the television and the children were playing outside, Mungo went upstairs and uncovered his father's khaki and helmet. Imagine going out to die in shorts, he thought as he held them up. Why not? A corpse doesn't care how it's dressed. He took off his clothes and put on the uniform and to his surprise it was a tight fit. For some reason he expected it to hang off him, but then he realized that his father had only been twenty in 1943. He put on the helmet and ammunition pouches and stood to attention before the mirror, rifle in his left hand. There he was in the guard of honour, like his father, waiting to be inspected by Winston Churchill. Only twenty, little more than a boy, in one of the great battles of history. Yet he never spoke about it. The medals on the shelf in the wardrobe, dull with age and neglect, were testimony to his presence and perhaps his courage. His mother had never spoken about it either – had refused, in fact. It stank of mothballs.

'What are you doing done up in that?' Connie asked quietly. He swung around, and stared at her.

'It's my father's uniform,' he said then.

'I know that. But what are you doing in it?'

'Just curious. I'm thinking of bringing it to Dublin to sell.'

'Good idea. I was going to throw it out. I don't want Aidan to get any romantic ideas about war.'

She left. Maybe she had a point, though it was a shame not

to show him his grandfather's uniform. It was his own history, after all. It was Mungo's, too, and yet he was going to demean it at a party. He took it off and put it away.

When he went down to the living-room Connie was watching the news. A reporter was commenting on the Presidential campaign, and Connie made some disparaging remarks about the woman candidate, who she regarded as a communist because of her liberal record. Mungo said nothing. He had already made up his mind to vote for her.

The next day he made the appointment with the solicitor. Even if it cut into his time with Tess, he felt better covering his tracks. In Monaseed he bought apples and nuts and a large turnip, which he hollowed out, with eyes and nose and mouth, and put a candle in it. Connie helped him to set things up, putting streamers in the kitchen, pennies in a basin of water which they had to retrieve with their mouths, and hanging apples from the ceiling by a thread, which they had to eat with their hands behind their backs. Then they blacked out the kitchen, lit the candle, and called the children, who wore the masks and old clothes which would disguise them when they went begging for money or nuts or whatever indulgent neighbours would give them.

For the first time in too long Mungo saw Connie laugh so hard at the children's attempts to bite the elusive apples and retrieve the submerged pennies that she held her belly. If only they could be like this even occasionally. If only laughter would soften them to each other. He was shouting a mixture of encouragement and jovial abuse as he thought this, as the children's enthusiasm spilled over into mayhem which would not have been allowed at another time.

Connie drove him to the station. The children were still excited and in their costumes but for once she was indulgent, curbing them only when they interfered with her driving, at which point Mungo supported her. At the station he kissed the children good-bye in the car and wished them happy pickings for the night. Connie leaned over and kissed him on the lips. 'You were great,' she said, her hand on his cheek.

'So were you,' he said, and she smiled and got ready to turn the ignition.

It was easy to get a seat on the train. He had more luggage than usual. In a holdall he had the carefully folded uniform and helmet of a Desert Rat.

When he arrived in Dublin he went to The Ranch and, pretending to look at the menu on the window outside, he saw Tess, in uniform, wait on a table. He was tempted to go in and order a meal, but instead went to a local pub and had a toasted cheese sandwich and a pint. Already the bar was full of the young and beautiful, some of them in fancy dress as priests, nuns, wizards, French maids, stocking-and-garter nurses, and weedy-looking Supermen. Mungo felt much older than his age, although there was a sprinkling of his contemporaries. They were probably actors, and artists from the local studios. One group was talking about the presidential election. The Tánaiste, one of the presidential candidates, had been sacked from the government. Obviously, to his surprise, the campaign was stirring interest among more people than Connie. There was no doubt who was the favourite here, and now, with this latest news, she was the favourite to win.

This time Tess spotted him as he peered in from the dark street. Some customers were still in the restaurant, but she winked and put up her hand, fingers splayed. Five minutes. Accustomed to no more than a few bottles of beer on warm evenings, he was a bit drunk after a few pints. It felt good, though. He was relaxed and optimistic and smiling to himself. She was nearer to fifteen minutes, and when she came out, carrying a bag, she kissed him quickly and took him by the arm back to the pub from which he had come. She'd had a quick glass of wine earlier to get her in the mood, but now she needed a long cool pint followed by whiskey. The bar was now difficult to get into, and she shouted to him to get her a drink while she changed. With the leavening of drink and fancy dress, the atmosphere was intoxicating. He had never seen so many garters, so much revealed flesh, anonymous behind masks and make-up, but he felt an outsider and gulped back a lot of his pint to equalize things somehow. When Tess returned he didn't recognize her in her snake crown, her golden make-up, her false beard, spiral earrings and long golden dress off one shoulder.

'Who are you?'

'Nefertiti. I saw a bust of her in Berlin. Give me that pint before I die.' She drank several mouthfuls. 'What about you – did you bring the uniform?'

'Yeah, it's in my bag.'

'Well change! I want to see my soldier boy.'

'Here?' He cringed at the thought.

'Can't you see that everyone's dressed up?'

'Not everyone.'

'You're the only one with clothes on a nudist beach. I'll mind your drink.'

He took his bag and went down the narrow stairs to the toilet where a bishop and a Roundhead were urinating. He went into the water closet.

'Father, forgive me,' he muttered, his eyes raised to where he presumed his father's spirit dwelt. It was a struggle to change in the toilet, as apart from being cramped the floor was wet, but there was a hook on the back of the door, so at least he could hang his bag there. He took off his jacket and shirt, being careful of his wallet and keys, and put on the army shirt. That was simple enough. The smell of stale urine was getting to him and he thought that if he got out of this place without a tropical disease he'd be lucky. He rolled off wads of toilet paper and put them on the ground, largely solving the problem if he could keep his balance. It proved relatively easy, but he lost his balance once because of a light head and fell against the wall with his khaki shorts half on. Balancing on one leg, he got himself upright again and strapped on the ammunition pouches, into one of which he stashed his wallet, and the other his keys. It had been too awkward to bring the rifle, but he strapped on the heavy revolver. If some smart fucker jeered him once, he swore, he'd pull it on him. He had a piss while he was there. There was no mirror in the toilet, but he peered into the dull chrome of the hand drier. He had forgotten the helmet. He strapped it on and peered again. That was better. He'd probably end up needing it.

As he went up the stairs, he momentarily startled a young man who was coming down. Then there was a nod of amused recognition, and Mungo passed him stiffly, his eyes, he imagined, glinting like steel in the desert sun.

'Hey, you look great!' said Nefertiti, handing him his drink. He needed it. They bought a bottle of whiskey to take away.

The atmosphere on the street was electric, like a souped-up Saturday night. He spotted French maids and Mandrakes dodging between cars, hopelessly looking for taxis. Above the noise of the traffic he could hear laughing and shouting. Tess looked very young, and, he realized, very upright. She was walking like a queen.

'Here,' he said, 'give me your bag. It's ruining the effect.'

'Thanks,' she said out of the corner of her mouth.

'The only thing I don't like is the beard. It isn't very feminine.'

'I have to wear it to look right,' she said. 'It's a symbol of authority.'

By the time they reached Heytesbury Street the party was in full swing, with bodies, singly or in pairs, sprawled in the hall and on the stairs. Loud music with an insistent bass pounded the house. Tess brought him to her room and closed the door.

'Well, aren't you going to kiss me?'

'Not with that beard on,' he said, putting down their bags. She put her arms around him and kissed him, her tongue deep into his mouth. Then she grabbed the bottle of whiskey, took two glasses and brought him to one of the larger flats downstairs. Throughout the night she kept introducing him to people who lived in the house, but there wasn't much point, as he forgot their names instantly, and as they were disguised there was no way he could remember their faces. People began to cluster in small groups and couples. One couple was leaving little to the imagination; several were necking. Mungo and Tess were necking too. It was after three a.m. and they were very drunk.

'Let's go to your room,' Mungo said.

'Yes, let's,' she agreed, but when they got there, a naked man with a eagle mask on the back of his head was lying between the legs of a similarly attired woman. Another couple, who seemed not to have quite made it, was lying on the floor.

'Fuck it.' Tess was crying with frustration, the tears incrementing the chaos of her make-up. 'Fuck it, I need to sleep. Do you still have a place?' He nodded. 'Let's go then.' She was gone and, unsteadily, he followed her. It needed all his concentration to negotiate the sprawled bodies on the stairs, and by the time he reached the door she was crossing the street. The traffic was sparse but she looked neither left or right and strode on, her head in the air. The taxis were full and they had to walk. His mind wandered and he recalled the argument in the pub earlier in the night.

'Who're you going to vote for?' he asked her.

'Who do you think? And you?'

'Oh, the same.' He had made up his mind and it pleased him.

'I can't wait,' she said.

They walked down from Dame Street, into Parliament Street and reached Grattan Bridge.

'Where are we going?' he demanded.

'Wherever,' she said.

'Hey, we hardly danced at all tonight,' he said, his eyes closing. 'Let's dance.'

So they danced off the pavement to some tuneless waltz, onto the middle of the bridge. A passing taxi driver blew his horn, but they were oblivious.

'Hold on a minute,' she said abruptly and trotted to the parapet. 'I don't believe it,' she shouted. 'The fuckers!'

'What? What don't you believe?'

'They've knocked my lovely house down, that's what I don't believe. Wankers!' she shouted. 'Wankers!'

'Let's dance,' he said, his arms stretched out to her.

'My lovely house.' She was crying and without warning she

ran towards the demolished building, and Mungo's arms were left with nothing but air between them. Nevertheless, arms outstretched, he resumed the dance, waltzing onto the middle of the bridge again. The tanks had opened up, and day turned to night as the tracks churned up the sand. He was scared of dying, his stomach capsized in fear, and he vomited over the parapet into the Liffey.

That sobered him a little and he looked around for Tess. He found her along the quay, sitting on the pavement, sniffling, her shoulders shaking in irregular spasms, staring at the gap which had once been her home. He sat down beside her and put his arm around her and she leaned into him.

'I loved that place. It's the only place I was ever free.'

He looked up to where they had first gone to bed, and he had been so confused when she stopped him he had put his trousers on back to front. And then, the other times when they had got used to each other and their passion had ignited. And then their tall tales, told to each other so intimately. The ghosts of so much embarrassment and lust and happenings he knew nothing of, floating about up there. And their own ghosts. Did they leave any mark on the universe at all?

'Let's go,' he whispered, 'before we get our death,' and she got up without protest and followed him along the quays.

Coming towards them, a couple were fighting, screaming and shouting at each other. A cruising squad car pulled over and a guard warned them to be quiet. The man turned on him and abused him with a stream of oaths, at which the guards moved in to arrest him. The man struggled and his girlfriend cursed the guards. Then the man went limp as a guard opened the backdoor of the squad car to bundle him in, but he suddenly came to life and broke away. The guards ran after him, one of them shouting into his radio, and the girl followed, screaming, across the road and into a laneway. Mungo and Tess followed at a discreet distance. The guards had the man on the ground, punching him, but he was fighting back, loudly encouraged by his girlfriend. Two more guards came running down the street, then another squad car with two more, and between them the six guards quietened him and dragged him to the second squad car and bundled his hysterical girlfriend in beside him. Mungo decided it was time to leave and spotted a free taxi on the quays. As it turned in, the second squad car accelerated, followed a few moments later by the one on the quay.

When the Desert Rat awoke beside Nefertiti her beard was on her cheek. He too was fully dressed, and he did not know which hurt more – his feet or his head. Looking down at his boots, he saw for the first time the cracks in the shining leather. Nefertiti stirred, instinctively removing her beard. Through bloodshot eyes she looked at the Desert Rat and groaned.

'We're in trouble, Tess. Our clothes are back in your place.'

'Shit.' She closed her eyes. 'So are my keys.'

'That's wonderful news. And I've an appointment with a solicitor in fifteen minutes.'

'Has he a sense of humour?'

It was a mistake to get up quickly, as his head spun and he was flooded with nausea, but he managed to steady himself. After he had been to the bathroom he went back upstairs to assess the situation. His helmet was on the floor and perhaps it was a good idea to take off his gun. Apart from his stubble and bloodshot eyes, he convinced himself that his image in the mirror was no worse than that of an eccentric tourist.

'I can't go out on the street like this,' she groaned.

'Sure no one'll recognize you, Tess. But what the fuck are we going to do?'

'Francine. You met her last night.'

'Did I?'

'Bell seven. Keep ringing till she answers. She works with me. If you're not back in two hours I'll hang myself.'

At least he had his wallet. He picked up the helmet as if it were a hat, glanced at her and left. He was half-way to the solicitor's before he realized he was still wearing the gun, and when he put his hand gingerly to his head there was a tin hat on it. It was only then he noticed that people were staring at him. Didn't they realize he was a refugee from a fancy-dress party? Then he remembered that time on the Ha'penny Bridge twelve months before, and lengthened his stride. If it wasn't for his throbbing head, he wouldn't have a care in the world.

After a moment's surprise, both the secretary and solicitor treated him as if he were wearing a three-piece suit. The secretary even allowed him to make a phone call. It rang for a long time.

'Francine?'

In less than two hours Mungo had rescued Tess in a taxi and she made him breakfast.

'It was a colourful night, huh?'

'Yeah. I have to go in a few minutes. Do you want to see me again?'

'Why? Don't you want to see me?'

'Yes. Very much.'

'Well then. Ring me.' She stretched out her hand and he squeezed it.

He rang from Hollyfort or Gorey every few days. Brief calls. If there was talk of anything, it was about the presidential election. It seemed to be an obsession with Tess. Connie and Mungo argued over the woman candidate, the first in Irish history. He couldn't believe that Connie was so emotional about her, so critical, so vehemently against her. His mother's voting card arrived, but neither Connie nor Mungo was registered in Wexford. Connie said she wouldn't have voted anyway, but he declared his intention of going to Dublin. Connie was incredulous that he would waste a day like that. Tess was delighted.

'She's going to make it, you know,' she said fervently.

He thought so too, and it put him in a buoyant mood. It led to a damaging row with Connie. A lot of old hurt poured out, and when she had nothing else left, she cast up the fire which had scarred Aidan. That killed him off, as she knew it would, and she walked in victory out of the room.

'You bitch,' he said faintly. 'You bitch ...'

He packed a bag with enough fresh clothes to last for several days and hitched to Gorey and caught the afternoon train. Tess was not expecting him till the following day so he would have to wait for her outside The Ranch. He went to a boring picture and had a few drinks in the pub nearby. By eleven he was waiting across the road from the restaurant. He noticed a tall young man check the name of the place and then look inside the window. It must have been a trick of the light, but he could have sworn he saw Tess wave at him. Whether it was Tess or not, the young man waved back and then walked a few paces on, evidently pleased with himself. Within minutes Tess had left work and was in the young man's arms, and for the second time in several hours, Mungo was shaken to his heart.

Somehow he endured. There was nothing for it but to endure. On Grattan Bridge he looked over the side and re- membered Hallowe'en. Idly, he thought he should jump, it looked black and deep enough, but dismissed the idea as melodramatic. He looked up at the dark air where Tess's flat had been, and for an instant he felt crushed again, but pulled back. He was determined to endure, to put his pain into a strength that would help him take hold of life again. It was unrealistic to expect her to survive on his periodic embrace. She was a mature woman, and needed more. Yet, when he reached the house that was no longer his, he could not bear to lie in the bed that she, and before her his spiteful wife, had lain on. Instead, he lay down on Aidan's bed and fell into a deep sleep.

The next morning he woke late. He lay in bed, reluctant to get up. His neck, for some reason, was stiff. There were voting cards on the floor in the hall which he had overlooked the pre- vious night. It gave him a sweet satisfaction to vote in Aidan and Ethna's old school. The place was full of young voters, and women with small children, and for the first time he could remember, Mungo felt an excitement in the polling centre. One woman was agitated because her child had scrawled all over her polling card, but she had identification, so to her immense relief, they let her vote. Mungo hung around the yard for a while. It was hard to believe that Ethna and Aidan had so recently played in this yard; that he had waited so often outside the gates to meet them. There were too many ghosts accumulating of late.

He bought some provisions and made himself breakfast. Tess was expecting him to call and he wondered now if he should, but he had always found it impossible to break an appointment, however unpleasant, and he knew it was inevitable that he would ring. He would not ask her about her young man. That was her affair. They had made no promises of fidelity to each other. And in reality, or what passed as the real world, in sharing the difficulties and pleasures of ordinary life they had never been close, and never could be. That was sobering, and it was sad. And yet, somehow, her fickleness didn't matter. What mattered was that in telling her his stories, and in listening to hers, a loneliness which he had been barely aware of all his life had gone. He drank back the dregs of his tea, and laughed. Imagine! They were friends. Even as he thought this, he knew he felt more than friendship, but knew also that he would settle for it. With Tess as his friend, perhaps he could survive his life in Wexford. That seemed to be the way things were turning out, presuming he could swallow the row with Connie, and he had only to think of Ethna and Aidan to know that he would.

His hand shook as he held the receiver, but he went through with it.

'I've just voted. How about you?'

'First thing. God, if she doesn't make it, I'll die.'

'She will.' His voice was soft, but to his surprise it was also steady. They talked on for a while, quietly, like two people who know each other very well. She asked him to meet her outside The Ranch after work.

'I'll be there.'

When he put down the receiver he wondered if Francine and the other waitresses knew if Tess was keeping a couple of men on a string. He supposed they did, and that they laughed about it, but he didn't care. He supposed it must be good for Tess's ego, which he knew was fragile.

She looked tired, and that wasn't surprising; but she looked genuinely happy to see him. After a few drinks her tiredness seemed to disappear and she became more and more affectionate. He became more confused. They took a taxi back to her place and she insisted on paying. He had taken more taxis in the last few months than he had taken in his life, but so what. She nestled into him, breaking into his loneliness.

When they got to her flat she went to the bathroom for a few minutes, then immediately stripped and got into bed. He went too, then joined her, but although he muddled through the motions of responding to her kisses, his mind was elsewhere, and he broke away from her.

'I'm sorry Tess. I can't. I had a big row with Connie before I left.'

'Don't worry about it. We'll do it another night.' She ran her fingers through his hair. 'I'll tell you what – why don't you tell the rest of your story. Your Spanish story.'

Yes, he thought. That was the one thing he could rise to, the one thing that mattered that was still untold. As usual, he paused to find the thread.

'There isn't much left to tell. Connie and I came home and got married. Aidan was born about two years afterwards. I had qualified as a carpenter before I went to Spain and I took it up again when I came back. I never liked it but I was a man with responsibilities now so I did it. Ethna came a few years after and I worked like a dog, overtime, nixers, anything I could get. We wanted for nothing, had our few drinks at the weekends when the kids got strong, and I'd saved so much I managed to pay off the house, which we'd got cheap anyway. Everything in the garden was rosy. I was too tired during the week, but Connie seemed satisfied with sex on a Saturday night.

'Then we went back to Barcelona on a holiday, as much to lay old wounds to rest as anything else. Connie went back to the hospital, took a look at the ward she was in, and cried for about two days. It was good for her, and she was a lot happier. Then we moved up the coast, to the Costa Brava, to a small village which looked nothing but it had a lovely, deserted beach. The main road to Barcelona passed through the village and there was the constant noise of the traffic, but the beach was worth it and we spent a few lovely days there.

'On the Sunday morning we decided we'd go for a walk into the country, which really meant into the hills. It was ridiculous really. Poor Ethna was exhausted by the first hill, but Aidan insisted on continuing, so Connie said she'd go back with Ethna and gave me her water bottle as it was already hot. Aidan and I watched them go down the hill and I've often wondered about that moment, as if it was one of those times where your life divides into before and after and there is no turning back. The sea was glinting, and far out you could see the squat black shapes of the US Fleet, just as I had from the train years before.

'The countryside was beautiful in its way, but brown and somewhat monotonous to Irish eyes. I was afraid it would get too hot, but Aidan spotted a lizard and was so amazed he insisted on going on so that we might see another. I was about to insist that we turn back when we heard music, and in the distance we saw a file of people led by a priest, a trombonist and a drummer. That settled it. As we came up to them, we saw that a few in the procession were carrying an enormous wicker basket of flowers. We were heading towards an old church, which blended into the background on a rise. Some of the group looked at us, then said something in Catalan, smiling and nodding an inclusive approval. Aidan smiled up at me as if to say, well, wasn't I right? and I smiled too and clapped his back. We had to cross a small footbridge, no more than a footstick, really, over what turned out to be a surprisingly vigorous stream.

'The church had been abandoned a long time, maybe over a century before, and I longed to ask why but didn't have any Catalan. There was nothing inside except heaps of dried bushes and vegetation and whatever the wind had blown in, along with a thick layer of dust. A lizard basked where a window had been, and Aidan pointed in pleasure.

'They placed the basket of flowers in the centre and the priest walked around it sprinkling holy water and blessing it. Then he led the pilgrims in prayer, and the little band struck up, played something very haunting, and it was over.

'Outside they broke into small groups of men and women, the priest talking to the women. The men lit cigarettes and offered one to me, but I declined. They smiled at us and we smiled back. Then the party set off down again and stopped at the stream to cool themselves, splashing the water on their faces and washing their hands and feet. It seemed part of the ritual, probably born of ordinary physical need, and we did the same. They smiled at us again, and as we went down the hill one of them tried to engage me in conversation, and with the help of my rusty Castilian we talked the usual small talk in such situations. We had gone some way before I noticed that Aidan was missing and I made my excuses and went back up the hill, calling him. There was no sign of him at the stream and then I thought I heard a faint crackling, and when I looked up I saw smoke coming from the church. I wanted to call him, but I had lost my voice. I was running, but no matter how hard I tried it was as if I was a film in slow motion. Then suddenly I was inside the church and what I saw I will never forget.'

Mungo paused.

'Aidan was standing beside the basket of flowers, surrounded by burning bushes. He was screaming to me, but I could not hear him above the roar of the flames, which had covered the entire floor of the church apart from the circle at the centre of which Aidan and the flowers were a part. Then a flaming bush floated up to a rafter and I couldn't help looking up. It had a captivating beauty as it wafted upwards until it was blocked by the rafter, which it seemed to play with, until the rafter ignited with an angry burst. Then at last I heard Aidan's voice, and I wasn't sure if the fire was in the church or in my head, but I screamed and braced myself to run through the flames. Maybe fear is the first path to intelligence, but some voice told me I should throw dust on the flames and that is what I did, like making a path through the sea, until I reached him. You'd think I would have run with him the way I came, but no, I picked him up and both of us were sobbing with fear, and I squeezed him to me. Then Aidan, his face smudged with smoke and tears, reached back from me and took a large white flower from the basket and said, "Come on, Daddy, come on," and we started back, choking on the smoke, Aidan swinging the flower from side to side, beating back the flames to make a way. Then the rafter collapsed and fell before us, a shower of sparks flying away from it. A gust of hot air blew against us and, choking, I dropped Aidan and he fell ... he fell ...'

Mungo was panting and covered in sweat, unable to say it, and yet he had to. If he did not say it now, he never would. He would turn in on himself and wither away, and he knew this, so he groaned and gathered himself for a last effort. Tess stared at him.

'He fell into the flames, which were no higher than the length of a hand, but they were flames, and his shirt caught fire. I don't know if it was the best thing to do, it may be what scarred him in the end, but I rolled him over and covered his torso with dust. It was hot but it smothered the flames. Aidan was screaming, beating my face with pain and fear, and I was terrified myself and sure we were going to die. I thought for a moment it was wishful thinking, a mirage that would help us die, but as if by a divine hand the fiery rafter was moved to one side and the flames on the floor had nothing left to devour and died away, and I heard shouting in Catalan as Aidan passed out. A woman took him from me and others supported me and brought us down to the river, bathing Aidan in it with great gentleness as the priest prayed over him. In the distance I could see a young man running like a hare to the village, so I knew I could trust them to take care of Aidan, just as I knew that nothing would ever be the same again.'

- *Fifteen* -

It was after midday; that much she knew. As usual, she dressed before waking Larry. He looked at her coldly. She supposed he thought it was the manly thing to do. Oh yes, keep the woman insecure, that was the way these young lords thought; keep her begging for you. Well, it wasn't like that at all. It helped her to maintain a clear conscience, in fact. She could have his perfect body without giving a damn for his feelings. And boy, how greedy he was when she let him near her. That was the sexiest thing of all, holding him off until he was half crazy, so crazy that he was blind to her flaws and blemishes, with only one imperative in his steaming brain.

She went to the toilet along the hall and as, when she returned, he hadn't stirred, she made tea and toast and brought them to him. He accepted his breakfast without a word, and she watched his lean, stubbled jawbone as he masticated, and the way his black hair casually fell over the nape of his neck. She smiled. At last, at long long last, she had learned enough to be in control. And he really was so beautiful, with those long smooth hands which had never known work, with his long smooth body to match.

One night she had gone for a drink with the girls in Camden Street and had lain her eyes on him, but from the first moment, though she wanted him badly, she had arranged it so that he thought he was the one who had spotted her. How subtle women can be, she mused, when we don't really care. He, on the other hand, had been crude and direct, as she had guessed he would. He was young, drunk and handsome, so she allowed him to think himself immortal and perfectly potent, and that a woman like her was his plaything as of right.

She still relished how his face dropped when she answered him as if he had asked her the time. 'Yes, I'd love a ride,' she said. There are moments in life which, if we pounce on them, make us free. She hadn't blushed and her heart had barely quickened, because as she said it she knew it was all a matter of flattery and a game.

'More tea,' Larry said.

She brought him the tea and sugar and milk without resentment. He was fifteen years older than Arthur. She turned on the radio. In fifteen years time would Arthur be like this, lording it in an older woman's bed and treating her like dirt, unaware that his machismo was her best defence against him? And would she warn him? No. No, it had to happen like this. He had to learn the hard way.

The radio was tuned to some music station, but they paused to mention the presidential election count.

'It's looking like Mary Robinson will be the next President of Ireland,' drawled the mid-Atlantic voice. Tess stared at the radio, then with shaking fingers searched the airwaves for more substantial news. She had forgotten about it, as if she hadn't realized that every last vote had to be counted and that real people did this.

'Is she in?' came from the bed.

'Not yet,' she said quietly.

'It'd be cool to have a woman President,' Larry said as he dressed.

Tess looked at him sharply. Cool! Now she wished that Mungo was here in his stead. He was the only one she could think of who would understand the near-panic she felt in case Robinson didn't make it. History was not in her favour, but maybe, just maybe, something odd was happening to history.

'Kiss your hero good-bye,' Larry said, leaning over her. She caught the whiff of stale sweat, all that remained of his wild heaving the night before, and was mildly disgusted.

'No,' she said.

'Oh. In a bad mood, are we? That time of the month, or something?'

'Oh fuck off, Larry.'

He threw up his hands and made a face. 'I reckon it's time for a tactical withdrawal. See you tonight?'

'No. I want to be with adults tonight.'

'Ah you're not that old,' he said, lifting the underside of her hair in his hand.

'Out. Out now, and don't come back. I mean it.'

He laughed. 'I'll give you a call,' he said. The door closed behind him.

Right now she truly meant it. She didn't want to see him again, but from somewhere a voice warned her that winter was setting in and there might be cold dark nights when she would long for the flattery of his attentions which would rid her of her own leaden presence.

Where was Mungo now that she needed him? The analysis continued on the radio. She had, it seemed, held her own in conservative rural areas. It was down to the transfers. Tess fidgeted. Why the hell was this so important to her? Her life would go on as before, of that she had no doubt. She thought about it for a while and came to a tentative conclusion. It was something to do with the way she could see herself. That was it. Something about the way she regarded herself, even without having to think of it.

'Come on!' she groaned at the radio.

The telephone rang downstairs and after some hesitation she answered it.

'Mungo! Thank Christ. Where are you?'

'In a phonebox on Ormond Quay. She's going to win, Tess.'

'Oh God I hope so. There's talk in the house about a party if she does. Would you come?'

'Of course.'

'I've to go shopping before I go to Fairview. Will you meet me tonight?'

'Outside The Ranch, ten-thirty. Win or lose, I'd like to get drunk.'

'How are you, Mungo?'

'I'm okay.'

But his tired voice suggested otherwise.

It was much later than she thought and already dark as she walked into town. She joined a crowd gathered at a shop window. The several television screens were tuned to the same images, the three candidates and their political sponsors waiting in a line on a stage for the announcement. She could see by their expressions that the men were beaten and that, although she wasn't smiling, the woman had won. Then, noiselessly,, those around her smiled and clapped as she was pronounced President-elect.

'A commie in the Park,' one man said. 'I never thought I'd live to see the day.' But no one paid him any heed. As the cameras zoomed in and the woman smiled as she turned to accept congratulations, Tess realized she had wet herself.

She was baffled by depression. It had happened more than once before: when she'd had most reason to be happy her emotions went into reverse, leaving her miserable. She was late, but as Arthur watched television and she cooked dinner, she picked up a little. Then Brian came home from work.

'She made it,' he said.

'You seem happy.'

'Why wouldn't I be happy? I voted for her, didn't I?'

'Did you?' Somehow, had she thought about it she wouldn't have guessed.

'Well, she's for divorce, isn't she? And you and I want a divorce, isn't that so.' She was surprised by the friendly, almost sympathetic way he said that.

'She doesn't have the power, as President.'

'Maybe she doesn't – but then again, maybe she does. The news'll be on in a minute. Are you coming in to watch it?'

'What about the dinner?'

'Why don't we bring it inside?'

He tested the potatoes before draining them in a cloud of steam as she stood by, uncertain. He seemed to have taken over and she felt superfluous, but then she gathered up the plates she had set. He had by now drained and buttered the peas and checked that the chops were well done, and now he served the food onto the plates she held out. He carried in Arthur's plate and cutlery as well as his own and she followed with hers.

'We're eating in here this evening, Arthur pet. To see the new President.'

Arthur said nothing but seemed pleased to stay on his belly beside the fire. They ate in silence as the Angelus bell rang on the television. As she watched Brian with a curiosity she had not felt in years, she felt that the battle between them had, by some process or miracle, come to a peaceful end.

It was a rush back to work. They were busier than usual that night and Tess wondered if it was a coincidence or whether some had come out to celebrate. Wanting to think, she had walked to work and as her shift drew to a close her concentration faltered several times and it was only luck that she didn't drop anything. All night the customers had talked about the new President, and finally she realized what had left her bewildered earlier in the day. There were others, many others, who had yearned for her to win. It was like being found naked in the middle of the street and being greeted with friendly approval instead of being clapped into jail. Of course she had known that others would vote for her. Of course she had known that. But what she had not realized was that it was so important to others, and that they could, and would win.

She finished late but Mungo was waiting for her and she hugged him, pressing her cheek against the thick cloth of his overcoat, holding him as tightly as she could, and to her relief he hugged her back in like measure.

'Would you mind if we didn't go to any party?' she asked him.

'I'd prefer if we didn't, as a matter of fact.'

'Good.'

'Will we get a bottle of whiskey?'

'Yes. Let's do that.'

Party or no party, she wanted to be in her own room. It didn't matter about the noise, in fact it would be fine, but as it turned out the house was quiet apart from a television in one flat. Mungo opened the whiskey while she made the bed, flapping the sheets vigorously in case there was any lingering odour belonging to Larry, or some stray masculine hair in a fold.

She brushed the hair out of her eyes as she accepted the glass.

'Have you a toast?'

'To the next generation,' he said after some hesitation, and then he smiled.

'To the next generation,' she echoed doubtfully. Their glasses clinked, and they drank.

'Mungo, there's something sad about you this last while. I mean you were sad when I met you, but you're like that again.' Even as she said it, she realized that he somehow knew about Larry, and although she dreaded his reply she found herself asking if there was anything he would like to tell her. He looked at her with those lovely eyes and she could see that, oh yes, he knew, but he would not cast it up to her, he wouldn't accuse her of anything. In a way, she wished he would.

'It's Aidan,' he said after what seemed a long time. 'I have to make my peace with Aidan. I'm going back to Wexford tomorrow.'

'How will you do that?'

'I don't know. Remind him, perhaps.'

'Aren't you afraid he's too young?'

'Yes. But there's something urgent about the present. I'm afraid that if I wait, the chance won't be there.'

She held him as she had done on the street, but now she could feel the warmth of his body. He left his glass down and held her in return, and she closed her eyes tightly, wanting to lose herself in this.

They continued drinking in front of the two-bar electric fire, sometimes talking, sometimes falling silent for minutes on end. They were so easy with each other that she had to fight back the urge to confess about Larry, not out of guilt but to say that it was a frivolous affair, now over, which only served as a contrast to her feelings about Mungo, her only true friend.

He had lightened up and now began to tease her. She countered, and soon they were laughing continuously as every nuance assumed a double meaning. A lot of it was crude, but very funny, and even as she laughed she was aware of how desperately she wanted to laugh like this; and then they were on a roll, the repartee coming instinctively, and she was lost in it; she had given herself up to what she would afterwards recall as pure happiness.

He was happy too and when their laughter died away, and they were groaning at the aches and tears it had left in its wake, he suddenly held her tight, as if he wanted to cling to something he saw in her. Then he relaxed and broke into a smile.

In bed they giggled, tickling each other until they were shouting and laughing again. She wasn't sure when the laughter stopped and passion began, but she ached for him as his fingers slipped between her moist lips, and this was all she wanted.

* * *

Had they finished the bottle or what? Mungo was feeling shaky; his stomach was sour and his skull seemed as if it would split just over his eyes, in the middle.

Yet he hummed as he left his bag, and the two rods which he had bought in Mary's Abbey, on the overhead rack. As the train pulled out of Connolly Station he hummed again, this time to the percussion of his fingers on the table. It had turned out to be a night which would console him in the

- 225 -

troughs of despair which he knew lay ahead, but whose future reality he now ignored. There had to be happiness. It was as valid, as necessary and as true as its dark twin. And to make sense of living, to balance all the heartbreak which he saw around him and in himself, he had a duty, and if it wasn't too grandiose, he had a duty to life itself to fight his way towards being happy. It would be a contribution towards balancing things out, as it were.

These thoughts didn't come in a rush. They had wandered into his head, between waves of forgetfulness, growing like connective tissue, as the train passed Sandymount Strand, and as it went slowly around Killiney Bay. It wouldn't be easy.

He walked briskly from the station in Gorey, up the Avenue and out the Hollyfort road. There was a light drizzle and the clouds were oppressively low and grey and he feared that it would be dark before he could hitch a lift; but just past the town boundary, the first car going in his direction stopped.

'The bould Mungo,' Jim Begley greeted him. He knew Jim from primary school. 'Are you going fishing or what?'

'Good man Jim,' Mungo said with feeling, as he put the rods and his bag into the chaos of the back seat. 'I got a rod for the young fella in Dublin.'

'God I haven't seen you since the funeral,' Jim said. 'How's the oul' farmin' treatin' you, anyway. A big change from the Big Smoke.'

'Tough enough, to tell you the truth.'

Jim looked him over, assessing the unusual admission. 'Huh,' he said then as he leaned forward over the steering wheel and glared ahead. 'Farmin' – the last car on the road.'

'Ah,' Mungo said, looking out the side window at nothing in particular, 'I'm not cut out for it. In the city you do your job, five days a week, and you get your cheque at the end of it.' He had almost added – if you have a job. 'I'm doing it for the children, really. They need the freedom and the fresh air.'

'You mean the cleanin' out the dung and the smell of silage!' Jim guffawed, as if he had been waiting for the chance to say that for years.

And so they talked. As they turned up from Hollyfort, through the great canopy of trees and rhododendron leaves, up past the Protestant church, Mungo asked him about a good place to fish, as he wanted to be away from the ghosts of their own place with Aidan.

'The Bann down there used to be as good a place as any, but sure it's gone to a trickle now. Hould on for a good sup of rain, I'd say.'

Jim was continuing on to Monaseed, so he left Mungo off at the crossroads and he walked the rest of the way, his collar up against the drizzle. The day was fading as he arrived, and the yard lights were on, the squeals of pigs telling him where Connie was. He went around the back and sure enough she was in the pig house looking tired and harassed by the buffeting pigs. She struggled out of the pig house and bolted the door, the buckets still in her hands. In her old clothes and wellingtons, a scarf around her head and her hips noticeably widening, she looked like a drudge, and it was his fault. She crossed the yard and he waited for her to look up. Her reaction was instant.

'Oh you decided to come home. How kind!' She flung the buckets from her without breaking stride and disappeared into the house. He picked up the buckets, sticky with wet meal, and rinsed them under the yard tap before going in. He left his bag and the rods in the kitchen and went upstairs.

As he changed into his working clothes he heard Ethna calling and running upstairs to greet him.

'Daddy!' She burst into the room and into his arms. He raised her to his face and her eyes locked onto his, possessing him totally.

'Did you miss me miss?' He pinched her nose gently and carried her downstairs, where Aidan was waiting, half-smiling, agitated but silent. Mungo ruffled his hair and led him, hand on his shoulder, to the kitchen, asking him what needed to be done before dark.

'Did you bring me anything daddy?' Ethna butted in.

'We'll see,' he said, relieved that he had. 'We'll see. We have to help Mammy first.'

'You needn't bother,' Connie said, standing at the door. 'It's all done.' She kicked off her wellingtons and barefoot, washed her hands and took meat from the fridge. Steam from the pot of potatoes had settled on the window and drops of moisture trickled down behind the half net curtain. The children lowered their eyes as Mungo took off his wellingtons again.

'Well, let me see what we have here,' he said as cheerfully as he could manage, and opened his bag with a theatrical flourish. The children raised their heads again, with hesitant smiles. Connie put the chops on the pan and stepped into her shoes, anger sitting on her like a troll.

'I think we have something for Ethna!' Mungo said, reaching into the bag down to his elbow before producing a large box of crayons.

'Colours!' she exclaimed, and grabbed them.

'And what else?' She had a crayon half out of the box, but left it aside and looked in what seemed like alarm from Mungo to the bag and back again.

'More colours!' Mungo declared. It was a kaleidoscope, and he put it to his eye and revolved the lens against the light.

'Let me Daddy, let me,' she squealed, and he surrendered it.

Aidan had been patient, perhaps because he had guessed what his present was. He smiled as he unwrapped and examined it. Mungo was ready to tell him how to assemble it, but he had already worked that out.

'And who's the other one for, Da?'

'For me of course. I had to get myself something. We'll have to go on a fishing trip now, I suppose. There's no use having fishing rods if we don't fish, is there?'

'When?'

'The first wet Saturday. And this,' Mungo said, laying a slim, gift-wrapped box on the table, 'this is for Mammy.'

Connie was tending to the chops, and looked over her shoulder.

'Well, we might as well have something out of that house,' he said softly. 'Go on. Open it.'